Silas W. Mitchell

The Collected Poems

Silas W. Mitchell

The Collected Poems

ISBN/EAN: 9783337206475

Printed in Europe, USA, Canada, Australia, Japan

Cover: Foto ©Andreas Hilbeck / pixelio.de

More available books at **www.hansebooks.com**

COLLECTED POEMS

THE COLLECTED POEMS

OF

S. WEIR MITCHELL

M. D., LL. D., HARVARD AND EDINBURGH

NEW YORK

THE CENTURY CO.

1896

THE DE VINNE PRESS.

CONTENTS

✠

DRAMATIC POEMS

MISCELLANEOUS POEMS

	PAGE

POEMS OF OCCASION

DRAMATIC POEMS

FRANCIS DRAKE

A TRAGEDY OF THE SEA

TIME 1578

At sea, off the coast of Patagonia, on board the *Pelican*, the *Elizabeth*, and the *Plymouth*.

———

DRAMATIS PERSONÆ:

FRANCIS DRAKE.
THOMAS DOUGHTY, his friend.
FRANCIS FLETCHER, Chaplain.
JOHN WINTER.
LEONARD VICARY, } Captains. ·
WILLIAM CHESTER,
GENTLEMEN-VENTURERS.
SEAMEN.

FRANCIS DRAKE

Deck of the Elizabeth.   Fleet in the offing.

JOHN WINTER.   THOMAS DOUGHTY.

DOUGHTY (*coming aboard*).   Good-morrow, Winter.
    Still the winds are foul.
I would they blew from merry England shores.
    WINTER.   I would they had not blown you to my ship.
None are more welcome elsewhere.   Strict commands
Forbid this visiting from ship to ship.
    DOUGHTY.   These orders are most wise, — I doubt not
    that;
Yet must I learn that any here afloat
Is master of the gentlemen who venture
Their ducats and their lives.   Let him make laws
To rule rough sailors; they are not for us.
    WINTER.   Yet one must be the master.   Ill it were
If, drifting masterless, this little realm
Of tossing ships obeyed not one sure helm.
I shall but serve you if I bid you go.
    DOUGHTY.   The *Pelican* is twice a league away.
'T is time the several captains of the fleet
Should learn how little mind the seamen have,

Ay, and the gentlemen, to hold our course.
Now, were we all of us of one firm mind,
This cheating voyage should end, and that full soon.
This in your ear.   Did I dare speak of Burleigh —

                                                 [Winter recoils.

WINTER.   Have you a mind to lose us both our heads ?
I would not ill report you, but your words
Sail near to treason, both to Queen and Friend.   ,

DOUGHTY.   I pray you but this once be patient with me.
My actions shall not lack support in England.
If I might dare say all, you best of any
Would know the admiral has no better friend.
The ships decay; the sailors mutiny;
Before us lies a waste of unknown seas;
Methinks authority doth beget in men
A certain madness.   Think you if we chance
To ruin peaceful towns and scuttle ships,
And rouse these Spanish hornets on their coasts,
Think you the dearest counsellor of the Queen —
I may not name him — will be better pleased
With him that hurts or him that helps this voyage ?

WINTER.   I think your enterprise more perilous
Than half a hundred voyages, good friend —
I pray you risk not losing of the name,
For you are greatly changed from him I knew
This some time past of gentle disposition;
In danger tranquil; gay, and yet discreet;
Learned in the law, a scholar and a soldier.

DOUGHTY.   An old-time nursery trick : comfits before,
And after comes the dose; then sweets again.

WINTER.   Be not so hasty; hear me to the end,
And be my careful friendship early pardoned.
I have heard you say of late you lack advancement.

There is advancement no man need to lack
Who makes his Duty like a mother's knees,
Where all his prayers are said.   This man you were.
What other man is this I hardly know :
One that of all his natural endowments
Makes but base use to stir the meaner sort,
To darken counsel with a mist of words,
To scatter falsehood, and to sow distrust;
And all as lightly as a housewife flings
The morning grain amidst her cackling crew.

   DOUGHTY.   You have done well to ask my pardon first.
   WINTER.   Nay.   I do hold the bond of friendship
       strong;
And he who wills to keep his friends must know
To stomach that they lack.   I would indeed
You had not spoken as you have to-day.

   DOUGHTY.   What matters it ?   My words are safe with
       you.
   WINTER.   Safe as my countenance will let them be;
Safe till the admiral asks, and, like a boy,
I stand a-twiddling of uneasy thumbs,
On this foot, now, or that, red in the face.
By Heaven! what fetched you on this hated voyage ?

   DOUGHTY.   A trick.   A fetch indeed !
   WINTER.   Nay, that 's not so.
Trick or no trick, this is not English earth,
Nor Drake the man who on the Devon greens
Sat half the night a-talking poesy.
I have seen many men in angry moods,
But this man's wrath is as the wrath of God,
Instant and terrible.   Pray you, be warned,
And if your soul be capable of fear —

   DOUGHTY.   Fear!

  1*

WINTER.   Ay, a healthful virtue in its place.
Had I been but the half as rash as you,
My very sword would tremble in its sheath.
    DOUGHTY.   And yet I have no nearer friend than he.
    WINTER.   You judge men by their love, as maidens do.
    DOUGHTY.   And not an ill way, either, as earth goes.
The admiral in his less distracted times
Hath some rare flavor of the woman in him.
    WINTER.   Oh, that 's the half of him : no lady wronged,
No pillaged church, no hurt of unarmed man,
Will stain his record at the great account.
Have then a care.   The gentle, just, and brave
Are ill to anger
    DOUGHTY.   What I say to you
I not less readily shall say to him,
Trusting the friendly equity of his love.
    WINTER.   A certain devil lurks in every angel,
Else had there never been a strife in heaven.
Now on my soul I wonder at the man.
Thrice has he warned you as a brother might,
And once removed you from a high command.
'T is very strange to me how men may differ.
No doubts have I ; along these savage coasts
Magellan sailed.   Are we not English born ?
    DOUGHTY.   I neither have forgotten nor forget.
Thanks for your patience.   There is more to say
That might be said.   ·
    WINTER.   I would it had been less.
I think it well no other hears your words.
    DOUGHTY.   Oh, fear not I shall rashly squander speech.
    WINTER.   Spend not your thoughts at all.   Be miserly.
These wooden walls have echoes ; to and fro
Some wild word wanders, till, on each return,

We less and less our own mind's children know.
All gold they say is of the devil's mint;
But words are very devils of themselves.
I do commend you to a fast of speech.
 DOUGHTY. It might be wise—but you 'll not talk of this.
 WINTER. Nay, that I will not. It is you will speak.
A restless tongue is ever no man's friend.
Come, let us shift the talk. 'T is perilous.
       [*Winter, as he speaks, walks to the rail.*
How huge and bloody red the moon to-night!
This utter quiet of the brooding sea
I like not over well; nor yon red moon.
So, there 's a breeze again, and now 't is still.
We shall have storms to-morrow.
 DOUGHTY.   Reason good
Before our ships are scattered far and wide,
That I should speak what others dare not speak.
 WINTER. Nor I dare hear. My mother used to say
That silence was a very Christian virtue.
When I talk folly, be the Moon my friend;
There are no eavesdroppers among the stars.
 DOUGHTY. Her sex they say are leaky counsellors;
And, too, she shares thy secrets with a man,
Red i' the visage now. Here 's three to keep
Thy pleasant indiscretions.
 WINTER.   Happy Moon!
That ere a day is dead shall England see.
Ah, gentle dame, shine on our island homes;
Kiss for my sake a face as fair as thine;
Go, tell our love to every maiden flower
That droops tear-laden in our Devon woods.
 DOUGHTY. I dreamed last night that never more again
Should I see England.

WINTER. That 's as God may will.
I dare not think on England. Why should you?
What ails you now that you should look behind
When honor cries come on?
DOUGHTY. To be a child!
Is that your largest wisdom?
WINTER. Yes, well said!
Child, woman, man — the nobler life hath need
That man be all of these.
DOUGHTY (*is silent a moment*). I would that I
Were always near you, Winter. Drake has power
To tempt resistance as no other can.
With you, dear friend, my soul abides in peace.
WINTER. Seek you such peace as comes to those
    alone
Who have for friend the duty of the hour.
DOUGHTY. Enough of preaching.
WINTER. Well, so be it then;
But guard that restless tongue. When night is come,
And all these mighty spaces overhead
And all this vast of sea lie motionless,
God seems so near to me, ill deeds so far,
That all my soul in gentled wonder rests.
                        [*They are silent a time.*
DOUGHTY. Mark how the southward splendor of the
    cross
Shines peace upon us. When the nights are calm,
I joy to climb the topmast's utmost peak,
And, hanging breathless in the unpeopled void,
Note how the still deep answers star for star.
WINTER. See, the wind freshens. Get you to your ship.
Come not again. This seeming quiet sea
Is not more dangerous than a man we know.

DOUGHTY. 'T is not the danger checks me; yet be sure
I shall not spare to think upon your words.
You have my thanks. Good night, and merry dreams.
See that you keep my counsel.

WINTER.   Said I not
'T was safe with me?

DOUGHTY (*goes over the rail to his boat*). Good night,
and better winds.

WINTER.   Good night to you.
The devil take the man.

Cabin of Pelican.

DRAKE. VICARY. WINTER.

WINTER.   It sorts not with my honor that I speak.
DRAKE.   Enough to know John Winter will not speak;
A cruel verdict is the just man's silence.
I have been patient, but the end has come.
What breeds these discontents? I know the man.
Were he twin brother of my mother's womb
He should not live to mar my Prince's venture.
(*To Vicary.*) Are you struck silent, like my good John
          Winter?
What substance is there in this mutinous talk?
VICARY.   Too little substance, not enough to eat;
A prating parson, and some empty bellies.
A very mutinous thing 's an empty paunch.
DRAKE.   Now here 's a man has never a plain answer.
Out with it in good English.
VICARY.   As you will,
I pray you pardon me my way of speech;

I cannot help it.   I was born a-grinning,
Or so my mother said.   If death 's a jest,
I doubt not I shall never die in earnest.
    DRAKE.   Now on my soul this passes all endurance;
Grin, if it please you, but at least speak out.
    VICARY.   I never had as little mind to speak.
    DRAKE.   I have heard you jesting with a Spanish Don
When sore beset and well nigh spent with wounds.
I think some counsel lies behind your mirth.
    VICARY.   Were I the admiral I would preach a sermon.
    DRAKE.   A sermon !
    VICARY.   Ay! and that a yardarm long,
And to conclude, a parson and a rope.
Also good rum 's a very Christian diet,
And vastly does console a shrunken belly.
DRAKE (*smiling*). Well, my gay jester, is there more to say?
    VICARY.   I sometimes think we carry on our ships
Too large a freight of time.
    DRAKE.   Talk plain again.
It takes three questions to beget an answer.
    VICARY.   Now, as the world runs, that 's unnatural
        many.
    DRAKE.   I think you will not speak.
    VICARY.   No, I 'm run dry.
I am as barren as a widowed hen.
    DRAKE (*laughing*). Out with you.   Go !
    VICARY (*aside*).   And none more glad to go.
                                    [*Exit Vicary.*
    DRAKE.   One that must needs be taken in his humor.
    WINTER.   'T is a strange disposition that hath mirth
For what breeds tears in others.
    DRAKE.   No, not strange.
But I 've no jesting in my heart to-day.

The straits lie yonder, dark and perilous;
The Spaniards' villainies sit heavy here.

                                   [Strikes his breast.

Their racks are red with honest English blood;
The dead call, "Come."   Ah, Winter, by my soul,
When Panama is ours, when their galleons lie
Distressful wrecks, and England's banner flies
Unquestioned on the far Pacific sea,
Then —
    WINTER.   Is it so?   Runs your commission thus?
    DRAKE.   Once past the straits, and all shall know my
        errand.
Here is the warrant of Her Majesty,
And here the sword she bade me call her own.
    WINTER.   Did Doughty know of this?
    DRAKE.   Ay, from the first.
    WINTER.   A double treason.
    DRAKE.   Counsel me, John Winter.
The sailors murmur, and the gentlemen
Sow quarrels and dissension through the fleet.
My dearest friend betrays my dearest trust.
What means this gay boy's chatter about time?
    WINTER.   A riddle easily read, if you but think
What use the devil has for idle hours.
    DRAKE.   I have long meant to make an end of that.
Go tell these lazy gentles Francis Drake
Bids them to haul and pull as sailors do;
Ay, let them reef and lay out on the yards.
I 'll bid 'gainst Satan for their idleness.
Belike they may not care to go aloft;
Then, on my word, I 've bilboes down alow.
    WINTER.   Thou wouldst not set a gentle i' the stocks?
    DRAKE.   Gentle or parson, let them try me not.

'T is said a gibbet stands on yonder shore:
There brave Magellan hanged a mutinous Don.
Let them look to it.   See I be obeyed.
None shall be favored.   Fetch me now aboard
This traitor Doughty, and no words with him.
    WINTER.   Ay, ay, sir.
    DRAKE.   Go.   Let there be no delay.

          [*Winter in his boat beside the Plymouth.*
    DOUGHTY (*descending*).   What means this summons?
    WINTER.   Hush!   I may not speak.
Give way there, men.   (*To Doughty.*)   Have you your
    tablets with you?
                 [*Takes them and writes:*
"Take care.   Be warned.   The devil is broke loose."
    DOUGHTY.   Why am I bidden?
    WINTER.   '   Way — give way there, men!
    DOUGHTY.   Will you not answer me?
    WINTER.   Not I, indeed.
Way there, enough!   Ho, there, aboard!
          [*Doughty goes aboard the Pelican.*
    DOUGHTY.   Good day.

Deck of Pelican.

DOUGHTY.   FLETCHER.

FLETCHER.   I think there is some mischief in the air.
'T is said the admiral has sent for you.
    DOUGHTY.   I 'm haled aboard with no more courtesy
Than any meanest ruffian of the crew.
Were I in England he should answer me.
    FLETCHER.   This is not England.

DOUGHTY. Oh, by heaven! no!
(*Aside.*) Time must be won. I 've been a loitering fool.
(*Aloud.*) I would that I could clear my mind to you.
FLETCHER. Why not to me? What other is so fit?
Is not confession like an act of nature?
DOUGHTY. I am like a wine thick with confusing lees.
To-day they settlé, and to-morrow morn
Another shakes me, and I 'm thick again.
  [*Fletcher watches him. Both are silent for a moment.*
Thou art both man and priest.
FLETCHER. Add friend to both.
DOUGHTY. You said, most reverend sir, both man
    and priest.
Had you been more of man, yet all of priest,
Confession had been easier.
FLETCHER. More of man!
Grant you I lack the courage of the sea,
Think you it takes none to be now your friend?
I have the will, ay, and the resolution,
To help you when I think you most need help.
I guess the half your lips delay to tell.
DOUGHTY (*looking about him*). Enough. Time passes,
    and you should know all.
My Lord of Burleigh much mis-likes this voyage.
Who helps to ruin it will no loser be.
Had I but known this ere my florins went
To help a foolish venture!
FLETCHER. But the Queen —
DOUGHTY. Hath ever had two minds, as is her way.
(*Points north.*) Now there advancement lies. (*Points
    south.*) And that way death.
FLETCHER. Art in the service of my Lord of Burleigh?
Not more than thou am I this admiral's man.

DOUGHTY.   And I am no man's man; I am the Queen's.
I shall best serve my God in serving her.
Shall it be Prince or friend?   I may not both.
   FLETCHER.   Is he thy friend?
   DOUGHTY.   Of late I doubt it much.
Now hath he closer counsellors than I.
   FLETCHER.   He loves thee not.   This ill-advised voyage
Goes to disaster in these unknown seas
Where some foul devil led the sons of Rome.
'T is said that demons lit them down the coast.
This nine and fifty years no Christian sail
Has gone this deathful way.   The admiral
Knows not the sullen temper of the fleet.
(*Looks at* DOUGHTY *steadily*).   There should be one — a
      friend — to bid him turn
And set our prows toward England.   Think on that.
   DOUGHTY.   But who shall bell the cat?   What mouse
      among us?
   FLETCHER.   If but we English mice were of one mind!
   DOUGHTY.   Soon shall we be so.   You have unawares
Made firm my purpose.   'T is not in thy kind
To court such peril as our talk may bring.
The more for this have you my thanks.   Enough.
The counsel given me —
   FLETCHER (*alarmed*).   I gave you none.
   DOUGHTY.   Oh, rest you easy.   It is safe with me.
As you are priest, so I am gentleman;
Now in the end it comes to much the same.

Enter CHESTER.

   CHESTER (*to* DOUGHTY).   The admiral would see you
      instantly.   [*Exit.*

Cabin of Pelican.

DRAKE. I would this man had been less dear to me;
Another I had long since crushed. The rat
Which gnaws the planks between our lives and death
I had as lightly dealt with. For love's sake
And all the honest past that has been ours
Once shall I speak. Once more: [*A knock.*
            Ho, there.   Come in.

Enter CHESTER *and* DOUGHTY.

CHESTER. The land lies low to westward, and the
    wind
Blows fair and steady.   [DRAKE *looks at the chart.*
    DRAKE.   Ay, St. Julian's isle.
                  [*Exit* CHESTER.
(*To* DOUGHTY).   Pray you be seated.
    DOUGHTY.   I am ordered hither.
'T were fit I stand.
    DRAKE.   Yes, I am admiral;
But there are moments in the lives of all
When the stern conscience of a too great office
Appals the kindlier heart that fain would be
Where indecisions breed less consequence.
I said, be seated.   [DOUGHTY *obeys.*
        Are you not my friend?
Forget these rolling seas, the time, the place,
This mighty errand which my Prince has sped.
Think me to-day but simple Francis Drake,
And be yourself the brother of my heart.
    DOUGHTY.   There spoke the old Frank Drake I seemed
    to lose.

DRAKE. Let us try back. We are like ill-broken dogs.
Our lives have lost the scent.
DOUGHTY.   Nay, think not so.
DRAKE. Ah, once I had a friend, a scholar wise,
A soldier, and a poet; dowered, I think,
With all the gentle gifts that win men's hearts.
Of late he seems another than himself;
Of late he is most changed, and him I knew
Is here no more. Ah, but I too am double,
And one of me is still thy nearest friend,
And one, ah, one is admiral of the fleet.
Let him that loves you whisper to your soul
The thing he would not say. You understand.
Ah, now you smile. A pretty turn of phrase
Did ever capture you. 'T was always thus.
We have seen death so often, eye to eye,
That fear of death were idle argument;
Yet in such words of yours as men report
A deathful sentence lurks. Oh, cast away
These mad temptations, won I know not whence.
Last night I fell to thinking, ere I slept,
Of those proud histories of older days
You loved to tell amid the tents in Ireland.
Trust me, no one of these that shall not fade
Before the wonder of this English tale
Of what El Draco and his captains did.
And when, at twilight, by our Devon hearths
Some old man tells the story, shall he pause,
And say, But one there was, of England born,
That sowed the way with perils not of God,
Breeding dissension, casting on his name
Dishonor —
    DOUGHTY (*leaping up*). Now, by heaven! no man
        shall say —

DRAKE (*smiling and quiet, puts a hand on each shoulder
of* DOUGHTY). Hush! you will waken up that
other man.
Read not my meaning wrong. I am sore beset.
Before me lie dark days. The timid shrink;
The gentlemen, who should have been my stay,
Fall from me useless. Yet, come what come may,
For England's glory and my lady's grace,
I go my way. Well did he speak who said,
" Heaven is as near by water as by land."
And therefore, whether it be death or fame
That waits in yonder seas, I go my way.
Yet, if I lose you on this venturous road,
Half the proud joy of victory were gone.
I have been long; you, patient. Rest we here.
  DOUGHTY. Yes, I am more than one man; more 's
    the pity.
If I have sinned, forgive me, and good night.
  DRAKE. Thou shalt stay with me on the Pelican.
  DOUGHTY (*aside*). So, so. A child in ward! (*Aloud.*)
    Again, good night.   [*Exit.*
                        [*Enter* VICARY.
  VICARY. The water shoals. A land lies west by south.
There seems good anchorage in the island's lee.
  DRAKE. We shall find water here, good fruit and fish.
Send in a boat for soundings. Signal all
To anchor where seems best; and Vicary,
Set thy gay humor to some thoughtful care
Of him that left just now. I hold him dear.
  VICARY. I would to heaven he were safe in England.
  DRAKE. And I, and I. He is more like a child
Than any man my life's experience knows.
Yet he is dangerous to himself and us;

Too fond of speech; too cunning with the tongue;
That tempts to mischief like a sharpened blade.
   VICARY. Ah, words! words! words! Ye children of
       the fiend,
On all your generated repetitions
Is visited your parents' wickedness.
He keeps boon company with each man's humor,
Is gay with me, is chivalrous with you,
At Winter's side a grave philosopher.
I shall set merry sentinels for his guards,
And there my wisdom ends.
   DRAKE.   My thanks. No more.
                      [*Exit* VICARY.

*Deck of Pelican. Ships at anchor near the north end of the
       island of St. Julian.*

     DOUGHTY. WINTER. SEAMEN.

WINTER. These are my orders.
   DOUGHTY.   I may not to shore;
And for the reason? Drake shall give it me.
                  [*Turns to the men.*
I hear there is no water on these shores.
   1ST SAILOR. That in the casks is but mere mud of
vileness; rot in the mouth, and stenches in the nose.
   2D SAILOR. And for the biscuits, they are moldy
green, and inhabited like an owl's nest with all manner
of live things.
   3D SAILOR. It will be worse in the lower seas. There
the men are eleven cubits tall.
   2D SAILOR. Nay, feet, and that 's enough.

4TH SAILOR.   Where scurvy Dons have gone, good
English may.

DOUGHTY.   We gentles are no better off than you.
Here is an order we shall pull and haul,
And lay aloft.   What!   Lack ye meat to-day?
Here are grubs to spare.   These caverned biscuits hold
Small beeves in plenty.   Here 's more life, I think,
Than we are like to find on yonder coast.

1ST SAILOR.   A Portugee did tell me once there was
no day in the straits where we must sail, and all the sea
be full of venomed snakes.

DOUGHTY.   Nay.   That 's a foolish fable.   True it is
that in the straits are mighty isles of ice, with sail and
mast.   They beat about, men say, like luggers on a wind,
and never man to handle rope or sail.

FLETCHER.   The boats are come again, and no water,
none!   Alas, this miserable voyage!

Enter VICARY *from boat.*

VICARY.   Not so, good chaplain.   Underneath a cliff
I found a spring as sweet as England's best.
Good store of shellfish, too, and these strange fruits.
(*To* DOUGHTY).   You 're but an old wife at these fireside
tales.   Lord, lads! there 's wonders yonder.   It is twice
as good as a fair in May.   There 's a merry-go-round
that 's called a swirlpool.   Round you go, a hundred
years, ship and all, not a farthing to pay, and then home
to bed, with addled pates, as good as drunk, and no man
the poorer.   [*The men laugh.*

1ST SAILOR (*aside*).   He do lie to beat a rusty wea-
ther-cock.

2D SAILOR.   But men do say there 's hell-traps set
along the rocks, and all the waters boil like witch's pots.

VICARY (*laughs*).   The tale is gone awry.   When last
I sailed this way, no fire would burn, and all the little fiends
were harvesting of mighty icicles to keep the daddy devils from frosted toes.

1ST SAILOR (*aside*).   He be a lively liar.   He be a very
flea among liars.   [*All laugh.*

VICARY.   The seas be rum, and all the whales mad
    drunk.   [*Laughter.*
I thought my laughter trap was baited well.

4TH SAILOR (*aside*).   He don't starve his lies.   A very
pretty liar.   His lies be fat as ever a Christmas hog.

VICARY.   Tom Doughty, I 'll match lies with you, my
    lad,
The longest day of June.   A song, a song!

SAILORS.   A song, a song!   The captain for a song!

VICARY.   Here 's for a song.   The admiral bids say
Your rum is doubled for a week to come.
So here we go.   Be hearty with the burden.

SONG.

Queen Bess has three bad boys,
    Such naughty boys!
They sailed away to Cadiz Bay
To make a mighty noise.
    Heave her round!
    Heave her round!
    Such bad boys!
    Yo ho!

There 's wicked Master Drake,
    As likes to play with guns;

He sailed away to Cadiz Bay
To wake the sleepy Dons.
          Heave her round! etc.

These be three captains small,
None taller than a splinter.
One does admire to play with fire,
That 's little Jacky Winter.
          Heave her round! etc.

There 's one does love to fight,
It might be Billy Chester.
And they 're away to Cadiz Bay
Before a stiff sou'-wester.
          Heave her round! etc.

Don Spaniard sings, Avast!
What 's doing with them grapples?
We 're just Queen Bess's naughty boys,
We 're only stealing apples.
          Heave her round! etc.

They filled their little stomachs,
They had a pretty frolic.
The boys as ate the apples up
Was n't them as had the colic.
          Heave her round! etc.

Small Frank he shot his gun,
And Willy played with fire.
To see those naughty boys again
No Spaniard do desire.
          Heave her round! etc.

VICARY.   Well tuned, my lads.   Now who of you 's
        for shore ?
DOUGHTY (*aside to a mate*).   There 'll be no songs
        down yonder.
WINTER (*leaning over him*).   What, again ?
More mischief, ever more ?   Dark is the sea
Where you will sail.   What fiend possesses you ?
This in your ear.   The priest is no man's friend.
If I do know the malady of baseness,
There 's one that needs a doctor.
        DOUGHTY.   You are wrong.
I have no better friend, none more assured.
        WINTER.   Indeed, I think you are too rich in friends.
Better you had a hundred eager foes
Than this man's friendly company.   One step more,
One slight excess of speech, some word retold —
And thou art lost to life.
        DOUGHTY.   He dare not do it !
        WINTER.   Dare not ! I think it oft doth chance a man
Knows not his nearest friend as others do.
As for thy priest — I greatly fear a coward.
The day will come when honest Francis Drake
Will shake all secrets from him as a dog
Shakes out a rat's mean life.   Beware the day !
Well do I know the admiral's silent mood;
Then should men fear him, and none more than you,
Because he dreads the counsel of his heart.
                                    [*Exeunt both.*

Deck of the Pelican.   Evening, a week later.   The fleet at anchor near the south end of the island of St. Julian. Sailors at the capstan.

WINTER.   Now, then, to warp her in.   Round with
    the capstan.
Sailors and gentlemen, bear all a hand!
    DOUGHTY.   Not I, by heaven! Not I! My father's son
Stains not his sword-hand with this peasant toil.
    GENTLEMEN.   Nor I! nor I! nay, never one of us.
    WINTER.   Do as I bid you!
    DOUGHTY.   Not a hand of mine
Shall to this sailor work.
    WINTER.   That shall we see.
    [*Walks to the cabin.*   *Boatswain whistles.*
             Men man the capstan, singing:

        Yo ho!   Heave ho!
    Oh, it 's ingots and doubloons,
    Oh, it 's diamonds big as moons,
          As we sail,
          As we sail.
      Yo ho!   Heave ho!

    Oh, it 's rusty, crusty Dons,
    And it 's rubies big as suns,
        As we sail, etc.

    Oh, it 's pieces by the scores,
    And it 's jolly red moidores,
        As we sail, etc.

> Oh, we 'll singe King Philip's beard,
> And no man here afeard,
> As we sail, etc.

Enter VICARY.

VICARY. Well sung. Well hauled, my lads. (*To*
DOUGHTY.) A word with you.
You will attend the admiral in his cabin.
(*Aside to* DOUGHTY.) Ware cat, good mouse! The
claws are out to-night!
DOUGHTY. 'T were better soon than later. After you.
[*Exit.*

Cabin of Pelican.

DRAKE. WINTER.

Enter VICARY, *followed by* DOUGHTY.

DRAKE. Pray you be seated. (*To* DOUGHTY.) Nay,
not you, not you.
(*To* WINTER.) Arrest this gentleman.
WINTER.   Your sword, an 't please you.
[*Receives it.*
DRAKE. I charge you here with treason to the Queen.
You shall to trial with no long delay.
DOUGHTY. What court is this with which you threaten
me?
DRAKE. Now, by St. George, your lawyer tricks and
quibbles
Shall help you little. I am Francis Drake,
The Queen's plain sailor, and the master here.
DOUGHTY. Master!

DRAKE.Ay, master! Traitor to the Queen,
This long account is closed.   All, all is known,
Since when, at Plymouth, on the eve we sailed,
My Lord of Burleigh bought you; what the price
The devil knows — and you.
DOUGHTY.My Lord of Burleigh!
I pray you speak of this with me alone.
What I would say is for a secret ear.
DRAKE.   No, by my sword, not I!
DOUGHTY.Then have thy way.
No law can touch me here.   This is not England.
DRAKE.   Where sails a plank in English forests hewn,
There England is.   This deck is England now,
And I a sea-king of this much of England.
Put me this man in irons!   See to it!
Let him have speech of none except yourselves.
[*Exeunt* WINTER *and* DOUGHTY.
(*To* VICARY.)   I have too long delayed.
VICARY.That may well be.
DRAKE.   I hear he hath great favor with the crews,
A maker of more mischief than I guessed.
VICARY.   Men love him well.
DRAKE.He hath too many friends.
This is the very harlotry of friendship.
Go now, and pray that when command is yours
You have no friends.   See that strict guard be kept.
[*Exit* VICARY.
(*Alone.*)   I would that God had spared me this one hour.

Pelican.   DOUGHTY *in irons on the deck, seated upon a coil
of ropes, leaning against a mast.*

WINTER (*to the guards*).   Back there, my men!
DOUGHTY.You are most welcome, Winter.

I am very glad of company.   My soul
Is sick to surfeit of its own dull thoughts.
I like not lonely hours.   What land is that ?
   WINTER.   St. Julian's cape.
   DOUGHTY.   Is that a cross I see ?
It seems, I think, the handiwork of man.
   WINTER.   No cross is that; there stout Magellan
      hanged
Don Carthagene, vice-admiral of his fleet.
   DOUGHTY.   Wherefore?
   WINTER.   'T is said he did dislike the voyage,
And had no mind to pass the narrow straits.
   DOUGHTY.   The strait he chose was narrower; mayhap
He had no choice — as I may not to-morrow.
[Is silent a few moments.
A little while ago, the scent of flowers
Came from the land.   Their nimble fragrance woke,
As by a charm, some sleeping memories.
I dreamed myself again a fair-haired boy,
A-gathering cowslips in my mother's fields.
[Pauses.
There is no order that I shall not sing ;
I can no mighty treason set to song.
   WINTER.   Sing, if it please you.   I 'll be glad it doth.
What song shall 't be ?

   DOUGHTY.   Ah me, those Devon lanes !
[Sings.

SONG.

I would I were an English rose,
In England for to be ;
The sweetest maid that Devon knows
Should pick, and carry me.

To pluck my leaves be tender quick,
A fortune fair to prove,
And count in love's arithmetic
Thy pretty sum of love.
[*The men come nearer.*

Oh, Devon's lanes be green o'ergrown,
And blithe her maidens be,
But there be some that walk alone,
And look across the sea.

1ST SAILOR.   'T is a sad shame so gay a gentleman
Should lie in irons.
2D SAILOR.   Ay, the pity of it.
WINTER (*to the men*). Off with you there! (*To* DOUGH-
TY.)   The devil 's in your tongue!
Why must you sing of England?   Follow me.
I think you would breed mutiny in heaven.
[*Exit.*

Cabin of Pelican.

DRAKE.   *Enter* FLETCHER.

FLETCHER.   I come as bidden.   What may be
your will?
DRAKE.   Think you a man may serve two masters?
FLETCHER.   Nay,
'T is not so writ.
DRAKE.   Yet there are some I know
Would have me serve a dozen, and my Queen.
Shall I serve this man's doubt, and that man's fear?
Who bade these cowards follow me to sea?
And you, that are Christ's captain,— what of you?

Were I a man vowed wholly unto God,
I should have courage both of God and man;
And fear 's a malady of swift infection.
    FLETCHER.   I think my captain has been ill informed.
    DRAKE.   Ah, not so ill.   Look at me, in the face;
A man's eyes may rest honest, though his soul
Be deeper damned than Judas.   Thou art false!
False to thy faith, thy duty, and thy Prince!
Now, if thou hast no righteous fear of God —
By heaven! here stands a man you well may fear.
    FLETCHER.   Indeed I know not how I 've angered you.
    DRAKE.   Thou shalt know soon. And — look not yet
        away —
You have hatched treason with the larger help
Of one that hath more courage. Spare him not
If you have hope to see another day.
What of your plans? I charge you, sir, be frank.
What has he told that you should fear to tell?
    FLETCHER. We did but talk. Perchance I may have said
I do not love the sea, that some aboard
Would be well pleased to stand on English soil.
    DRAKE.   If you have any wisdom of this world,
A coward heart may save a foolish head.
I asked you what this traitor Doughty said,
You answer me with babble of yourself.
Speak out, or, by my honor,—no light oath,—
I shall so score you with the boatswain's lash
That Joseph's coat shall be a mock to yours.
    FLETCHER.   You would not — dare —
    DRAKE.   I think you know me not.
You have my orders. Is it yes, or no?
    FLETCHER.   I pray you, sir, consider what you ask.
No priest of God may, without deadly sin,

Tell what in penitence a troubled soul
Has in confession whispered.   Ask me not.
   DRAKE.   If I do understand your words aright,
Save for the idle talk of idle men,
He hath said nought to you except of sin
Such as the best may in an hour of shame
Tell for the soul's relief.   If this be so,
Nor I, nor any man, may question you.
   FLETCHER.   I do assure you that I spoke the truth.
   DRAKE (*perplexed, walks to and fro.   Turns suddenly,
     offering the hilt of his sword*).   Swear it upon the
     cross-hilt of my sword.
Swear!   (*Fletcher hesitates.*)   As my God is dear, thou
     art more false
Than hell's worst devil.   Ho!   Without there!   Ho!
   FLETCHER.   Nay, I will swear.
   DRAKE.   Too late.   Without there!   Ho!
Send me the boatswain's mate.   Without there!   Ho!
If I confess thee not, thou lying priest,
May I die old — die quiet in my bed.
Ho there!   And quick!
   FLETCHER.   I pray you — let me think.
It may be that I did not understand.
It might be that he talked to me, a man,
As man to man.   I think 't was even so.
   DRAKE.   Out with it — quickly!   Speak!   Out!   Out
     with it!
   FLETCHER.   I think he said the purpose of this voyage
Was hid, and all of us are cheated men.
It seems he said that if the gentles here
Were of one mind, and stirred the crews to act,
We might see England and our homes again.
   DRAKE.   What more?

FLETCHER.　　　　　As who should take to bell the cat;
As that the Queen your errand did not guess.
　　DRAKE. So! Said he that? Go on; thy tale lacks wit.
　　FLETCHER.　Also, that storms and ever-vexing winds
Did show God's will.
　　DRAKE.　　　　　I think you trifle, sir.
Did he talk ever of my Lord of Burleigh?
　　FLETCHER.　I fear to speak.
　　DRAKE.　　　　　　　Fear rather to be silent.
Here lies the warrant of her Majesty:
'T is she, not I, commands.
　　FLETCHER.　　　　　He seemed to say
They would best serve my Lord of Burleigh's wish
Who marred this venture, ere the power of Spain
Was roused to open war. I can no more.
　　DRAKE. See that your memory fail not on the morrow!
Go thank the devil in your prayers to-night
For that your skin is whole. Begone! Begone!
　　　　　　　　　　　　　[*Exit Fletcher.*
Now know I what it costs a woman-prince
To keep her realm. The great should have no friends.

Enter VICARY, WINTER, *and* CHESTER.

　　DRAKE. Call all the captains and the officers.
The court shall meet to-morrow morn, at eight.
There shall be charges ready in due form;
You, all of you, shall hear the witnesses.
And, Winter,—we are far from England now,—
See that this trial be in all things fair,
As though each man of you, an ermined judge,
Sat in Westminster. Let no words of mine
Disturb the equities of patient judgment.

I would not that, when you and I are old,
Uneasy memories of too hasty action
Should haunt us with reproach.   But have a care.
My duty knows no friend; be thine as ignorant.
Our fortunes and the honor of the Queen —
I should have said her honor and our fortunes —
Rest in your hands.   See that my words be known.
WINTER.   To all?
DRAKE.   To all, sailors and gentlemen.
                          [*Exeunt the captains.*

WINTER, VICARY, *and* CHESTER *without.*

CHESTER.   I 'm like a child that fain would run away
To 'scape a whipping.
WINTER.   There are none of us
More sore at heart than Drake.
VICARY.   I know of one.
I would a friend were dead ere break of day,
And all to-morrow's story left untold.
I think that I shall never laugh again.
                          [*They reach the deck.*

CHESTER (*pointing to the gibbet on the shore*).
It may be yon long-memoried counsellor
Made hard the admiral's heart.
VICARY.   That might be so.
I wandered thither, yesterday, at eve,
And found a skull.   Didst ever notice, Winter,
How this least mortal relic of a man
Does seem to smile?   Hast ever talked with skulls?
They are courteous ever, and good listeners.
And never one of them, or man or maid,
That is not secret.   There 's another virtue;

For what more honest and more chaste than death ?
Now, then, this skull that grins an hundred years —
Pray think how mighty must the jest have been ;
And then, how transient are our living smiles.
    WINTER.   Ill-omened talk.   A graver business waits.
    VICARY.   Give me an hour.   I am not well to-day.
I will be with you very presently.   [*Exit* VICARY.

Evening of the day of the trial and condemnation of
    DOUGHTY.   *Time, sunset.   Ashore on St. Julian's
    Island.*

            WINTER.   VICARY.   DRAKE.

        DRAKE *walking to and fro under the trees.*

WINTER (*coming up and walking beside him*).   What
        orders are there ?
DRAKE.   See the prisoner,
And bid him choose the hour and the day.
    WINTER.   And for the manner of the execution ?
The court said nothing ; sir, it lies with you.
What is your pleasure ?
    DRAKE.   Say my will, John Winter.
The gallows and the rope !
    VICARY (*returning*).   Must that be so ?
'T is a dog's death, and not a gentleman's.
    DRAKE.   I have at home a very honest dog.
    VICARY.   Wilt pardon me if once again I plead ?
    DRAKE.   Plead not with me.   No plea the heart can
        bring
My own heart fails to urge.
    WINTER.   I made no plea.
The man I loved this morn for me is dead.

But there are those in England — far away —
Mother and sister —
    DRAKE.   Sir, you have my orders!
Henceforth no friends for me!   This traitor dies,
As traitors all should die, a traitor's death.
The man's life judges him, not you, nor I.
    VICARY.   Indeed, the manner of a man's departure,
Whether upon a war-horse or an ass,
Doth little matter, as it seems to me,
If those he leaves feel not the fashion of it.
Now, many a year that rope will throttle me,
Who am no traitor, and who like not well
What treachery this man's nature moved him to.
    DRAKE.   It seems to me that good men's lives are spent
In paying debts another makes for them.
I have my share.   Take you your portion, too.
Be just, I pray you, both to him and me.
Now, here 's a man that was my closest friend.
In Plymouth, ay, in London, ere we sailed,
Against the pledge myself had given the Queen,
He told the purpose of my voyage to Burleigh,
Pledging himself to wreck this enterprise,
Lest we should rouse these Spanish curs to bite.
That I do hold the warrant of the Queen
None but this traitor knew, and, knowing it,
Has set himself to brewing discontent,
Stirred mutiny amidst my crews, cast wide
The seed of discord, till obedience,
That is the feather on the shaft of duty,
Failed, and my very captains questioned me.
One man must die, or this great venture dies;
This man must die, or we go backward home,
Like mongrel dogs that fear a shaken stick.

WINTER.   Yet none of us have asked his life of you.
    DRAKE.   I ask it of myself; shall ask it, sir,
Knowing how vain and pitiful my plea.
I have said nothing of the darker charge,
The covert hints, the whispering here and there
Of how my death might please my Lord of Burleigh,
And settle all these mutinous debates.
I think 't was but an idle use of speech;
I think he meant not it should come to aught.
    WINTER.   Nor I.
    VICARY.   Nor I.   He hath confessed to all
Except this single charge.   That he denied.
    DRAKE.   And now no more!   And hope not I shall
            change.
Yet will I well consider all your words.
Rest you assured if there be any way
That both secures the safety of this voyage
And leaves this man to future punishment,
I shall not miss to find it.
    WINTER.   That were well.
I somewhat fear the temper of the men.
And these grave statesmen, closeted at home,
Have slight indulgence for the sterner needs
That whip us into what seems rash or cruel.
    DRAKE.   Ah, many a day 'twixt us and England lies,
And the peacemaker's blessing rests on time.
If death await me in the distant seas,
I shall not fear to meet a higher Judge.
If fortune smile upon our happy voyage,
No man in England that will dare to say
I served not well my country and my God;
The Queen will guard my honor as her own.
But, come what may, sirs, I shall act unmoved

By any dread of what the great may do,
Though we should prick this sullen Spain to war.
    VICARY.   Now, by St. George, could we but stir the
        Dons
To open fight!   The Queen has many minds,
But when the blades are out, and Philip strikes,
As strike he will, these wary counsellors
Will lose her ear amid the clash of swords.
    DRAKE.   Pray God that I do live to see the day
When all the might of England takes the sea,
And we, that are the falcons of the deep,
Shall tear these cruel vultures, till our beaks
Drip red with Spanish blood!
    VICARY.   May I be there!
    DRAKE (*gravely*).   Trust me, we all shall live to see
        that hour.
God gives us moments when the years to come
Lie easily open like a much-read book.
Oppressed with weight of care, in these last days
I seem to see beyond this bitter time.
We shall so carry us in yon Rome-locked seas
That all the heart of England shall be glad,
And the brown mothers of these priest-led Dons
Shall scare unruly children with my name.
And then, and then, I see a nobler hour.
A day of mightier battle, when their fleets
Shall fly in terror from our English guns,
And through the long hereafter we shall sail
Unquestioned lords of all the watery waste.
Oh, 't was a noble dream!
    VICARY.   But what were life
Without the splendid prophecy of dreams?
    DRAKE.   At least, a moment they have given release

From sadder thought of that which has to be.
The night is falling.   Get we now aboard.
To-morrow you shall have my final judgment.

*A cabin in the Pelican.   Early morning.   The day after
the trial and condemnation of* DOUGHTY.

DOUGHTY.   *Enter* WINTER.

DOUGHTY.   Is there an hour set?   When shall it be?
WINTER. That rests with you. Alas, too well you know
That, being charged with certain grave offences,
Of which, to our great grief, you are not cleared,
The court decreed your death.   Now, I am come
To offer you thus much of grace —
DOUGHTY.   As what?
WINTER.   Either to be at morning left ashore,
Or to be held till, at convenient time,
A ship may carry you to England, there
To answer for your deeds the Lords in Council;
Or will you take to be here done to death
As runs our sentence?
DOUGHTY.   Would I had no choice.
That 's a strange riddle!   Here be caskets three.
'T is like the story in the Venice tale.
Thank Francis Drake for me.   I 'll think upon it.
And send me Leonard Vicary with good speed.
WINTER.   Is there aught else a man may do for you?
DOUGHTY.   Yes, come no more until I send for you.
WINTER.   Have I in anything offended you?
DOUGHTY.   No, thou hast too much loved me; that is
    all.
The sting lies there.

WINTER.				I do not understand.
DOUGHTY.   And I too well.   Wilt send me Vicary?
WINTER (*aside*).   As strange a monitor for a mortal
     hour
As e'er a sick life's fancy hit upon.				[*Exit.*
     DOUGHTY (*alone*).   This is a sad disguise of clemency.
Death seemed a natural and safe conclusion.
As one serenely bound upon a voyage,
I had turned my back on all I did hold dear,
And looked no more to land.   I think, indeed,
Almost the very touch and sound of life
Seemed fading, as when sleep comes wholesomely.
Now I am in the wakened world again.
And all the blissful company of youth,
Love, friendship, hope, the mere esteem of men,
Beckon, and mock me like to sunlit fields
Seen from the wave-crests where a swimmer strives,
Struck hither, thither, by uneasy seas.
Christ to my help!   Ah, counsel always best.

How should I bide upon these heathen shores?
Knowing how frail I be, how strong a thing
Is the contagion of base men's customs.
Alas! alas!   I ever have been one
That wore the color of the hour's friend.
What! risk my soul, that hath an endless date,
For days or years of life?   That may not be.

What! home to England?   I, a tainted man;
That 's the gold casket where temptation lies.
There is no unconsidered blade of grass,
No little daisy, and no violet brief,
That does not hurt me with its sweet appeal.
				[*Walks to and fro.*

3*

I mind me of an evening — O my God!
No!   That way anguish waits.   I 'll none of that.
Twice, in my dreams last night, I saw her come;
And twice she cried, *"First Honor, and then love !"*
And came no more.   O Jesu, hear my prayer,
And let me never in that other world
Meet the sad verdict of those troubled eyes
I kissed to tears the day we sailed away.

Enter VICARY.

You are most welcome; sit beside me here.
I found my sentence in a woman's eyes.
   VICARY.   I understand.
   DOUGHTY.   How ever apt you are ;
That took my fancy always.   Now, it saves
The turning of a dagger in a wound.
I have chosen death.
   VICARY.   And chosen well, I think.
There was not one of us that said not so;
Not one but wishes life were possible.
   DOUGHTY.   Set that aside.   It is not possible.
And put no strain upon your natural self
To be another than the man you are.
Do you remember once a thing you said,—
How for the wise the soul has chapels four ?
One, that I name not.   One, a home of tears.
One, the grave shrine of high philosophy.
And one, where all the saints are jesters gay.
Smile on me when I die.   In that dim world
I am assured men laugh, as well they may,
To see this ant-heap stirred.   Oh, I shall look
To see you smile.

VICARY.   I pray you talk not thus.

DOUGHTY.   And wherefore not ?   A moment, only one,
The thought of England troubled my decision;
But that is over.   Yet, a word of home.
There is a maid in Devon — (*hesitates.*)   Pardon me.
When, by God's grace, you see her, as you must,
Tell her I loved her well — and what beside
I leave to you.   I shall not hear the tale.
Be gentle in the way of your report.
Ah me! by every cross a woman kneels;
I doubt not, Leonard, that some Syrian girl
Sobbed where the thief hung dying.   Now, good-by!
Go! and remember — I shall hold you to it.

[Exit VICARY.

Oft when the tides of life were at their full,
I have sat wondering what the ebb would be,
And what that tideless moment men call death.
I think it strange as nears the coming hour,
I willingly would fetch it yet more near.

VICARY (*without, as he goes on deck*).   He asks a smile
        where nature proffers tears.
I have laughed tears before, and may again.
Here dies a man who, like that heir of Lynne,
Has madly squandered honor, friendship, love,
And hath no refuge save the dismal rope.
Shall that bring other fortunes than he spent ?
Ah me! I loved him well, — and I must smile —
That will seem strange to men.   I sometimes wish
I could feel sure that Christ did ever smile.

Enter DRAKE.

DRAKE.   I come to hear thy choice.
DOUGHTY.   My choice is made.

Death, and no long delay.   And be not grieved;
You will — ah, well I know you — feel the hurt.
Were you to say, "Take life, take hope again,
Take back command," and bid me mend my ways,
The mercy were but vanity of kindness.
Never could I be other than I am;
Yet think of me as but the minute's traitor.
You have been merciful.   'T is I am stern.
Not you, but I, decree that I shall die.
A sudden weariness of life is mine;
Let me depart in peace —
    DRAKE.   Must it be so?
Another court may clear you.
    DOUGHTY.   Urge me not.
Another court!   There is but one high court
May clear my soul of guilt.   I go to God.
There shall be witnesses you cannot call.
Let this suffice.   No man can move me now;
And rest assured I never loved you more.
    DRAKE.   I thank you.   Now, what else?
    DOUGHTY.   I choose to die.
Go we ashore at noon, and eat at table,
Like gentlemen who speed a parting friend
Upon a pleasant and a certain voyage:
And I would share with you the bread of God.   [*Pauses.*
There is but one thing more —
    DRAKE.   Speak!   Oh, my God!
Except — except mere life, there is no thing
I would not give you; yea, to my own life.
    DOUGHTY.   You cannot think that I would ask my life?
    DRAKE.   Pardon, sweet gentleman, and sweeter friend.
    DOUGHTY.   There is a maid in Devon — oh, Frank
        Drake!

It must not be the gibbet and the rope!
The axe and block, men say, cure all disgrace.
   DRAKE.   So shall it be.
   DOUGHTY.   I knew you not unkind.
I pray you leave me now.   God prosper you.
You cannot know how kind a thing is death.

*Island of St. Julian.   Table spread at noon, under the
   trees.   DRAKE seated with DOUGHTY and other officers.
   In the background, a block, with the headsman, sailors,
   and others.*

        VICARY *and* WINTER *approach the table.*

VICARY.   Didst hear, John Winter, what he said to him?
WINTER.   I had but come ashore.   What said he,
     Leonard?
VICARY.   First, he would have the admiral take the
     bread;
Then, when in turn the priest did come to him,
He said, I would another man than you
Were here to give me of this bread of God.
Yet, as for this dear body of my Lord,
A pearl that 's carried in a robber's pouch
Doth lose no lustre; and with no more words
Took of the sacrament; and so to table.
                [*They approach sadly and in silence.*
   DOUGHTY (*looking up*). Come, come, I 'll none of this!
     Here are bent brows;
You go not thus to battle.   Shall one death
Disturb our appetites and spoil our mirth?

Am I not host? They 'll not be bid again
Who come not merry. (*Aside to* VICARY.) See you fail
      me not.
Some men ask prayers. I only ask a smile.
(*Aloud.*) Come, gentlemen, I put this hardship on you.
There might be many questions, much to say.
      DRAKE. I shall sit here forever, if you will,
But talk I cannot.
      DOUGHTY.   Nay, but that is strange.
'T is the glad privilege of the gentle-born
To see in death an honest creditor,
That any day may ask the debt of life.
What! must I make the talk? That 's naughty manners.
I never was a happier man than now.
There 's few among you shall have choice of deaths.
And you, Frank Drake,— if God should bid elect—
What way to death wouldst choose?
      DRAKE.   I do not know —
Not in my bed, please God.
      DOUGHTY.   Speak for him, Leonard.
I think my friend has shed his wits to-day.
Once he was readier —
      VICARY.   Were I Francis Drake,
When waves are wild and fly the bolts of war,
And timbers crash, and decks are bloody red,
Then would I pass, slain by my loving sea,
As died the hurt Greek by a friendly sword.
      DOUGHTY. Full bravely answered. Winter, what of
      you?
      WINTER. As God may will. I have no other thought.
      DOUGHTY (*to* VICARY). And what, dear jester, Leonard,
      what of you?
      VICARY. Oh, between kisses, of a morn of May,

Or in the merriest moment of a fight,
When blades are out, and the brave Dons stand fast —
Upon my soul, I can no more of this,
You ask too much of man.   I can no more!
[Leaves the table.

DOUGHTY.   Now, here 's a dull companion.   Go not
    yet —
Or go not far, and let not sorrow cheat me.
    VICARY.   Oh, I shall smile.   Rest you assured of that.
[Moves away.

DOUGHTY.   I thought he had been made of sterner stuff.
There 's a too gentle jester.   (*To* DRAKE.)   Think you,
    Frank,
That we shall meet in heaven ?
    DRAKE.   Such is my trust.
[They talk in whispers.

DOUGHTY (*aloud*).   The wind lies fair to south.   Friends,
    gentles, all,
It were not well to lose a prospering hour.
God send you kindly gales and gallant ventures!
Strike hard for me, John Winter!   When the Dons
Are thick about you and the fight goes ill,
Cry, This is for remembrance!   This, and this!
And you, dear Leonard, when the feast is gay
Drink double for your friend.   Be sure my lips
Shall share with yours the laughter and the cup.
[Rises, as do all.

Now, then: The Queen and England!   (*Drinks.*)   (*To*
    DRAKE.)   Take my love.
Still let me live a friendly memory —
Come with me.
    DRAKE.   No, I cannot, cannot come!
[Moves away.

Doughty (*To* Vicary, *as they walk to the block.*)   What,
    not a smile?   Not one?   That's better, Leonard,
Albeit of a rather sickly sort.
Come hither, Francis Drake. (Drake *approaches.*) Good-
    by, dear friend.
    [*Kisses him on both cheeks.   Kneels, and the axe falls.*
Vicary.   God rest this soul!
Winter.   Amen!
Drake.   Christ comfort me!

PHILIP VERNON

THE INN

July 21, 1588

When Bess was queen, and the Bishop of Rome and the King of Spain were troubling our England, the cowls were many in the land, and knew how to pull the lamb-skins well around them.

One of these wolves, of a summer morning, walked, halting a little, to and fro under the great oaks between the Vernon Arms and the road. His sheep's clothing was a burgher's gray hose and doublet; but he was not right, red English, having of late come out of Spain, yellow-cheeked and lean. He looked down the highway to the bridge, and then with his eyes followed the river curves to the sea, whence, he smiled to think, the great Armada would come, in time to help certain wicked schemes, and set the cowls again in high places. Then, less pleased, he cast looks at a gallant in blue with yellow points, who sat at a table a little way from the inn. This gentle had a good leg and was high-colored and young. At times

he drummed on the table, or uneasily cast down his
cap, and once half drew his sword, then presently, as
if impatient, drove it back into its sheath.   But whether
he yawned or sat quiet in thought, Hugh Langmayde,
the priest in gray, lost naught of what he did; and at
last, still watching the gallant, he fell to open talk with
himself after this fashion:

" Soon shall you stretch those sturdy limbs, my boy,
And for your rapier find a brave employ.
I am too old, too feeble,— you alone
Shall do this sacred errand of our Lord,
Avenge his murdered saints, and from her throne
Cast down this Jezebel, of men abhorred.
I thought not, when I taught thy youth to know
One creed, one king, and questionless to go
Where Church or king decreed, that you and I,
As if we were but one, like head and hand,
Should free this England which doth fettered lie,
And give to God another Christian land.

" What if my weapon fail me ?   Restless grown,
He asks now this, now that, would have me own
My purpose,— hath the waywardness of youth,—
Is wilful, petulant, or grave.   In truth,
It shall mean little when he comes to learn
What splendid bribe an eager hand may earn,
And at my will he goes my way to win
God's gold or this world's guerdon.   Is it sin
To shudder thinking death may be his lot ?
My task were easier if he loved me not.
God's priest should die unloved; should have no fears,
Live without memories, and know not tears."

Herewith the young gallant, Philip Vernon by name,
calls out to a servant of the inn:

  " Fetch me some ale, good fellow. Set it here —
  Two brimming tankards. See 't is cool and clear.
  How fresh the air! I like this breezy shade
  The better since by sunshine it is made.
  Our Spanish saying aptly hits my mark:
       Soar with the hawk,
       Sing with the lark;
       Eyes for the sunlight,
       Lips for the dark.
  St. James! I 'm weary of my unused self,
  Left like a dull book on a dusty shelf.
  I hate this corner life! Now, by the Cid!
  I must be more discreet. I 'm sternly bid
  To hide my name because my name may lead —
  I know not why — to questions that exceed
  Our skill to answer fitly.— Master Hugh,
  Come taste with me our host's last autumn brew."

Hearing his call, the priest, smiling, sits down beside
the young man he had been gravely watching; and
taking of the ale,— but with a wry face, for in Spain
he had learned dislike of such honest English drink,—
he lays a hand on the lad's knee, and says to him:

  " What troubles you, my Philip ? "

PHILIP VERNON.   We have strayed
  Now here, now there, in England, while you played
  A game, good Father, somewhat like the chess
  Our prior loved. You smile on me,— my guess

    Has hit the butt ?   Here moves a pawn, and there,
    Haply, a bishop.   Then the queen —

HUGH LANGMAYDE.   Beware !
    You chatter lightly, call me " Father "— try
    To lose the habit; that way dangers lie.
    One careless word, and rack and axe or rope
    Await us; and so dies the saintliest hope
    This misruled kingdom knows.   To die were gain
    For me; and yet God's work, the Church, our Spain,
    The king, our master, own me till this strife
    With evil ends.   Be patient !

PHILIP VERNON.   Oh, this life
    Of masquerade, and lies, and daily fear
    Of what I know not, wearies me !

HUGH LANGMAYDE.   -   Not here
    The time or place for truant tongues.   Speak low,
    Or, better, change the talk.

PHILIP VERNON.   Soon I must know.

The priest, emptying his tankard and pushing it from
him, looks askance at his companion, and therewith
says, as if to quiet his mind with other thought:

    " Poor stuff is this beside our convent wine.
    You need but squeeze the ripeness of the vine
    To drain its reddest blood : — torment the grains
    God meant for bread, and lo! you get for pains
    This boorish drink."

And now is heard a quick rattle of horse-hoofs, and a
score of gentles come down the road at speed.   Some

are armed, and more are clad in gay doublets, with
plumes unmeet for riding — sign of haste, perchance.
Red, blue, and purple, with glint of steel, flash through
the yellow dust, aglow with the sun of noon, as the
riders go by the inn. But three draw rein beneath
the oaks; whereon this Philip Vernon leaps up, over-
setting a flagon of good ale, and crying:

> "Look, look, ye saints!   That roan,
> And that dark chestnut,— his who rode alone,—
> Are worth a prince's ransom!   See — they stay
> To breathe their horses.   He with plume of gray
> Hath the best seat.   Red Doublet 's all untrussed:
> He must have ridden hard; and, see — the dust!
> Why ride they thus? "

As he speaks the servants and landlord come hastily
forth from the inn.

HUGH LANGMAYDE.   Hush!   Out comes all the hive.
   You shall know shortly.

RED DOUBLET.   Ho! are none alive?
   The Armada 's off the Lizard.   Look aright
   That all your headland beacons blaze to-night!
   These be Lord Howard's orders.   Ho, there, quick!
   Ale, ale — three flagons!

GRAY PLUME.   Wine, wine!   I am sick
   With dusty thirst.

RED DOUBLET.   And I could drink a tun.

   As they sit in the saddle, the fair maid of the inn
   brings to each his flagon of ale.

4

One Armed in a Cuirass.   Keep me some kisses.

Red Doublet.   I shall ask but one.

Maid.   Oh, my good lords, there shall not lack a prayer
      From one poor wench that God your lives will spare.
      Alas! alas! I 'm mightily afraid
      Scarce will be left a man to kiss a maid!
      This dreadful war! —

Gray Plume.   Now, by the gods! but *he*
      Will truly have his hands full.— This for thee!
      — The admiral rides hard, and we must sup
      Aboard the ships.— Thanks for the stirrup-cup.

            A hand on the bridle,
            A cup of good sack;
            Pray keep those lips idle
            Until I come back.

Red Doublet.

            Here 's a curse on Romish rats!
            Here 's good luck to English cats!

Then he who wore a cuirass, as they ride away, sings
lustily:

            " 'T is always pleasant weather
            In the company of wine;
            And the mile-stones run together,
            And the roughest road is fine,
            In the company of wine.
            For no man owes a shilling,
            And all the land is thine.
            And every lip is willing,
            In the company of wine."

LANDLORD.   God keep our England merry!

PHILIP VERNON.   Who be they
    Who ride so hotly at full noon of day?

LANDLORD.   Howard of Effingham, Lord High Admiral,
    A lover of the Pope, and yet withal ·
    A sturdy gentle, English to the core,
    And hates a Spaniard.   What can one say more?

HUGH LANGMAYDE.   Where rides he now?

LANDLORD.   To Plymouth Port.   The coast
    Is all astir.   The great Armada's host
    Is come at last.   God help our little fleet!

HUGH LANGMAYDE.   God help the right and England!

LANDLORD.   Aye.

PHILIP VERNON.   Retreat
    Could scarce fly swifter than these gallants ride.
    I would, good Father, I were at their side.

Hereon Hugh Langmayde and Philip together leave
the inn and highroad, and as they slowly climb a little
hill, and begin to enter into a wood of oak, the priest
makes this answer to the lad's vexation of spirit:

    " Peace, boy!   Thy ways are in a nobler path.
    They ride to death.   Already God's stern wrath
    Is gathering for their ruin on the seas.
    Come with me, Philip.   There among the trees
    Talk will be safer.   Come,—the hour of fate
    Is near at hand.   You shall no longer wait
    To hear the tale I ofttimes promised you

When, the day's lessons done, at fall of dew
Above Grenada from the convent wall
We watched the paling gold of evening crawl
From peak to peak, while o'er the Vega's plain
The dusking shadows marched. Thus, not in vain,
When all the lower world is dim and gray,
God sets the promise of another day
On those his Church has taught to live above
Man's mist of passions — aye, and earthly love."

THE CHASE

As they move through the wood the priest pauses at
last where from a hillside the more open forest commands a broad view of green fields, the river with
hills beyond, and to left the distant sea.

PHILIP VERNON.   How still it is, how full of peace, how far
From the rude hurry and alarm of war !
See what an airy build the mountains show
When over them the broad-winged shadows go.
A land to love !

HUGH LANGMAYDE.   Ay, and a land to serve
With noble deeds that may indeed deserve
This splendid recompense. A land to win
Back from its damned covenant with sin.
Sit here, my son. Once this great fallen tree
Looked o'er the land, and could no equal see.
Lord of the forest, underneath its shade
The wanderer rested. Here both man and maid
Found shelter. High among its eaves

The birds sang hymns which God alone had taught,
Or nested peaceful in its spreading leaves,
Where sun and rain His mystic wonders wrought.

PHILIP VERNON.   I see not clearly, Father —

HUGH LANGMAYDE.   No, my son,
A nation wandered from the fold, undone,
Sunk in delusion, waits full many a year —
Waits for God's hour to read that riddle clear.
Once, in this land, the Church spread broad and high
The mighty leafage of her destiny —
Why mince my meaning?   Lo! a brutal king
Struck, and the splendid trunk lies moldering.

PHILIP VERNON.   And still I see not wherefore —

HUGH LANGMAYDE.   Ah! The rest
Attends your hearing.   Soon this land oppressed
Shall know deliverance.   O'er yon waiting sea
Great Philip's viceroy comes.   To you, to me,
God grants on land as sure a victory.
And now, my Philip, hear me to an end.
In happier times I shall be glad to mend
My broken story of your life.   To-day
Accept a briefer tale.   I have grown gray
Now many years, since through these woods I fled,
A hunted priest, this land where God seemed dead.
Pursuit was hot; my boat lay off the shore;
A bullet caught me as I plunged; a score
Flew over.   Still this crippled leg, my lad,
Keeps me a memory not wholly sad;
For, as I bleeding strove, a boy's white face
Rose in a black wave's hollow.   By God's grace

I clutched your hand, my son. The boat's crew caught
The pair of us, half drowned ; and so God wrought
This great deliverance. I think the tide
Trapped you at play on yonder sands. I tried
To set you safe upon the coast. 'T was vain ;
I could not do the thing I would. In Spain
The fevered life I scarce had hope to save
Came back as if new born, as if the grave
That was so near had taken half away
Your boyhood's recollections. Need I say
Love to my heart came easily ? I yearned
To win the love my double help had earned.

PHILIP VERNON.

You have it in full measure. Now at last
I shall know all. Is this to end that past
Of doubts, and dreams, and fears ? Before my eyes,
Lo! as you speak, faint memories arise.

HUGH LANGMAYDE. Trust them not wholly.

PHILIP VERNON.   I 've a vision wild
Of ravening seas ; and them beyond, a child,
I live again glad days. I seem indeed
Like one who, waking from a dream, has need
To piece it out with thinking. Who is he —
A stately gentleman, I strive to see,
And cannot clearly, though he smiles ? Stay, stay !
Was that my father ? As you love me, say !
Was it my father ? Ah ! so much is dim ;
But that has substance. Let me go to him —
Yes, you and me together. I can hear
How he will thank you.

Hugh Langmayde.   Wherefore should I fear
    To know at last if I have truly read
    The soul I trained?

Philip Vernon.   Why hesitate?   You dread
    To speak some truth!

Hugh Langmayde.   You do not ask to know
    Your name and station?

Philip Vernon.   Let that matter go.
    Where is my father?

Hugh Langmayde.   Can I give the dead?

Philip Vernon.   Dead!   And how long ago?

Hugh Langmayde.   Two years, 't is said.

Philip Vernon.   Dead!   Two years dead!   Know you
    the hour, the day?

Hugh Langmayde.   I know them not.

Philip Vernon.   And I may have been gay,
    And laughed, or diced, the hour he passed away!

As he ceases, the priest, who has watched him moodily,
touches his arm as if in appeal, whereupon the young
man exclaims:

    " Nay, do not speak.   How very often here
    He must have wandered, and when death drew near
    Thought of this son in heaven!   Some might fear
    To cheat the living and the dead.   Despair

> Seems but a thing of earth. How could you dare
> To cast its shadow on a world beyond ? "

HUGH LANGMAYDE.

> My more than child, ah, when this earthly bond
> Of love is severed, surely God has power
> To heal the sorrows of earth's little hour.

As if not hearing the priest, and with yet more of anger,
the younger man continues :

> "My God ! Those years of youth when I in Spain,
> And he in England, took our ignorant pain
> To God, and never knew what statecraft stole
> Of nature's honest store ! You took the whole —
> All, all of love two lives had ! By my soul,
> I think that you must see forevermore
> A gray-haired man who walks beside the shore,
> And of the silent ocean asks his dead ! "

HUGH LANGMAYDE.   You wrong me, Philip.

PHILIP VERNON.   No, I should have fled —
> Oh, long ago — had I known all, but now
> 'T is past the cure of word or deed. Ah, how —
> How could you hurt me thus ?

HUGH LANGMAYDE.   I did God's will —
> His, and the king's.

PHILIP VERNON.   The king's ! Could he fulfil
> What home and father would have given ?

HUGH LANGMAYDE.   My son,
> Pray you consider. Could I aught have done
> Against the king's command ?   I did not dare.

What lack you else the gentle-born should bear?
Head, hand, and eye have had such anxious care
As only Spain can give.   What English peer
Has court or camp trained better?   Do you fear
To cross a sword with any?   Who, I ask,
Can match you mounted?   Mine the graver task
To see you lack not learning.   Pause, reflect;
Not without prayer I acted.   You suspect
Some treason? — Philip, where you stand to-day
The soil is yours.   That castle old and gray,
The river's sweep, hill, forest, town, and lake,
In God's good time are yours, my son, to take.
See where yon eagle o'er the mountain soars!
Scarce can he look beyond what land is yours.
Set foot in stirrup, draw your father's sword:
A thousand men will follow you, my lord!
Low at your word will bow that tavern churl,
And I shall bid you welcome, my Lord Earl!

PHILIP VERNON.   Earl! Lord!   These manors mine?
    You could not jest?

HUGH LANGMAYDE.
    Not I, my lord; you match with England's best.
    The proofs that give you these the Church will guard
    Till one proud day of triumph and reward.

PHILIP VERNON.
    'T is a strange tale, and sad as it is strange.
    I would a braver love had bid you change
    Those home-reft years I have forever lost.
    You should have counted well the cruel cost,
    And saved my life this pain.   Oh, bitter day!

Vexed with a convent life, made next to play
A page's part, or squire's, left to say
I knew not who I was, or high or base,
Until, worn out, I smote a snarling face
That mocked my birth as knowing some disgrace;
For text of thought he got a rapier thrust.
Alas!   I gave you all my boyhood's trust,
And thus you used it!

HUGH LANGMAYDE.   Philip, that same breath
With which you question me, I gave; the death
From which I saved you set a silent grave
Between the lost life and the life I gave.
You have a father.   Have I seemed to be
Less than a father?

PHILIP VERNON.   None were that to me.
I have been hurt enough: 't were well to spare
These convent subtleties.   In England fair
I tread where men are free, breathe lighter air.
Much have I learned no Spanish cloister taught,
More have I heard that Spain had never thought.

HUGH LANGMAYDE.
Ill have you heard.   Not all my tale is told.
Let but the Church her lifting hand withhold,
And you are lost!   Be her true son, be bold,
And these broad lands are yours to win when she
Who rules this kingdom dies.   For you, for me,
The path lies straight.   But yestermorn in prayer
I asked of God a sign, and found it where
At close of eve I sat and saw the sun
Set in a sea of blood ere day was done—
A cloud-born cross above.   Oh, dark shall be

The Church's reckoning when yon loathing sea
Its unrepentant dead spits on the shore,
And the long torment of the galley's oar
Shall chain the souls that live! What seek you more?

PHILIP VERNON.
What more indeed!   I went your way, not mine,
Knew but one prince, sought never to divine
Your reasons, nor the policy of state
That without explanation ruled my fate.
Answer my manhood outright!   Be more true
To one who loves you!   Give me all love's due.
What keeps us here?   I will not be denied.
An English noble!   Wherefore should I bide
Upon your will my father's lands to claim
While pope and king play out a doubtful game?

HUGH LANGMAYDE.
You ask untimely.   Shall the arrow know
The stern commission of the bended bow?
In God's good time—

PHILIP VERNON.   The hour that is, is good;
No other answers.   Ah, I think you should
Have known me better.   Speak!   By good St. James
I 'm very weary of these priestly games!
I take it that, as well as one can see
Through this dim, wordy haze of mystery,
I rest mere Philip Vernon until death
Strikes with your hand, or mine, Elizabeth.
Is that your meaning, Father?   If 't is so,
We part to-day.   Oh, I must clearly know
What the cowl's caution hid from me.   Be frank,

As you were wont.   Give me new cause to thank
The man within the priest.

HUGH LANGMAYDE.   Go, if you will.
If God and king, my danger, and these years
Of love lack force to teach you duty still,
Go!   Leave me here to peril and to tears.

PHILIP VERNON.
Love is not bondage; and, for that harsh king,
I owe him hate alone.— Oh, do not wring
My heart with more of grief!   Tell me the tale
Of who and what I am.   There cannot fail
To be some light, some guidance, some poor path
Out of this mystery!

HUGH LANGMAYDE.   The Lord's just wrath
Will punish this revolt.

PHILIP VERNON.   I do not change
As shifts the weather-vane!   Hold you it strange
I should learn English ways?— but yesterday
I fell to talking with a gallant gay —
Upon my soul, a rare, sweet gentle he,
Hidalgo born, a flower of chivalry,
Simple and courteous, melancholic now,
And now as merry as a May-day queen,
With chat of court and camp and state, a brow
Just helmet-dinted, o'er an eye serene
That made swift capture of my inward thought
Before a word my tardy tongue had wrought.
Sir Philip Sidney he!   We talked full long
Of Spain and England, of what cruel wrong
My jailor Philip did, and soon we passed

To speak of Spain's Armada.   "Now," at last,
"Thank God for war!" he cried.   "The die is cast!
And you, a gentleman, young sir,"— to me,—
"Sit in a tavern sad, while history
Is in the mighty making."   Then he quaffed
A cup of wine.   "Is it a woman?"—laughed
Because, shame-flushed, I, angry, answered not.
"Pardon," he added.   "Cast the iron lot
Of war, and take with us the splendid chance.
God and the queen, a sword, a horse, a lance!
Your name, fair sir?"   I could but hang my head.
What could I answer?   "I have none," I said.
—You bade me hide it, you were well obeyed.
He touched my shoulder kindly: "Many a man
Has found a proud name where the red blood ran.
Aimless and nameless?   Get you aim and name
Where two great nations play war's royal game.
Come with me on the morrow."

HUGH LANGMAYDE.   And you cried,
    Vade Sathanas!

PHILIP VERNON.   Nay, I naught replied,
    Or scarce a word.   By Heaven, I had been right
    To follow loyally that gallant knight
    Where England calls her sons!

HUGH LANGMAYDE.   What, must I fail
    For this boy folly? — You shall hear the tale —
    Aye, all of it a tender heart withheld
    To give more gently in the happier hour
    God's victory will bring.   Ah, then dispelled
    Were half its anguish!

PHILIP VERNON.   Speak!　I have the power
　To bear life's very worst.

HUGH LANGMAYDE.   Is this the lad
　I saved from death ?　Defiant, reckless, mad,
　You ask you know not what.

PHILIP VERNON.   But I will know,
　And on the minute, or by Heaven! I go
　To claim what rights are mine.

HUGH LANGMAYDE.   Take then the fate
　That bides for him who does not know to wait
　On God's maturing hour.　Alas, poor fool!
　Art nameless ?　Yes!　This, on my oath to rule
　A froward nature, by the rood I swear!
　Didst hear ? — the rood !　Thou art a bastard born !
　Art fitly answered ?　Didst thou think to dare
　To cross my purpose,— thou, a child of scorn !

PHILIP VERNON.
　What fool's device is this ?　A little while
　I was my lord, am now a bastard vile.
　Another man this pleasant tale should rue
　All the brief life I 'd leave him.

HUGH LANGMAYDE.   Still, 't is true.

PHILIP VERNON.　By Heaven, thou liest!

HUGH LANGMAYDE.   Have I ever lied ?

PHILIP VERNON.　God knows, not I.

HUGH LANGMAYDE. I should have naught replied.
　A priest, and lie !　It seems a challenge cheap.

Tears! — that is wiser.   Oh, I did but keep
My better tidings back.   Alas, no friend
Could hide this ill news long, or know to mend
A wrong of birth; but when, in God's good time,
Your arm has freed a land, and yonder chime
Rings in our king, rings out this fated queen,
Then she who owns this broad domain has seen
Her last of greatness.

PHILIP VERNON.   Who?

HUGH LANGMAYDE.   Your cousin,— she,
Your father's heir, your steward now till we
Win Philip's battle, and his potent hand
Strikes from your shield the bastard's shameful band,
Gives all I promised, honor, wealth, and place,—
All that men covet in this earthly race.
Go! I have done.   Think on it for the week
We linger here.   Be prudent, slow to speak,
Watchful and wise.   God's hand is on the helm,
And I, the church, the king, this woeful realm
Will need your help.

PHILIP VERNON.   I would that I could doubt
One who has never lied.   I stand without
The pale of honor and the hopes of men,
A nameless creature, bred to turn again
And rend the race that gave me, with this stain,
Intrepid honor, proud desires,— in fine,
The manly virtues of a noble line.
Poor useless jewels! all in vain their worth.
I had been happier made of meaner earth.

HUGH LANGMAYDE.

 Nay, nay; but that 's not so. Land, title, place,
 Are yours to gain when, by God's helping grace,
 That Spanish dagger at your side strikes quick.
 Oh, I can see — can *see* this heretic
 Roll bloody in the dust, and hear the land
 Ring joy from spire to spire!

PHILIP VERNON. .   I understand
 At last too well. No more for me the prayer
 To be delivered from temptation's snare.

HUGH LANGMAYDE. Sad words, my son!

PHILIP VERNON.   Yet heed them well: they say
 The malice of dishonor. If I prey
 Like maggots on the carcass whose decay
 Begot my baseness, who shall blame the banned?
 What would'st thou of me? Is it head or hand?

HUGH LANGMAYDE.

 How beautiful the evening is! Behold
 The dim, green meadows take the dewy gold,
 While in the hollows little pools of mist
 Are gathering slowly where the cattle list
 The milky summons of the twilight horn.
 Look! 'T is your heritage! Some men are born
 Ignobly great; some in one matchless hour
 Scale at a bound the heights of human power.

PHILIP VERNON.

 A bastard lord! Not I! Awhile ago
 You took from life its beauty and its glow.
 How could you mock my fancies with a tale

Such as my boyhood dreamed, and let it fail
In such a slough of shame ?   Love, honor, hope —
You took them all, and offer now a rope !
'T is kind !   I was a man, and you have made
A fiend of whom you well might be afraid
If you had lied.— You could not.— Take me !   Use
My strength,·my will, my hate, as you may choose.

HUGH LANGMAYDE.   There 's time to think.

PHILIP VERNON.   Not I !   What next ?

HUGH LANGMAYDE.   Wilt swear ?

PHILIP VERNON
    Aye, for an oath is only empty air.
    Once 't was a thing to spend a life for.   I
    Am but a hireling now mere gold may buy,
    Or any Judas coin.

As Philip speaks he makes a move as if to go, but, of
a sudden returning, looks the priest steadily in the
face, and with a troubled countenance says to him :

                    " One word to close
An hour the damned might pity.   I suppose —
— There was a mother —
                    — Well ? "

HUGH LANGMAYDE.   Long, long ago
    Your mother died.

PHILIP VERNON.   'T is all I care to know.
    Loved, sinned, and died !   May God's sweet pity rest

5

Upon the shameless woman from whose breast
I drew the milk of sorrows!

Hugh Langmayde.   Sleep and prayer
Will bring you peace, yet leave you power to dare
A deed with which the world shall ring. Good night.
In three days I return again. To right
Your pathway lies toward the inn. Invite
No comment. Guard yourself. Good night.

As the priest moves away Philip Vernon replies tardily:

                                   "Good night.
What night is good to me? Alas, what day?"

THE GARDEN

Walking slowly away, Philip Vernon takes his sadness
deeper into the woods, and wandering far, comes at last
to a great garden wall.   There he stays awhile, until sweet
odors, rising, seem to call him; and with no more thought
of what may lie beyond, he leaps the wall, and stands
amid the flowers, waist-deep in hollyhock and golden
plume.

"I wonder somewhat was my life then gay
When here I chased the butterflies, and trod
These garden lanes, or rolled upon the sod,
A thoughtless boy?   I 'll take, for memory's sake,
One rose of home."

Hither into the garden at this moment comes Lord
Francis Grey, in red velvet, with a face aflame to match.

Seeing this gallant across a hedge of sweet-peas, he slips
the collar of his humor and sets it on to bite in this wise:

      "Ho! Who are you who break
These castle bounds at will? Ho there! Take heed!
Didst hear me?"

PHILIP VERNON.   Yes. Your words, I think, exceed
 The owner's power to back his tongue at need.

LORD GREY.
 My cousin is the chancellor's ward; none dare
 Avenge an insult here.

PHILIP VERNON.   Then wiser 't were
 To keep the tongue in ward. You question one
 That hath lost touch of fear beneath the sun.
 The chancellor? What care I? Your cousin? Mine?
 Now, why not mine? Suppose, to cap the jest,
 We fight for cousinship: who wins is best.
 And is she fair, this woman? Doth her talk,
 Like thine, lack breeding? This smooth garden walk
 Is broad enough to serve us. Draw, on guard!
 And let my rapier teach your tongue such ward
 As hasty manners lack.

LORD GREY.   Have then your will!
 Or mad or foolish, you 're a man to kill!
 Yet to cross blades with one unknown or base —

PHILIP VERNON.
 Base! By my soul! Were you his very Grace,
 This same lord chancellor, his mighty face
 Should know my glove!

Lord Grey, having already drawn his sword, advances
and lunges smartly at Philip, at the same time crying out :

"By Heaven, you are dead!"

PHILIP VERNON.
    A thing, observe, less easily done than said.
    A step more near, a trifle yet more quick,
    And you had boasted shrewdly. Oh, the trick
    Is stale. In Spain we lunge this wise, and then
    A thrust in tierce — Well parried! — Good, again!
    I take it firmly close to hilt; the wrist
    Well up; then deftly, with this cunning twist,
    Give point. Your sword-arm? By the Cid, 't is sad!
    That stops the sport.

LORD GREY.   'T is not so very bad
    But that a day will cure it.

At this he sees men break through the shrubbery and
come running toward them, whereon he says to Philip :

"Get you gone!
    There, by the terrace, and across the lawn."

PHILIP VERNON.   And wherefore?

LORD GREY.   Hasten, leap the brook and fly!

As Philip stands with no mind to escape, the steward
and many servants gather around them.

STEWARD.
    What means this brawl?   My lady asks, not I.

LORD GREY.
    'T is but a trifle. Come with me. The blame
    I shall stand father to. This way. The dame ?—

STEWARD.   Is in the eastern gallery.

LORD GREY.   ·   Best it were
    You tarry here awhile. My cousin fair
    Has many humors: which shall be our share
    No man has skill to tell. Her No, or Yes,
    A hundred years' experience could not guess.

With these words Lord Grey leaves Philip Vernon at the
entrance of the castle, where, with sudden interest in his
face, he looks about him, and at last says:

    " How most familiar 't is ! There the great hall,
    The windowed gallery, and on the wall
    The gray stone dial. There the poplars tall.
    Now, as I live, the willows and the brook !
    And there my father sat the while I took
    His great horse o'er it — much I feared the leap.
    How memory wakens as if from a sleep !
    The stair ! Sir Lancelot's armor ! That brave lance
    Lord Arthur carried to the wars in France.
    One night I touched it — on the floor it crashed,
    And the fierce strife of Crécy round me clashed
    With din of spear and steed, and shock and blow,
    And clang of knights that set my heart aglow."

A SERVANT.
    My lady bids me say for her, Sir Knight,
    She waits you in the gallery. Here, to right.

5*

Philip Vernon enters the picture-gallery, and sees at the
far end Elizabeth Vernon speaking with Lord Grey.

LORD GREY.   The errant knight waits yonder.

ELIZABETH VERNON.   Let him wait;
    'T is a man's business.   Now, I pray you, state
    What means this quarrel?

LORD GREY.   Ask of yonder man.

ELIZABETH VERNON.
    Man!   Why not gentle, cousin?   Never ran
    Mean blood in one like him, who there, at ease,
    In courteous silence stands.   Now, an you please,
    What more, my lord?

LORD GREY.   I found the man you see
    A-picking roses 'neath your balcony.

ELIZABETH VERNON.
    Why, this should hang him on the nearest tree!
    And my blunt cousin picked, for company,
    A quarrel.   That is easier than a rose.
    He found a thorn, as rather plainly shows
    That crimsoned sleeve.

LORD GREY.   Now look you, Cousin Bess,
    Your jest is but ill-timed.   Let me confess
    I made this quarrel when, my heart aflame,
    You left me stinging with your words.   The blame
    Is yours, fair cousin.   Shafts in anger sent
    May find mad errands ere their force be spent.

ELIZABETH VERNON.   Now, by our Lady!

LORD GREY.   Nay, but hear me still;
    And let your servants know at least your will
    That yonder venturer go on his way,
    And no such words escape as haply may
    Breed risks for me.

ELIZABETH VERNON.   I shall consider first
    When I have questioned him, nor shall the worst
    Be worse, my lord, than what has chanced. You
        claim
    Such license here as men may justly blame.
    Best choose a fitter place, a feebler prey,
    To hawk at with your anger.

At this Lord Grey, turning to one side, mutters to himself
as he glances down the hall at Philip:

                              " He shall pay
    His debt and yours, my lady.   Those who court
    Tongue-tilts with wounded creatures, find the sport
    A doubtful venture.   ' By the Cid,' he swore;
    Mocked me with Spanish sword-play.   Ah ! my score
    Is easily settled."

ELIZABETH VERNON.   You are silent, sir ?

LORD GREY.
    I school my hurt heart to soft words, for her
    Whose lightest word my very blood can stir;
    And if in aught I have exceeded, rest
    Assured I meant it not.   Were it not best
    I set this errant knight without your gate ?

Elizabeth Vernon.
    No.   I would speak with him.   Pray do not wait:
    My temper 's of the shortest.   On your way
    Send me the gentleman ; and, cousin, stay! —
    I 'll have no gossip.

Lord Grey, sullenly walking down the hall, pauses beside
Philip Vernon:

                  "We shall meet again!
    My lady waits.   And for those tricks of Spain
    I shall be readier.   Good day."

Philip Vernon.   'T is plain
    I was imprudent.

As he moves up the hall toward Elizabeth Vernon, she
watches him, speaking to herself the while:

                "Where saw I those eyes,
    Large, gray, and watchful?   Some elate surprise
    Is in their gaze.

            I pray you pardon us
    This most uncourteous hour.   It is not thus
    We welcome unknown comers.   I have heard
    You would be nameless : so is every bird
    That wings my garden.   And 't is said you stole
    A rose or two.   If that be all — the whole
    Of this last hour's sin — I hold you shriven ;
    Ay, and that lesson to a fool forgiven."

Philip Vernon.   I thank you, madam.

Elizabeth Vernon.   Am I, sir, a book,
    That you would read me with that eager look ?

PHILIP VERNON.
    Oft have I read you.   I am wont to share
    My idle hours with you.

ELIZABETH VERNON.   Indeed, sir?
PHILIP VERNON.   Where
    The chase o'erhangs your garden, oft I sit
    And read you page by page, nor want I wit
    To comment on your sweetness.

ELIZABETH VERNON.   You are bold
    Past nurtured manners.

PHILIP VERNON.   Pardon me, I told
    But half my heart says.

ELIZABETH VERNON.   Sir, an hour ago
    We were but strangers.

PHILIP VERNON.   Ere the sand shall flow
    Another hour, we shall be strange once more,
    And ever strange.

ELIZABETH VERNON.   Is this some Quixote, mad,
    That loved and lost, and cannot live it o'er?
    — By all the saints, I think it very sad
    To see good wits astray.

PHILIP VERNON.   Are mine astray?
    It seems they wandered wisely.   Let them say
    What saner wits would shun.   The shyest maid
    That ever loved, and, loving, grew afraid,
    Would braver be to set her love in words.
    Mine hath uncertain wings, like new-born birds,
    And may not think on heaven.   Forgive, forget!

Think me a lover wild of brain, once met
In some freaked tale of eld — a prince of fay
That came, and loved, and lost, and rode away.

ELIZABETH VERNON.   That 's a wild riddle.

PHILIP VERNON.   Time owns not the hour
    Shall give some buds the answer of a flower.
    You have been very gentle with a man
    Who dare not name himself, who never can
    Do more than thank your kindness.   I am one
    Accursed and nameless till my days be done.
    How you have helped me you may never know,
    Nor what you saved us both.   I came your foe;
    More than your friend I leave.   Just Heaven knows
    How sad my life has been.   Let this one rose
    I took for — well, no matter — let me guard
    This rose for memory.   It will make less hard
    The strife of days to come.

ELIZABETH VERNON.   You speak like one
    By some strange cruelty of fate undone.
    Be plain.

PHILIP VERNON.   I may not farther.

ELIZABETH VERNON.   Then take hence
    A woman's prayer for peace.   There 's no offence
    In honest words, and none did ever speak
    Words that more sadly touched me.   I am weak
    Where women should be.   There 's no need to say
    'T is but mere weakness.   Must you, then, away?

PHILIP VERNON.

>I dare not— must not — linger.   Here to stay
>Were to tempt folly.   Ah, you may divine
>All that my honor bids my heart resign.
>So fades another dream.   Alack! alack!
>Dreams are but dreams — we may not dream them
>>back.
>Take you an exile's thanks.   This gracious hour
>Shall live remembered.

As he walks away, Elizabeth Vernon whispers to herself:

>>>>" Still those eyes have power
>To tease dull memory with some strange surmise.
>And trouble expectation."

Philip, walking down the gallery and seeing the portraits
on the walls, stops abruptly ; whereupon Elizabeth Vernon adds :
>>>>" What surprise
>So moves this stranger ? "

PHILIP VERNON.   There 's the Lady Blanche,

>That held the castle ; there the baron stanch,
>Who rode to battle laughing.   Am I heir,
>Through him, of that mad merriment I share
>When swords are out and death is in the air ?
>My father's face !   So gracious too !— by Heaven !
>Now I can say, " Be all thy sin forgiven ! "
>And thank the gentle hand that swept away
>The desperate counsels of a darker day.

For a moment he stands before the portrait, and then goes
slowly down the gallery, and leaves the castle.

THE CHASE

Two days later, in the afternoon of the summer day,
Philip Vernon walks here and there in the great forest,
and at last, leaning against a tree, speaks thus to himself:

> " How wearily the hours go by!   This chase
> I haunt, as haunts a bird the lonely place
> That holds her pillaged nest."

Seeing him of a sudden, Elizabeth Vernon comes timidly
through the thickets.

ELIZABETH VERNON.   I thought, Sir Knight,
  You had been far from this.   I would quick flight
  Had set you miles away.   I more than fear
  My cousin's treachery.   What keeps you here
  Is much in question, and in days of war
  The questioned man is lost.   You should be far
  From this to-morrow.

PHILIP VERNON.   Not while dangers grow
  So thick about one frail old man.

ELIZABETH VERNON.   I know
  Of you, of him, no more than what I hear
  From one who hates you, yet enough to fear
  For you such peril as may cost too dear
  Some woman heart at home.

PHILIP VERNON.   Ah, there are none
  Will weep for me.   Of all that live not one.
  As alien ships that only meet to part,

Thy life and mine have crossed on stormy seas.
Learn to forget.   'T is a most wholesome art.

ELIZABETH VERNON.
    An art that women practise with less ease
    Than men.

PHILIP VERNON.
                    There 's time to learn it, for no more
    Shall we two meet.

ELIZABETH VERNON.   No more !

PHILIP VERNON.   Dear heart, no more.
    I said forget.   How could I say forget ?
    No, rather let some shadow of regret
    Still haunt thy better fortunes in glad hours
    When Spring is come again, and with her flowers
    Arise frail memories and thoughts long dumb,
    That are the wildings of the mind, and come
    With Nature's yearning season.

ELIZABETH VERNON.   Hush ! I heard
    Steps in the wood.

PHILIP VERNON.   No, not a leaf has stirred.

ELIZABETH VERNON.
    I am grown fearful.   If you would but go
    While the near hour is gracious —

PHILIP VERNON.   No ; ah, no !
    Not for the bribe of love.

ELIZABETH VERNON.   If, sir, you loved,
 My prayer were quickly answered. You 'd be moved,
 And fly.

PHILIP VERNON. You will not ask it. Those proud eyes
 Would turn with scorn from him whose honor dies.
 Men call me traitor: but, my lady fair,
 That died in me when all of my despair
 I cast before your feet. What mercy lies
 In the sweet equity of honest eyes
 I gladly trust.

ELIZABETH VERNON. Thank Heaven, I know not, sir,
 What sad temptation may have bid you err.
 I would not — will not — know. Do you forget
 I suffer while you linger here?

PHILIP VERNON.   And yet
 I cannot go. I would we had not met,
 Or God had given to me a kinder fate,
 A less uncertain birth, a nobler state.

ELIZABETH VERNON.
 Uncertain, said you?

PHILIP VERNON.   Yes, I said it — yes.
 For that time has no comfort, no redress,
 And you are worlds away. But here, alone,
 Once let me speak. The falcon love has flown
 Where the proud instinct of his haughty wings
 Takes love that soars. Beneath it earth's mean things
 Grow half unreal, and the morning rings
 With new-born light his world of wish and will.
 I love you — love you. Be it well or ill,

Still shall I love you.   None may ever doubt
Hope's dying words.   Alas! my treason 's out.
Oh, traitor heart!

Elizabeth Vernon looks at Philip, and of a sudden seating
herself upon a fallen tree, covers her face with her hands,
and is silent for a moment.

PHILIP VERNON.   You will not speak ?

ELIZABETH VERNON.   Wait, wait !
    — My God, I love him !— Sir, as sad a fate
    As yours will make my life and land the prize
    Of some debt-burdened noble.—It were wise
    We part at once.

PHILIP VERNON.   At once !

ELIZABETH VERNON.   Be merciful !
    Go while my blinded sight with tears is dull.
    You have been cruel.   Ah, I cannot see
    For tears of pity both for you and me.

PHILIP VERNON.
    And have I wounded you, my gentle dove ?
    That were most sad of all, to hurt with love.
    I have done wrong —

ELIZABETH VERNON.
                    Yes — no ! Would you were spared
    This most unhappy fortune !

As she ceases, Lord Grey comes abruptly into the open
space, and cries out:

> "Neatly snared!
> 'T is well I chanced to come.   And have you dared,
> A maid, a Vernon, thus to blot our fame,
> My mother's lineage?   Go!   Go, take your shame
> Where shame is common.   Off with you!   Fie! fie!
> Have you no blushes?   For this masking spy,
> Who lured you hither — "

PHILIP VERNON.   By my soul, you die!

They draw their swords as Hugh Langmayde, in haste
coming through the wood, steps between them.

PHILIP VERNON.   Out of my path!

HUGH LANGMAYDE.

> No! no!   In God's name, peace!
> The Church forbids you.

Lord Grey falls back, sheathes his sword, and says:

> "Easy 't is to cease
> When finer nets are spread.   A priest, indeed!
> And thus disguised.   In truth, it seems decreed
> My double debt shall wait.— You, madam, need
> No further words from me.   Begone with speed!"

ELIZABETH VERNON.   Oh, for one hour to be a man!

LORD GREY.   True, true!
> That had been better.   There were less to rue.

PHILIP VERNON.
 I shall be surely man enough for two ;
And you, whose tongue is quicker than your blade,
Shall lack no lesson.

Lord Grey stands smiling, while Hugh Langmayde seizes
Philip by the arm, and, drawing him away, says to him :

        "Why have you delayed?
I waited long. 'T is like we are betrayed.
Lose not a minute; and if fall of night
Find me not with you at the ford, take flight :
I shall be dead. Now God protect the right!"

Philip cries to Elizabeth Vernon as he follows the priest :

 "I may not wait. Heaven keep you!"

Then, turning to Lord Grey, says haughtily, and with a
bow :
        "We shall meet."
LORD GREY.
 Yes, where the gallows makes revenge complete.

With these words he walks swiftly away, while the priest
and Philip hurry through the wood in the opposite direc-
tion, leaving Elizabeth Vernon, who for a time stands
still in the deepening shadows, and looks along the path
where her lover has gone.

6

THE FORD

After dusk Philip Vernon, having waited long at the appointed ford, begins to walk to and fro uneasily, and says:

> "How long he tarries!   I have that to say
> Will sorely hurt him; and yet, chance what may,
> This treason ends.   Who 's there?"

HUGH LANGMAYDE.   Come!   We are gone!
> Lost men, I fear.   The wood, the wood!   Ere dawn
> We must be far from this.   One feeble fool
> Upon the rack betrayed us.   Oh, that school
> Makes ready scholars!   Death is close at hand.

As they leave the shore, the sound of men-at-arms comes from above and below, and always nearing them.

> "All ways are closed.   O sad, unhappy land,
> That was so near deliverance!   Here, my son,
> Take this, and go."

The priest, fainting and in haste, gives to Philip a packet.

>   "My earthly course is run."
PHILIP VERNON.
> I will not leave you.   Quick!   The garden gate
> I saw wide open.   Come!

The old man, helped, hurries through the chase.   As they cross an open space near the garden, the moon comes out, and from a thicket the flash of steel is seen, and the red blaze of half a dozen musquetoons.   The priest stumbles, and groans; men run forth, and, falling on Philip and his companion, stab the priest, who falls within the arched and open gateway of the garden of the castle, crying:

"Too late, too late!

 Curse on the heretic!   Fly, Philip!"

PHILIP VERNON.   No!
 Not I, by Heaven!

And, standing within the gateway, he cries fiercely as he fights:

"This for your coward blow,

 You this for vengeance, and you this, and go
 To hell that spawned you!"

As with cries and shouts the men fall back, there is a brief pause, while Lord Grey comes forward, sword in hand.

PHILIP VERNON.   Have a care, my lord!
 The place is somewhat narrow, and the sward
 Gives but ill footing.   Neither can I spare
 To teach you tricks of fence to-day.   Beware!
 Habet!   You have it.   Yes, this under thrust
 Is deadly dangerous.   Never put your trust
 In that weak parry — traitor! coward! take
 This for my love! this for that old man's sake!

As Lord Grey staggers and falls, he cries to those about him:

 "In on him! seize him!   Quick, the gate, the wall!"

Philip again attacks the men who are nearest, and as
they give way, retreating, he shuts the gate.   Then,
kneeling, he lifts the priest's head, and exclaims:

> "Ye saints, he 's dead!   Now let what may befall;
> No worse can come to me."

As Philip bends over the priest, he hears him groan and
mutter:

> "Strike sure!   You swore —
> Kill, kill the heretic!"

PHILIP VERNON.   Alas!

HUGH LANGMAYDE.   There 's more,—
> Christ, for a minute's life to speak!   I said
> Of her — your mother — something —

But even as the words are on his lips the priest's head
drops, and he dies.

PHILIP VERNON.   He is dead!
> God pity me, I loved him.   Wrong or right,
> I loved him well.   Christ rest his soul to-night.

As he rises he hears voices and shots, and, instantly
turning, flies through the shrubbery until, bewildered,
he comes upon a doorway in the side wall of the castle,
and, in the darkness stumbling in haste upon a narrow
stairway, opens a door cautiously, and enters the chapel
of the castle.

> "Ye saints be praised! for I am well-nigh spent,
> And here 's a little respite, Heaven sent."

Breathing fast and hard, he sinks exhausted on the chancel step.

    " The only friend I had this evening died;
    I would to God that I were by his side!
    But the mere brute in us will show his teeth:
    I fought as if·all life were glad.— Beneath
    This cross a child I knelt."

Of a sudden he leaps up at sight of one coming through the darkness.

                       " Speak, or you die!"

ELIZABETH VERNON.
    Mother of mercy!   It is I! 't is I!
    I thought you slain.

PHILIP VERNON.   I have one friend the less.
    They 've killed my only father; none may guess
    My utter loneliness.

ELIZABETH VERNON.   I hear men's feet.
    Get you behind the altar.

PHILIP VERNON.   Kiss me, sweet;
    That will make death seem easy.

ELIZABETH VERNON.   Go, make haste!

He obeys, and Elizabeth Vernon falls on her knees before the crucifix.

ELIZABETH VERNON.
    Oh, Mary Mother, pitiful and chaste!
    Save! save him!

6*

Here comes in hot haste the steward, with men-at-arms
and the Queen's officers.

STEWARD.   Peace!   She prays!

The Lady Elizabeth rising, he says, as he comes forward:

                              "We seek in vain
    The dead man's traitor comrade."

ELIZABETH VERNON.   Well, 't is plain
    He hides not here.   Search you the river-banks;
    The hills beyond the chase.   He shall have thanks
    Who finds this Spanish ruffler. Go! make haste!
    These ducats for his capture.   See you waste
    No time about the castle.   Shall it hap
    This Spanish fox would seek so plain a trap?

Upon this the steward and men leave the chapel, and as
the noise fades away Philip Vernon comes forward.

PHILIP VERNON.   Right bravely done!

ELIZABETH VERNON.   God guard you!

At this Philip Vernon gives her that packet the priest
had given him, and, much troubled, says:

                              "Here is this
    Sits heavy on my conscience.   Ere I miss
    Thy dear face, take it; for I have no mind
    To carry treason.   Should you chance to find
    Aught that may ruin men, I pray of you
    Destroy it; burn it."

Elizabeth Vernon.   Why not wait to view
    What costs a minute?   You have that to spare.
    This altar lamp suffices.   Rest you there.
    Some one might enter on us unaware.

As she opens the packet and reads therein a great surprise
possesses her.   ·

    "This holds no treason; none!   Where got you
        these?
    The Vernon arms?— a locket?— mysteries
    That much concern me."

Philip Vernon.   Answer I have none.
    The good priest gave me these ere life was done.
    I thought them dangerous.

Elizabeth Vernon.   Letters out of Spain!
    The king's grave attestation.   Still in vain
    I tax my cunning.   Who are you that brought
    This tale of wonder?

Philip Vernon.   Madam, I was taught
    To call myself plain Philip Vernon.   I
    Was that in Spain.

Elizabeth Vernon.   You Philip Vernon! Try
    To tell me more.   Is it indeed of you
    What I find written here?   Is — is it true?

Philip Vernon.
    How can I know?   The Jesuit, flying, found
    A tired boy-swimmer floating as if drowned,
    And kept him all these years in Spain.

ELIZABETH VERNON.   Think.   Strive
      Some memory of childhood to revive.

PHILIP VERNON.
      Ah, but what matters it to me ?   They bring
      No happy fortune.   What am I ?   A thing
      The sea refused to bury, which that priest
      Caught for mere pity ere it died — the least,
      Ay, least of men am I.   A waif forlorn.
      Only in name a Vernon.   I have borne
      That old man's silence long, till he of late
      Cursed me with knowledge of my bastard fate,
      To use my anguish in a desperate game —
      For what cared I, the unreckoned child of shame ?

ELIZABETH VERNON.
      A bastard ! bastard !   No, my lord; the pride
      Of twenty earls is in your veins.   He lied
      Who told you that.   Look ! look ! these papers ! See !
      I am the heir no longer; you are he.

Philip staggers back against a marble effigy of a boy on
a tomb just behind him, and cries out :

      "Christ help me !   How I loved him !   Yet he swore —
      Swore by the rood !   A priest !   The rood !   No more !
      It cannot be."

ELIZABETH VERNON.   It is.   If less the gloom,
      You might have seen, my lord, your very tomb
      Behind you there.   And fully on the scroll
      How, Philip Vernon drowned, " his precious soul
      Is with the saints."   Oh, I could laugh, were death
      Less neighbored to my mirth.   Also it saith,

"A youth of parts; well loved," that 's very truth;
"Witty and virtuous, also learned"—forsooth,
I think I must have loved you in your youth,
And ever since, my Philip. (——) What to do
I know not. Yes! let your sword counsel you.
Seek my Lord Howard, the High Admiral;
Tell him this·story boldly. Ay, tell all —
All this strange story. Let what may befall,
You cannot lose my love. Go, go, my lord;
Only to England could my soul afford
This new-born hope. Go now; the Spanish fleet
Is on the seas. Go, Philip. When you meet
Your boyhood's jailers, strike for brave Queen Bess,
And for this Bess, that is thy queen no less.
Go! I shall love you as no mortal man
Was ever loved of maid since love began.

PHILIP VERNON.
    My God, I thank thee for this hour of grace.

As he speaks he kneels, and sets her hand to his lips, and
then looking up, says:

    "Hope, honor, home, a land to serve, a face
    Dear as the summer sun to prisoned men,
    Life, trust, and love, I have them all again.
    Love! By my soul, I would I knew a word
    Unsoiled by this world's commerce — never heard,
    Save by some ardent angel, that should say
    My more than earthly love."

ELIZABETH VERNON.   Oh, haste away!
    Let love teach haste. This for the stirrup-cup!
    And now, God speed you! All the country 's up;

    The highway 's watched; I think none guard the
        shore:
    That way is safest. Here, this further door
    Leads to the strand. Go, set those wits to see
    What rose of honor you can pluck for me.

They go out of the chapel, and descend to the bank of
the river.

PHILIP VERNON.
    Good night! Sweet night, that marries hope to love.

ELIZABETH VERNON.
    Good night. God keep you, and all saints above!

She stands and watches him as his boat goes down the
river.

ELIZABETH VERNON.
    Oh, I could cry, could laugh; and if I knew
    A saint of laughter, I would pray that you
    Do keep me merry for good cause. Alack,
    Being but a maid, I would I had you back.

THE GARDEN

VERNON CASTLE OF A MORNING IN AUGUST, 1588

ELIZABETH VERNON walks amidst the flowers, an open
letter in her hand.

    " Oh, the sweet morning and the sweeter news
    That make me doubly glad! Ah, who would lose
    The hours of grief that won this leave to smile

Through one long careless day of joy, the while
I wait a larger joy!   Our smiles and tears
Have many meanings.   I could weep to-day
For very joy; and yesterday my fears
Fetched me strange laughter, though my life seemed
    gray
With age of longing.   Oh, be glad with me,
Ye English roses!   See, the morning sun
Asks for the lifted face of prayer.   The sea,
God's sea, laughs with us; we have won — have won!"

Thus speaking, Elizabeth Vernon walks to and fro among
the flowers, and sometimes pauses to shadow her eyes
with her hand, that she may look across the river all
aglitter with the sun.   But at last she kneels on the sod,
and, laughing, cries:

" I must kiss some one, something.   You, red rose,
Will never whisper it if I suppose
You are my Philip.   Kiss me, kiss me quick!
These be the lips I love.   I 'll shut my eyes
So not to know it is not he.   I 'm sick
For kisses.   Ah, but when he comes, and tries
To kiss me, I 'll be maidenly and wise,
And say, Fie on you, sir!"

Philip Vernon, coming of a sudden through the hedge:

                              "Sweetheart, take this!
I 'll play rose-lover with you, till I kiss
You one red rose with blushes.   He who brings
A galleon-freight of kisses, each with wings
Of gathered honor, cannot beggared be."

ELIZABETH VERNON.   My love! my lord!

PHILIP VERNON.   One kiss from thee outweighs
A hundred given.   Not all love's usury,
Not all the interest of unnumbered days,
Can keep us even.

ELIZABETH VERNON.   There 's for ransom, see!
Oh, I 'll be honest.   Tell me of the fight.
Indeed, I prayed for you both morn and night.
Now, tell me of it.   Did we hear aright ?
Hast seen the Queen ?

PHILIP VERNON.   Aye, and she mocked me, too,
Because these lands are cumbered, love, with you.
I had her pardon also.   My Lord Grey
Takes more to kill him than most traitors may.

ELIZABETH VERNON. The packet reached the chancellor?

PHILIP VERNON.   You did well
To send it.   I have no long tale to tell.

ELIZABETH VERNON.
Sit near me, Philip.   Now, the battle, pray !

PHILIP VERNON.
Oh, I 'll be brief; I 've other things to say.
We caught them in the Channel.   Day by day
We hung about them, like bold dogs that tease
Great lumbering bullocks; left them at our ease,
Then bit again, until each bloody deck,
Mast, sail, and timber, shorn to shattered wreck,

Their cannon silent, helpless, overpowered,
Northward they drifted, and a storm that lowered
Broke on their ruin, pitiless and swift.
The gray fog closed about them like a pall;
The great seas, leaping, smote them, and the lift
Grew dark above them.   One bleak funeral,
They passed from sight of man.   For us, we fled
To 'scape the storm's worst peril.

All is said

That may not till the morrow be delayed.

ELIZABETH VERNON.
Ah, never day like this has England seen!
Come, drink a cup to England and the Queen:
I 'll cast my love within the bowl.

PHILIP VERNON.   That pearl
Shall jewel every cup of life.

ELIZABETH VERNON.   Sweet Earl,
Thy people grow impatient.   Hark! the chimes
Ring in their new lord, and these gladder times.

RESPONSIBILITY

Thus, lying among roses in the garden of the Great Inn
after certain cups of wine, I, Attar El Din, sang of things
to come, when, I being dead a day, the Angels of Affirma-
tion and Denial should struggle for my soul.

> " I, Moonkir, the angel, am come
> To count of his good deeds the sum,
> For this mortal death-stricken and dumb."

> " I, Nekkir, the clerk of ill thought,
> Am here to dispute what hath wrought
> This breeder of song, come to naught.

> " Let us call from the valleys of gloom,
> From the day's death of sleep and the tomb,
> The wretched he lured to their doom."

> Then, such as my song had made weep
> Came parting the tent-folds of sleep,
> Or rose from their earth-couches deep.

Spake a Voice:
> " I sat beside the cistern on the sand,
> When this man's song did take me in its hand,
> And hurled me, helpless, as a sling the stone
> That knows not will nor pity of its own.

Within my heart was seed of murder sown,
So once I struck — yea, twice, when he did groan."

Spake a Voice:
  "Ay, that was the song
  Which I heard as I lay
  'Gainst my camel's broad flanks,
  Thinking how to repay
  The death-debt so bitter with wrong.
  I rose, as he sang, to rejoice
  With a blessing of thanks;
  For the song ruled my slack will and me,
  Like one who doth lustily throw
  The power of hand and of knee
  To string up to purpose a bow.
  Quick I stole through the dark, but delayed
  To hear how, with every-day phrase,
  Such as useth a child or a maid,
  From praise of decision to praise
  Of the quiet of evening he fell.
  Thus a torrent grows still on the plain
  To mirror how come through the grain
  The women with jars to the well.
  Swift I drew o'er the sands cool and gray,
  With my knife in my teeth held to slay.
  Hot and wet felt my hand as it crept —
  Lo! dead 'neath my hand the man lay;
  This other had struck where he slept."

  Then Moonkir, who treasures good deeds,
  To mark how the total exceeds,
  Said, " He soweth or millet or weeds

Who casts forth a song in the night,
As a pigeon is flung for its flight;
He knoweth not where 't will alight.
Lo, Allah a wind doth command,
And the caravan dies in the sand,
And the good ship is sped to the land."

SPAKE A VOICE:

" I lay among the idle on the grass,
And saw before me come and go, alas!
This evil rhymer.   And he sang how God
Is but the cruel user of the rod,
And how the wine-cup better is than prayer :
Whereon I cursed, and counselled with despair,
And drank with him, and left my field untilled,
Whilst all my house with woe and want was filled."

SPAKE A VOICE:

" And I that took no heed of things divine,
But ever loved to loiter with the wine,
Was straightway sobered.   From the inn I went,
And in the folded stillness of my tent
Wrestled with Allah, till the morning fair
Beheld this scorner like the rest at prayer."

Quoth I, this same Attar El Din,
Whose doubtful proportion of sin
These angels considered within :

" Ye weighers of darkness and light,
Ere cometh the day and the night,
Mark how, from the minaret's height,

The prayer seed of Allah is strown :
In the heart of the man it is sown.
He tilleth, or letteth alone.

" Behold at even-time within my tent
I wailed in song because a death-shaft, sent
From Azrael's fateful bow, had laid in dust
My eldest-born; I sang because I must.
For hate, love, joy, or grief, like Allah's birds,
I have but song, and man's dull use of words
Fills not the thirsty cup of my desire
To hurt my brothers with the scorch of fire
That burns within.   Yea, they must share my fate,
Love with me, hate, with me be desolate.
And so I drew my bowstring to the eye,
And shot my shafts, I cared not where or why,
If but the men indifferent, who lay
Beneath the palm-trees at the fall of day,
I could make see with me the dead boy's look
That swayed me as the bent reeds of the brook
Sway when the sudden torrent of the hills
From bank to bank the crumbling channel fills.

" Then one who heard me, and through stress of grief
Struggled with agony of loss in vain,
Into the desert fled, and made full brief
A clearance with the creditor called Pain,
And by a sword-thrust gave his heart relief.

" But one whose eyes were dry as summer sand
Wept as I sang, and said, ' I understand.'

"And one, who loved, did rightly comprehend,
Because I sang how, ever to life's end,

7

The death-fear sweetens love: and went his way
With deepened love to where the dark-eyed lay."

SPAKE A VOICE:
" My father's foe, a dying man,
Thirst-stricken near the brookside lay;
Its prattle mocked him as it ran,
So near and yet so far away.
While the quick waters cooled my feet,
Hot from the long day's desert heat,
I drank deep draughts, and deep delight
Of vengeance sated and complete,
Because the great breast heaved and groaned,
The red eyes yearned, the black lips moaned,
Because my foe should die ere night.
Then, as a rich man scatters alms,
This careless singer 'neath the palms,
With lapse, and laughter, and pauses long,
Merrily scattered the gold of song,
A babble of simple childish chants:
How they dig little wells with the small brown hand;
How they watch the caravan march of the ants,
And build tall mosques with the shifting sand,
And are mighty sheiks of a corner of land.

" Ah! the rush and the joy of the singing
Swept peace o'er my hate, and was sweet
As the freshness the waters were bringing
Was cool to my desert-baked feet.

"Thereon I raised mine enemy, and gave
The cold clear water of the wave;

And when he blessed me I did give again,
And had strange fear my bounty were but vain;
When, as I bent, he smote me through the breast.—
And that is all!   Great Allah knows the rest."

Said Nekkir, the clerk of man's wrong,
" Great Solomon's self might be long
In judging this mad son of song."

Then I, who am Attar El Din,
Cried, " Surely no two shall agree!
Thou mighty collector of sin,
Be advised: come with me to the Inn;
There are friends who shall witness for me —
Big-bellied, respectable, stanch,
One arm set a-crook on the haunch;
They will pour the red wine of advice,
And behold! ye shall know in a trice
How hopeless for wisdom to weigh
The song-words a poet may say."

Cried Moonkir, the clerk of good thought,
" Ah, where shall decision be sought?
Let us quit this crazed maker of song,
A confuser of right and of wrong."

" But first," laughed I, Attar El Din,
" I am dry: leave my soul at the Inn."

Newport, 1891.

WIND AND SEA

Scene I

*A June Afternoon.—Meadows.—A Farm, with distant
Woods; New Jersey Coast; Cape May.*

An idle group within the willow's shade
We lay and chatted, holding lazy tilts,
And many a lance of mocking laughter broke,
Or calmly settled creeds and governments
High on the pleasant uplands of content,
Till soon the westering sun peeped underneath
The fringes of our green tent skirts, and fell,
Where on the paling-fence the milk cans gleamed,
Red in the level gold, whilst suddenly,
Swift from the sea, the gay salt breezes came,
And, dipping like the swallows here and there,
With quick cool kisses touched the startled grain,
And fled ashamed, to seek new loves afar, .
Where in the dark damp marsh the lilies float,
And lustrous leaved the white magnolia lifts
Its silvery censers, and the frogs, like friars,
Intone their even-song along the marge.

HESTER (*rising*).
How sweet the air!   Wilt hear the song you made
Of this same gentle north wind's winter pranks?

The lusty north wind all night long
  His carols sang above my head,
And shook the roof, and roused the fire,
  And with the cold, red morning fled.

Yet ere he left, upon my panes
  He drew, with bold and easy hand,
Pine and fir, and icy bergs,
  And frost ferns of his northern land;

And southward, like the Northmen old
  Whose ships he drove across the seas,
Has gone to fade where roses grow,
  And die among the orange-trees.

ALFRED.
  That 's music for a poet's soul, his words
  Soft slipping from a woman's lips, the while
  Caressed by lingering sunshine wrapt she stands,
  A shining aureole round her fallen hair.

HENRY.
  A bid for equal flattery.   Let us go
  Across the sand dunes o'er the mazy creeks.
  Hear how old ocean calls us.   Come away.

FRANK.
  Dost thou remember that October day
  We three together stood and saw at eve
  The wanton wind yon sleeping waves arouse,
  Till at the touch of that coy courtesan
  Strange yearning seized them, and with shout and cry
  They followed fleetly, while she, laughing, fled
  Across the golden-rods above the beach?

7*

HENRY.

    Ay, then it was you, perched beneath an oak,
    To us, the long expectant heirs, set forth
    King Autumn's testament and royal will.

HESTER.

    I pray you tell again his dying thoughts,
    And we shall lie upon the meadow grass
    And be as heirs should be, stern visaged, grave,
    Whilst you within yon bower of wild grapes stand:
    So shall your words steal o'er the listening ear,
    Breeze broken, while the melancholy sea
    Moans his sad chorus on the distant shore.

FRANK.

    Brown-visaged Autumn sat within the wood,
    And counted miserly his ripened wealth;
    I, Autumn, heritor of Summer's wealth,—
    I, Autumn, who am old and near to death,—
    Do thus make clear my will: I dowered earth
    With fruit and flowers. I fed her hungry tribes,
    The bee, the bird, the worm, the lazy flocks,
    And like a king who unto certain death
    Goes proudly clad, in royal state I go,
    Through the long sunset of October woods,
    Where like a trembling maid the smooth-limbed beech
    Lets fall her ruddy robes, or where afield
    Red vine leaves fleck the cedar's sombre cone,
    Or where the maple and the hickory tall
    Shed the long summer's store of garnered gold.
    Mine, too, the orchard's raining fruit, and mine
    Round-shouldered melons fattening in the sun;

Mine the brown pennons of the rustling maize,
The squirrel's nutty wealth, the wrinkled gourd.
For I am Autumn, lord of fruits and flowers,—
God's almoner to all the tribes of man.
Here, then, to earth and all her habitants,
I, dying, leave what Summer's bounty gave:
Great store òf grain, ripe fruit, and tasselled corn;
Yea, last of all, and best, I here bequeath,
With loving thought, a special legacy
To all good fellows everywhere on earth:
To them I give the sun-kissed grapes of Spain,
The Rhine's autumnal treasure, and the fruit
Of knightly Burgundy and winding Rhone;
Nor less the grape of Capri's lifted cliff,
The purple globes that jewel Ischia's isle,
And that sad vintage weeping holy tears
On black Vesuvian slopes.   To them I give
The soothing sweetness of the Cuban leaf
Wherewith to hold good counsel, when life palls,
Wherewith to charm away some weary hour.
And when from thoughtful lips the pale blue
        wreaths
Curl upward, and, the wanderer's only hearth,
His pipe-bowl, glows with hospitable fires,
I charge them drink a single cup, and say,
He was a good old fellow—peace to him.
So died great Autumn, passing like a mist,
Where in the woodland verge the maples rain
Reluctant gold in hesitating fall.

ALFRED.
    What ho! good minstrel.   Let us seaward roam,
    'T is but a half hour's stroll past yonder hill.

FRANK.

> I well recall the way.   It lies within
> A wood of stunted cedars and of firs,
> Which heard in infancy the great sea moan,
> And so took on the wilted forms of fright.

HESTER.

> Well, too, I know it: when the tide is up
> 'T is barred and traversed by an hundred creeks,
> So populous with lilies, you might dream
> King Oberon's navy rode at anchor there.

FRANK.

> Let us away to it.   Our sculptor here
> Knows not the sea as we do.   He shall feast
> His eager eyes on it, and own to us
> That earth has glories other than the curves
> Of lithe Apollo and the queen of love.

SCENE II

Seashore.—Sand Dunes dotted with distorted Trees.

HENRY.

> Why never can the painter tell to us
> This awful story of a lonely sea,
> This terrible soliloquy of nature?
> Why must he slip us in the bit of red,
> The group of fishers or the tossing ship?
> Who asks for life or human action here?

FRANK.

> Nay, man is nature's complement.   The sea,
> The sky, the flowers suggest him.   Best I love
> The smiling landscape of a woman's face.

ALFRED.

> But he who worships nature, ought to be
> The ready lover of her thousand gods.

HESTER.

> Lo! what a thought is yon triumphant sea,
> A thought so perfect in its competence,
> That I would leave it to its loneliness.

ALFRED.

> Think what it was when unto God there came
> This great sea thought.

FRANK.   Here, friend, your chisel fails.
> 'T is powerless here.   Thank heaven, I at least
> Can some way capture it with feeble brush.

ALFRED.

> Alas, 't is no man's prize.   It mocks us all.
> Leave me but only man, and you may paint,
> And you may chisel.   I would sail alone
> The great Atlantic of the human heart.

HENRY.

> Do you remember how, last summer, here
> We played with fancies, and in idle mood
> Struck to and fro the shuttlecocks of thought ?

FRANK.

> Ah, well I do.   'T was such an hour as comes
> Once in the life of joy.   Just here we lay.
> As oft before, you led the playful race.

HENRY.
　　Watch now the waves; each has its little life,
　　High couraged triumph in yon crest of pride,
　　Some proud decision in its onward sweep,—
　　Destruction, failure,— 't is a history!

FRANK.
　　I like it best when of a winter day
　　The cold dry norther rolls athwart the beach
　　The gleaming foam balls into serpents white,
　　And all the sand is starred with rainbow lights.

HESTER.
　　It knoweth all the secrets of my moods:
　　To-day is gay with me, to-morrow grave.

FRANK.
　　For me its voice is ever sorrowful
　　As some God's grief beyond all earthly speech.

HESTER.
　　How wave on wave turns lapsing on the beach,
　　Like the great leaves of some eternal book.

ALFRED.
　　Unread forever since creation's dawn.
　　I pray you notice how the seaside trees
　　Seem flying headlong, all their withering limbs
　　Stretched landward, craving refuge from the sea.

FRANK.
　　As they might be remorseful murderers,
　　That heard the hoarse deep, like an angry foe,
　　Storm up the sand slopes — nearer, nearer still,
　　Crying, vengeance, vengeance, all the summer
　　　　night.
1865.

THE SHRIVING OF GUINEVERE

STILL she stood in the shunning crowd.
" Is there none," she said, aloud,
" None who knelt to me, great and proud,
Will say one word for me, sad and bowed ?
Alas ! it seems to me, if I
Were one of you, who, standing by,
Hear gathered in a woman's cry
The years of such an agony,
It seemeth me that I would take
Sweet pity's side for mine own sake,
And, knowing guilt alone should quake,
For chance of right one battle make."
But, no man heeding her, she stayed
Beneath the linden's trembling shade,
And peered, half hopeful, half afraid,
While passed in silence man and maid.
She, staring on the stone-dry street
Through the long summer-noonday heat,
And, stirring never from her seat,
Half saw men's shadows pass her feet.
" Ah me ! " she murmured, " well I see
How bitter each day's life may be
To them who have not where to flee
And are as one with misery."
But, whether knight to tourney rode,

Or bridal garments past her flowed,
Or by some bier slow mourners trode,
No sign of life the woman showed.
When as the priestly evening threw
The blessed waters of the dew,
About her head her cloak she drew
And hid her face from every view;
Till, as the twilight grew to shade,
And passed no more or man or maid,
A sudden hand was on her laid.
"And who art thou?" she moaned, afraid.
Beside her one of visage sad
Which yet to see made sorrow glad
Stood, in a knight's white raiment clad,
But neither sword nor poniard had.
"One who has loved you well," he said.
"Living I loved you well, and dead
I love you still; when joys were spread
Like flowers, and greatness crowned your head,
None loved you more. Not Arthur gave —
He will not check me from his grave —
So pure a love; nor Launcelot brave
With deeper love had yearned to save."
"Then," said the woman, still at bay,
"Why do I tremble when you lay
A hand upon my shoulder? Stay,
What is thy name, sir knight, I pray?
For wheresoever memory chase
I know not one such troubled face,
Nor one that hath such godly grace
Of solemn sweetness any place:
But, whatsoever man thou be,
What is it I should do for thee?"

Whereon, he, smiling cheerily,
Said: " I would have thee follow me."

Not any answer did he wait.
But turned towards the city gate;
Not any word said she, but straight
Went after, bent and desolate ;
And, as a dream might draw, he drew
Her feet to action, till she knew
That house and palace round her grew,
And some wild revel's reeling crew,
And dame and page and squire and knight,
And torches flashing on the sight,
And fiery jewels flaming bright,
And love and music and delight;
But slow across the spangled green
The stern knight went and went the queen,—
He solemn, silent, and serene,
She bending low with humble mien.
But where he turned the music died,
Love-parted lips no more replied,
And, shrinking back on either side,
Serf and lord stared, wonder-eyed,
Or marveling shrunk swift away
Before that visage solemn, gray,
Till, where the leaping fountains sway,
Thick showed the knights in white array.
Where'er he passed, though stirred no breeze,
The leaves shook, trembling on the trees.
Where'er he looked, by slow degrees
Fell silence and some strange unease,
Whilst whispers ran : " Who may it be ?
What knight is this ?   And who is she ? "

But only Gawain looked to see,
And, praying, fell upon his knee.
Then said a voice full solemnly:
" Of all the knights that look on me,
If only one of them there be
That never hath sinned wittingly,
Let him the woman first disown,
Let him be first to cast a stone
At her who, fallen from a throne,
Is sad and weary and alone.
Him, when the lists of God are set,
Him, when the knights of God are met,
If that he lacketh answer yet,
The soul of him shall answer get."

Then, as a lily bowed with rain
Leaps shedding it, she shed her pain,
And towering looked where men, like grain
Storm-humbled, bent upon the plain ;
Whilst over her the cold night air
Throbbed with some awful pulse of prayer,
As, bending low with reverent care,
She kissed the good knight's raiment fair.
When as she trembling rose again,
And felt no more in heart and brain
The weary weight of sin and pain,
For him that healed she looked in vain ;
And from the starry heavens immense
Unto her soul with penitence
Came, as if felt by some new sense,
The noise of wings departing thence.

1874.

THE SWAN-WOMAN

A LEGEND OF THE TYROL

I TOLD this story once to Kaiser Max.
If he believed it, that can no man say.
Within the Alte Kirche they have placed
His statue, kneeling, sword in hand, at prayer;
And though the cunning carver in his skill
Hath on that face a hundred battles set,
And dooms of men, and many a laden year
Of swift decisions, not those lips in life
Told more they would not than this face of bronze.

Hast been at Innspruck?   When the evening
    glooms,
Go see him girt about with lord and dame,
Arthur of England, Alaric, and the Duke.

In those days every great man had his fool,
And some men were their own, which saved some
    fools
Their share of fools' pay, cuffs; but so it was.
And now it chanced our ancient fool was dead
And gone to heaven, to be an angel-fool.
Thus, fool-craft prospering, they came by scores
To that bleak castle in the Tyrol hills,

And, while my lady and the knight above
Looked from the balcony, made sport below,
And jeered the men-at-arms, or mocked the page.
But most had wits like bludgeons, till my lord,
A smileless man, save when in shock of arms
He struck a blow that ever after quenched
The human laughter of some gentler soul,
Tired of their jesting, drove them roughly forth.
So out they went, until, one summer eve,
Came gayly singing up the castle hill
A man — scarce more than man, with cap and bells,
Head up, chin out, just a fool's carriage all;
And strutted gravely round the court, and smiled,
And kissed white fingers to my lady's maid,
Whereon, at last, the burly cook cried out,
" A silent fool; God send us many such ! "
But he, " Your Greasy Grace will pardon me, for I
Am but a lady's fool."   Quoth Hans the Squire,
" Ho then, 't will suit my lord, a lady's fool ! "
And so they giggling pushed him up the stairs,
And through the great hall where my lord at meat
Sat with my lady and a score of guests,
Pilgrim and merchant, and, above the salt,
A knight or two, and kinsfolk of my lord.
" What jest is this ? "

          " We 've found a lady's fool !
A silent fool, who can but grunt a joke
Like our old boar ; " but as he spake I saw
My fool's right hand twitch at his belt to left,
As one through habit seeking for his sword
When stung by insult ; flushing deep, he bowed,
Said, " By your leave, my lady," turned and fetched

Big Hans so rude a buffet on the ear,
The big squire tumbled half across the hall.
"Saint Margaret!" cried my lord, "the jest is good.
And this is what you call a lady's fool?
Canst gossip, mock, tell tales, sing songs at need?"
"Ay, noble sir, sing, jest, crack jokes or heads;
But that's a serious business, and spoils fools,
The cracker and the cracked.   Perchance my lord
Would try my folly for a month or two,
When, if it reach the level of my lord,
If I crack jokes as well as he cracks heads,
My lord shall set my wage."
                                        "So be it, fool.
Give him the dead fool's tower; and look you, fool,
Leave to thy betters the rough sport of blows,
Lest to thy grief I take to fools' trade too."
Low bent the fool to hide his troubled face,
Then meekly said, "King Folly's fool were I
To doubt my lord's success."   But while the Count,
Perplexed and grim, rose angrily, the dame,
Pleased with the tilting at her heavy lord,
Laughed a sweet girl-laugh outright, and for hint
Plucked at her dull lord's sleeve, while level-eyed
To meet whatever gaze might question his,
Our fool said carelessly, " I jest for dames.
A woman's fool am I, as who is not
Some woman's fool?"— then lightly, wrist on hip,
With something of too easy grace fell back
Smiling and gay.   And so we got our fool.
But I, that had been bred to be a priest,
And shut in convent walls had learned perforce
To read men's eyes for comment on their lips,
Saw some quick change in this man's as he turned,

Some lifting of the lids.   Orbs garnet-hued
In wide white margins set, and tender, too,
Methought a strange face for a fool, indeed.
Yet somehow from his coming all the house
Grew gay.   And never gentler jester was.
For when he laughed 't was like a baby's laugh,
Less at than with you; but he won them all,
Cook, page, and men-at-arms; and surly Hans
He charmed by teaching him the buffet's trick
And bought him a new dagger, and had gold
For them that wanted; yet my lord he shunned,
Or, meeting, puzzled him with jest on jest,
Some savage truth in wordy masquerade.
But above all, he was my lady's fool;
Sang for her,— ay, sang to her, I should say;
Told tales of Arthur in the chapel yon,—
Stories of ancient magic and quaint jests
Of masque and tourney and the Kaiser's court,
So that my lady, who was young and fair,
And yearning for some heart-hold upon life,
Like the loosed tendril of a wind-blown vine
That seeks and knows not why, smiled once again,
And blossomed like a bud surprised by June;
Then took to hawking, to my lord's delight,
With me, a page, for company, and the fool
To call the hawks, or tie their jesses on.
So many a day I followed them, as home
They rode, he talking strange things of the stars,
Or calling bird and beast with cries they knew.
Cursed goblin-tricks, not priest-taught, be you sure;
Could read you, too, the thing that was to be
By peering at your palm, until my lord
Bade one day tell him what would come about

When he, the Count, should issue forth to take
His turn at beating back the island lords.
I judged the fool reluctant, but he took
That square brown hand on his, and lightly traced
With fingers lithe and white its mazy lines,
Then paused, grew pale, and said, What God doth
    hide
Leave thou to time's wise answer; but the Count
Swore roundly that the fool was half a priest,
Yet started up in haste, and asked no more.

And so the fool, because men named him so,
Had leave to go and come; or at her feet
To lie, and wing with laughter some sweet words,
Or with fierce emphasis of ardent eyes
To look the thought he dared not put in speech.
So love, now bold, now put to timid flight,
Grew none the less for seeming shy retreats,
Like the slow, certain tides that are made up
Of myriad wave-deaths.

                              Yet she knew it not.
Then came the war.   To north the Margrave rose;
To south the great sea lords broke out anew.
So late in May our broad, bull-headed lord
Put on his armor, growling, since each year
He could not have it like a crab's case grow,
But guessed some exercise in cracking skulls
Might slack his belt, if helped by scant camp fare.
And scant it was, for some few marches thence
A robber horde fell on him from a wood,
Slew half his train, and plucked him from his horse,
And bore him with them as they fled away.
But Hans they loosed, sore hurt, and bade him take

His way across the hills, and tell the dame
What fate her lord should have if three days gone
No ransom bond came back to bring release.
But two days later fell the wounded squire,
Dust-grayed and bleeding, at the lady's feet,
And failing fast cried out, " My lord, my lord !
Ransom — thy lord — a castle in the hills —
Three days — and two are gone — the third he
        dies."
Then rose upon his elbow, said some words
None heard except the fool, and so fell back,
And ended honestly an honest life.
But as he spoke, in haste my lady turned,
Some masterful set purpose in her face ;
Bade double guards, called in more men for aid,
The castle put in siege shape, knowing not
What ill might follow next.   Then stood in doubt,
Till on the fool's stirred face her large eyes fell.
" And this must end," she cried.   " Sir, follow me ! "
And led him out upon the eastern tower,
Where many an eve they two had stayed to watch
Tofana's shadow cross Ampezza's vale.
Then of a sudden facing him, in wrath,
" Sir, was it knightly, this that you have done ?
What crime or folly bade you refuge here ? "
" Madam, a poor fool's fancy."   " Nay, 't was you,
'T was you who in the jousts at Ims, last year,
O'erthrew my lord, and won the tourney's prize,
Then round the lists with lifted visor rode,
Cast in my lap the jewel as you passed,
And known to none, unquestioned, rode away.
Nay, sir, the truth, the truth."   This once again
He set his face for company with a lie,

But looking, saw her red lips droop in scorn,
Nor dared to meet the judgment in her eyes,
So backward fell a pace, and murmured low :
" I came because I loved you, and I stayed
For like good reason; yea, my life had been
This and no more if I could but have lived
Beside you, near you.   For content were I
To leave my peers their strife for gold or land,
And in the quiet convent of my love
To let sweet hours grow to days as sweet,
And these to months of ever-ripening joy."
" Alas!" she moaned, " God help me in my need!"
Because the tender blazonry of joy
Lit face and neck with wandering isles of red.
" Ah, love!" he cried, seeing all her sweet dismay,
" The day is ours.   Fly with me — love is ours."
But then some angel memory came at call.
" Not so," she said.   " Pray sit you there awhile.
We both are young — too young to stain with sin
Of evil loves the weary years to come.
That bitter day the margrave stormed St. Jean,
There in the breach all that God gave to love,
Father and brothers, died.   None left, not one.
And then a hell of rapine and of blood
Swept all the town ; and I — well, this is all :
The man that is my husband now, he saved,
Alas! he saved me.   Yet I love him not."
Then like to one who, stranded on strange shores,
Awaking sees a color in the sky,
And knows not yet if it be dawn or dusk,
Agaze, he saw the rose-light leave her face,
And, being noble, knew the nobler soul.
" I go," he said,— " the thing I did was ill."

But on his motley sleeve a hand she laid.
" Now that I know how, loving me, love guides
To honour, not to baseness, I dare ask
The man's clear counsel, for my soul is set
To quit me of the debt of given life ;
Since then, perchance, I may myself forgive
For that I love him not, and shall not love ;
And if I ask of thee, because I must,
To do the thing is hateful to thy soul,
It will be only then to bid thee go,
Because I may not love thee, and I shall."
Then he paused, pondering, urged here and there,
Like some strong swimmer whom the waves at will
Hurl landward and take back ; till in strange haste,
As one who fears delay, he spake quick words :
" Now if thy soul be certain of itself,
If thou canst say, Thus will I, death or life,
I hold a charm which, to strong purpose wed,
Shall free thy heart from bondage to this debt.
Once on a forest verge, I, but a lad,
Set free a Jew some robber lord left bound,
And for remembrance got this little ring :
A face in gold, you see, and o'er its eyes
Twin hands clasped tight.   But if at midnight one
Shall turn it, and shall dare with purpose sure
To will that she shall be some living thing,
Or bird or other creature of the woods,
Three days the charm will hold, the fourth will break.
The winged wood-pigeon knows to find its mate,
And if thou wilt but give thy instinct wings
Thou too shalt find thy mate ; but I, if I
Should crown my follies with a larger jest,
And set my master free, the deed were thine,

Because thy own heart is not more thy own
Than I who love thee."   Then in dread he stood,
Fearing the devil in himself; but she,
" Not so! the debt is mine.   If death befall,
Death is an honest debtor, and God pays,"
Seized quick the ring, and of a sudden fled,
While slow the fool went down the turret stair.
" Alas!" he said, " can heaven be bought with hell
As hell with heaven thereafter?"   Then alone
Swift from the castle-gate he fled, and came
To where, long miles away, within the wood,
Three knights stood waiting, and a steed that neighed
To greet his master.   But he would not arm,
And saying merely, " Yea, a fool I am,"
Leapt on his horse, and swiftly through the wood
Rode, while they whispered, " Surely he is dazed."

At noon of night our gentle lady tied
A silken-threaded letter round her neck,
And on the turret stood and turned the ring,
And looked, and saw — for now the moon was full —
Strange sunsets glowing in the changeful gem,
And mists of color floating from its depths;
And crying, " Once he praised my swan-bowed neck!"
Put all her soul in one fierce wish, and felt
Such change as death may bring or life, and then
Half fear, half wonder, like a soul reborn,
Rose on white wings, that trembled as they rose,
And flared vast shadows o'er the old gray keep;
Till in the joyous freedom of her flight
Strong with delight of easy strength she soared,
And caught the warm gold of the unrisen sun
As souls unprisoned win new hopes and joys;

Saw with strange thrills the white wedge of her
      mates,
And falling gently through the morning light
Lit where the sedgy margins green and brown
Stirred, as with tawny webs they beat the wave.
Some bird-born pleasure luring, long she stayed
To bathe her bosom's silver in the lake,
Till all the summer day went by, and night
With sleep wave-rocked by cool wood-scented
      winds.
But when another morning brake, and glad
On eager wings she rose to greet the morn,
Too late she knew no tender instincts led.
Wing-weary, helpless, hopeless, sore beset,
Her gold eyes fell upon a train of knights,
And strong with joy that half was shame or fear,
Weak-winged she fluttered down, and saw below
The fool beside her lord, and knew, alas,
What gentle longings drew her to the earth.
There, sullen with the anger of the dull,
Her grim lord rode, or with wild oaths complained
Because with prison fare his arms were weak,
His eyes grown dim : then of a sudden spied
The wild white-winged thing over him, and snatched
A cross-bow from his saddle, set a bolt,
And loosed the string, and heard a human cry
So terrible that none who rode with him
Lived to forget it, or the thin red rain
That flecked the fool's white cloak, while slowly
      down
Light feathers flitted.   Then the fool turned short,
Caught the knight's saddle-axe, and cried aloud,
" Hast thou, O beast set free, no kindly sense ? "

And smote the great brute knight so fierce a blow
That man and steed rolled helpless; but the fool
Struck swiftly here and there, rode down a squire,
Cast wide his axe, and spurring wild his horse,
With eyes in air, grim-staring like a dog
His master calls, fled where the wounded swan
Fast faded in the yellow sunset's glow.
Homeward in wonderment the knight they bore,
Hurt, not to death, and ever as we went,
Cursing himself, and us, and most the fool,
And marvelling much why came not forth his dame.
None dared to tell him that three days had gone
Since any saw her face.   So all the house
Ran to and fro like to an ant-heap stirred,
While he, that loved her in his stolid way,
And blindly craved some sweetness never won,
Sought here and there in anger, like low souls
That turn to wrath all passions, and at last
Brake wildly out upon the turret-top,
'Midst man and squire and groom and wildered
        maids;
For there they found the lady, cold and still,
The sweetest dead thing that a man could see,
And in her bosom white a cross-bow bolt.

1883.

A MEDAL

PANDOLPHUS MALATESTA, ISOTTA.

MALATESTA.

WHY does it pleasure me, Isotta, why?
Canst guess,— I cannot,— wherefore such as I
Should crave to see myself in bronze or gold?
Matteo hath art's courage.   He is bold!
God-made or devil-fashioned, out I go
For comment of the world, or friend or foe.
What saith this face, Isotta? — what to you,
As to a gazer chance hath brought to view?
You smile,— dost dare?   The soul beyond thine
    eyes
Will bid you risk all other things save lies.

ISOTTA.

A jewel set in brass,— yet why, God knows,
If God knows anything of such as those
Like me, who fear you not as men know fear,
Being, see you, sir, so little and so dear.
Then lying is the luxury of the great.
The marge of perils sweet.   You dare me — wait;
Give me the wax.   This side face doth relate
More truth than most, my lord, may care to state.
And yet, not all; nay, with strange cunning hides

122

What little good or noble haply bides
For rare occasion.   Oh! you bade me try
At truth as of men dead beyond reply.
Be sure, my lord, I could not lie to you.
Why did Delilah love her great brute Jew,
Hated and loved him?   Riddle that, my lord.

MALATESTA.

Rare old Genosthos Platon, whom I stored
In yon stone tomb, might guess in vain for thee
Betwixt his dreams of Plato, but for me,
Too brief is life to riddle love or hate.
The face, the face,— what secrets shall it prate
When I am dead, and babbling students claim
In feebler days to know who set his name,
Ensigns, and heraldry on yonder wall,
With thine, my dame?   Dost fear to tell me all?

ISOTTA.

Narrow the forehead; bushy eyebrows set
O'er lizard lids, cross-furrowed; hair as jet;
The nose rapacious, falcon-curved, morose;
Cheeks wan, high-boned, o'er hollows; lips set close,
Like each to each, large, pouting, to men's eyes
Twin slaves of passion, apt for love or lies.
They who shall read in gentler days that face
Shall call thee mad, and wonder at thy race.

MALATESTA.

Dost think they tell my story?   Lo, how sweet!
The swallows flashing down the sunlit street;
A thrush upon the window,— he at least
Must hold me guileless as yon pale boy priest.
What more, fair mistress? How he seeks your eye!

Isotta.

    'Neath this stern brow forgotten murders lie;
    The red lip lines confess lust, scorn, and hate;
    Dark treacheries 'neath those sombre eye-caves wait.
    Ah, where, my lord, the scholar's studious pain,
    The zest for art, the Plato-puzzled brain,
    The high ambition for diviner thought,
    That joyed to see how well Alberti wrought?

Malatesta.

    The earthquake scars the mildly tended soil,
    And leaves behind no trace of man's slow toil;
    Lo, then, at last you find some alms of praise.
    Who sees a man full-faced must meet his gaze;
    This side face, mark you, lacks the quick eye's
        change.
    Unwatched, men see it.   Ever is it strange
    To him who carries it.   'T is like, you say.

Isotta.

    My good lord, so Matteo said to-day.

Malatesta.

    Now what a thing is custom!   You can scan
    This face and call me good.   See how a man
    May scourge through centuries with the whips of
        shame,
    And curse you with the thing that wins him fame.

Isotta.

    Minutes are courtiers.   The inflexible years
    To no man palter, know not loves nor fears.

Malatesta.

    Ah! none but you would dare in bitter speech

To front the Malatesta.   Doth naught teach
Thy careless tongue to fear loose talk of me?

ISOTTA.
Yet so the meanest churl shall prate of thee,
When axe or spear sets free thy soaring soul,
And its wild flight hath won an earthly goal.

MALATESTA.
Small care have I what man or gossip say,
When axe or spear-thrust come to close my day.
And yet, and yet, Isotta, when my face
Pales on some stricken field, and in my place
Another wooes thee, what wilt say, my maid?

ISOTTA.
Much as the rest.   The dead are oft betrayed.

MALATESTA (*aside*).
Not by the dead.   No other lips shall lay
Love's bribe upon thy cheek.
(*Aloud*).   Another day
Fades in the west, behind yon crumbling tower!
Give me my Plato.   Pray, how stands the hour?

1883.

THE HUGUENOT

1686

Dry-lipped with terror, o'er the broken flints
Stumbling I ran, my baby tightly held,
And of a sudden, coming from the wood,
Saw the low moon blood-dash the distant waves,
Felt the wet grass slope of the cliff, and heard
The hungry clamour of the hidden sea,
Nor dared to stir, but waited for the dawn,
And prayed and wondered why the beast alone
Some certain instinct guided in its flight;
When, God be praised! I saw my Louis stand
With slant hand o'er his brow, this wise, at gaze—
Just a mere outline, none but I had seen,
Set 'gainst the flitting white caps of the sea.
Then I said softly, " Louis," and he turned,
(I think that he would hear me were he dead),
But as he quickly drew across the cliff
I saw the sudden sadness of his face
Grow through the lessening night, and ere I moved
A strong arm caught me, while he cried in haste,
" Why didst thou add new sorrow to my flight?
Who has betrayed it?   Surely once again,
When these dark days are over, I had come
To fetch thee and my mother and the boy,

Where in free England we should find a home."
"Home! Home!" I gasped.   "Home! Mother!"
       for the words
Choked me as with a man's grip on the throat.
But he, hard breathing, held me fast and cried,
"Speak quickly,— death is near!" (but yet his
       hand
Put back my hair and soothed me).   So I gasped,
"As from our preaching in the wood we rode
With Jacques the forester, as is his way,
He fell to singing Clement Marot's psalm,
For them God calleth to the axe or rack.
I, liking not the omen, bade him cease;
Then saw a-sudden, far above the hill
A tongue of flame leap upward, heard a shot,
And then another, till at last our Jacques,
Bidding me wait, rode on.   An hour ago,
While yet the night was dark,— he came again,
And thrust our little one within my arms,
And sharply speaking, bade me urge my horse,
And on the way told all."

                          "Told all,— told what?"

"The dear old house is burned, thy mother dead!"

"Dead, Marie?"

                    "Dead! one fierce pike-thrust, no more!
She did not suffer, Louis!"

                                "But the babe?"

"Jacques found him near the dial, in the maze."
"My God! there 's blood upon his little hands!"
"Ay! it is thought she had him in her arms,

(Thy mother's, Louis !) and it must have been
She crawled, blood-spent, to hide the little man,
And seeking somewhere help, fell down and died
Beside the fountain."

                    "Oh, be quick! what more ?"
"This Jacques to me, as hitherward we spurred,
For, as we came, a noise behind us grew,
And, haply, I have only brought you death.
'T was but one man, we guessed; the rest, misled,
Rode toward St. Malo, and Jacques leaving me — "

"Hush ! listen ! "

                    " Nay, I see the boat, my lord ! "

" Be silent, Marie; kneel, here by the rock.
Let come what may, no word."   And so I knelt,
And trembling saw the fiery glow of morn
Shudder like some red judgment o'er the sea.
This while my dear lord bent and kissed the babe,
And then my cheek, my forehead, and my lips,
Unsheathed his sword, and gazing inland stood,
And slowly turned the ruffles from his wrist.
But then my heart beat fiercely in my breast,
For, on the sward between us and the verge,
Leapt of a sudden from the pines a man,
And paused a breath's time, for behind him dropped
An awful cliff wall to a stepless shore,
And steep the marge sloped to it, and before,
Close at his breast, he saw my Louis' blade,
Red like a viper's tongue, flash in the morn.
Then said my sweet lord, speaking tender low,
"Stir not, dear wife.   It is the Duke, thank God!"
So looking up I saw that traitor face,

With eyes of eager seeking, right and left,
Glance up the cliff, and then I heard a voice
Unlike my Louis', hollow, hoarse, and changed.
"Too late! They will not find thee. Quick, on guard!
The crows shall get thee graveyard room. On guard!"
Whereat the Duke turned short.   No better blade:
Thrice have I seen him, in our happier days,
Disarm my Louis in the armory play.
Whence, for a moment, as their rapiers met,
Fear caught and held me, till I looked and saw
My Louis' face grow passionless and calm,
As one decreed by God to judge and slay.
I crept apart, yet could not help but gaze,
Because the thing was terrible to see.
For my dear lord, his face unstirred and cold,
Now touched him on the shoulder or the breast,
Then in the chest an inch deep as he shrank,
Till, with each wound, the traitor, shrinking back,
Felt the sloped margin crumble 'neath his feet,
Then wildly thrust, whereon the rapiers coiled
Like twin steel serpents, and the Duke's flew wide.
My God! I cried, "Save! Save him! but my lord
In silence with his kerchief wiped his sword,
And coldly cast the good lace o'er the cliff.
Speechless, I saw the stiff knees giving way,
The long grass breaking in the hands' hard clutch,
Till on the brink — oh, that was terrible! —
A face — a cry — just "Marie!" that was all!
And then I heard my good lord sheathe his blade.
Ah, truly, that was very long ago,
And why, why would you have me tell the tale?
Sometimes at evening, underneath our oaks,
Here in our English home, I sit and think,

Stirred by the memory of a wild, white face.
Here come the boys you praised. My Louis'? No!
And this grave maid?   These are my baby's babes!
You did not think I am a grand-dame.   Well —
You 're very good to say so.

1880.

HOW LANCELOT CAME TO THE NUNNERY IN SEARCH OF THE QUEEN

THREE days on Gawain's tomb Sir Lancelot wept,
Then drew about him baron, knight, and earl,
And cried, " Alack, fair lords, too late we came,
For now heaven hath its own, and woe is mine :
But 'gainst the black knight Death may none avail.
I will that ye no longer stay for me.
In Arthur's realm I go to seek the Queen,
Nor ever more in earthly lists shall ride."
So, heeding none, seven days he westward rode,
And at the sainted mid-hour of the night
Was 'ware of voices, and above them all
One that he knew, and trembled now to hear.
Rose-hedged before him stood a nunnery's walls,
With gates wide open unto foe or friend.
Unquestioned to the cloister court he came,
And in the moonlight, on the balcony, saw
Beneath the arches nuns and ladies stand,
And in their midst a cowled white face he loved,
Whereat he cried aloud, " Lo, I am here !
Lo, I am here !— I, Lancelot, am here !
Would ye I came ?   I could not help but come."
Spake then the Queen, low-voiced as one in pain :

"Oh, call him here, I pray you call him here."
Then lit Sir Lancelot down, and climbed the stair,
And doffed his helm, and stood before the Queen.
But she that had great fear to see his face:
"Oh, sinless sisters, ye that are so dear,
Lo, this is he through whom great ills were wrought;
For by our love, which we have loved too well,
Is slain my lord and many noble knights.
And therefore, wit ye well, Sir Lancelot,
My soul's health waneth; yet through God's good
        grace
I trust, when death is come, to sit with Christ,
Because in heaven more sinful souls than I
Are saints in heaven; and therefore, Lancelot,
For all the love that ever bound our souls
I do beseech thee hide again thy face.
On God's behalf I bid thee straitly go,
Because my life is as a summer spent;
Yea, go, and keep thy realm from wrack and war,
For, well as I have loved thee, Lancelot,
My heart will no more serve to see thy face;
Nay, not if thou shouldst know love in mine eyes.
In good haste get thee to thy realm again,
And heartily do I beseech thee pray
That I may make amend of time mislived.
And take to thee a wife, for age is long."
"Ah no, sweet madam," said Sir Lancelot,
"That know ye well I may not while I breathe;
But as thou livest, I will live in prayer."
"If thou wilt do so," said the Queen, "so be.
Hold fast thy promise; yet full well I know
The world will bid thee back."—"And yet," he cried,
"When didst thou know me to a promise false?

Wherefore, my lady dame, sweet Guinevere,
For all my earthly bliss hath been in thee,
If thou wilt no more take of this world's joy,
I too shall cease to know the bliss of life.
I pray thee kiss me once, and nevermore."
" Nay," said the Queen, " that shall I never do.
No more of earthly lips shall I be kissed."
Then like to one stung through with hurt of spears,
Who stares, death-blinded, round the reeling lists,
At gaze he stood, but saw no more the Queen;
And as a man who gropes afoot in dreams,
Deaf, dumb, and sightless, down the gallery stairs
Stumbling he went, with hands outstretched for aid,
And found his horse, and rode, till in a vale
At evening, 'twixt two cliffs, came Bedevere,
And with his woesome story stayed the knight.
At this, Sir Lancelot's heart did almost break
For sorrow, and abroad his arms he cast,
And cried, " Alas! ah, who may trust this world!"

1886.

THE SKETCH

The sketch was done.   I laid it down
Athwart a rock with mosses brown;
Then backed a pace, and saw with shame
How dead my work.   The granite frame,
Grim record of earth's youth of power,
Mocked my slight venture of an hour.
How could I set that thing for praise
'Gainst its immeasurable days!
Lo, here and there, dull mica eyes
Stared from their cleavage mild surprise,
'Neath grim gray sockets lichen-browed.
Too well I knew, and laughed aloud,
For surely comes to us an hour
When sky or rock, or tree or flower,
Finds in our souls that certain tie
That binds God's whole in sympathy,
And bids us wonder, as we go
From large to less, from high to low,
If, past life's line of doubtful fence,
Is lost in rock or tree the sense
That stirs us, or if may remain
Some dulled diffusion of a brain.
At least for me this critic stone
Has thoughts which seem not all my own.
Then piece by piece the sketch I tear,

And cast it on the careless air,
In wonder at the mood could dare
To sit by that mysterious sea,
Nor tremble at its tragedy.
Around me stir the grasses green,
And thick the granite clefts between,
Like little maids that notice crave,
Lated daisies a welcome wave;
And cotton-weed, and golden-rod,
Shyly beckon, or gayly nod.
Here to left are timbers black
That knew the slave a century back;
As children steal through a place of graves,
Soft through its dark hold crawl the waves,
Part the seaweed, and sally out
In white-lipped hurry of tumbled rout.
The darkening sky is green o'erhead,
The solemn surge rolls ghastly red;
The leaping crimson of the sea
Dreams of the slave-ships' agony,
And slowly, on its westering course,
Crawls the dark nightfall of remorse.
My vision of that ancient sin
Is gone.
              Halloa! the tide is in.
Four hours to wait the outward flow:
Time to philosophize, I know.
What space that mocking moon decides
That I shall watch these moving tides
May serve some settlements to hatch
Of points —
                There goes my final match!
What test of philosophic might

Is like a pipe without a light?
Let 's see what kind of Eden isle
The tide will leave me in a while.—
Black lace, athwart a scarlet sleeve!
Can fate have here vouchsafed an Eve?
Half sad, I pause and think, oppressed,
How years have dulled adventure's zest.
A stern, set face; eyes cloudy blue,
That turn to meet my curious view.
A tree-like dignity of form
Might sway with breeze or mock at storm,
Full cloaked with snow-white hair to knee,—
Thanks, kindly wind, that set it free;
Thin hands that struggle with its grace,
Red sunlight through it, and a face
Ash pale against the fading gold;
The mouth 'so stern, the brow so old,
As if these servants of the heart
Had lost the sweetness of their art.
Her face disturbed me; but I set
The mood aside, and, smiling, met
The answering smile she turned on me.
" Well caged we are," she said. " I see
Yon jailer waves relentless be."
Then with strange echo of my thought,
" Time to philosophize of aught
That elsewhere mocks the puzzled will; "
And lightly laughing, " Shall it still?
If lonely darkness look to me
So fertile of philosophy,
How philosophic death must be ! "
" Just so," I said, in such surprise
As men will have when 'neath such eyes

Are asked impossible replies,
And, musing, guessed no rib of me
Had ever given this Eve to be.
Then on the granite ledge we sat,
Talked carelessly of this or that:
The wreck, the sky, the tide, the isle,
Of Browning, Lowell, Clough, the while
Her busy hands, with practised toil,
That strange white hair caught up in coil,
Till silence with the darkness fell;
And save for one drear wave-rocked bell,
And the lone nighthawk overhead,
All earth was still as are the dead.
At last she said, " What trick of fate
Kept you and me just here, so late;
Your sketch, my thoughts ?

                  I have not asked
Your name, nor shall."   And I, thus tasked,
Cried, laughing, " Not more curious I ! "
" Let pass," she urged, " that question by ;
Rest we unnamed as spirits are
That come and go from star to star."
" So be it," I said.   " What message bright
Wouldst have me fetch from yonder height ? "
" A question more," she added, " then
Leave we the world of things and men ;
And if irrelevant, again
You pardon me.   You leave, you say,
At nine, and to be long away ? "
" For years ! "

                A sadness in her tone
Sobbed through my brain.   I turned.   " Alone

Am I, and old; what love gave life
Death hath to-day,— child, brothers, wife."
Was it a tear fell on my hand?
"Thank you," she said,—" I understand.
The hurt are sorrow's priests.   *I* know,
Alas, no years will overgrow
With weeds of rank forgetfulness
The buried flowers of love's distress.
A stranger, on this silent rock,
What can I give you will not shock
Far more than help? "   Then suddenly
Rising, she faced the darkened sea.
" Help me a little.   If, some day
We meet, years hence, you will not say,
I knew that woman in a way:
Nay, not when death has made me glad.
Absurd you think me,— haply, mad:
Think as you will, or seek in vain
To know what ease the troubled brain
Gets when the anguished voice of sin
Prates to the grate-hid priest within."
I touched her hand.   'T was chill and wet.
I said, " If I should cry forget,
Forgive, no soul on earth has power
To drug the memories of an hour.
The phrase were idle: God is near,
Closer than any human ear.
How could I help you? — wherefore speak?
Why should the burdened language seek?
What gain is won?   The words we share,
The sin or grief stays surely there
Where God or chance, or some sad fate,
Has set it.   Will mere speech abate

Or jot or tittle aught of woe,
Or cool the hot lids' overflow ? "
" You think me answered.   Yet so much
You know of grief; have felt its clutch.
There is a grief you cannot feel,
The grief of sin that cannot kneel.
You say, to speak, confess, let loose
To man our hurt, lacks reason's use.
God hears; why speak ?   A straw you toss
To one who drowns; yet from the cross
Fell on the reeling world below
Some words of overmastering woe.
Have you no pity ?   See! my cheek
Burns through the dark that lets me speak.
Think! think!   A woman, hurt, at bay,
To you, God-sent, yearns here to say
Her soul's hell out.   All earthly shams
That burns away, all wordy alms
That shrivels when such speech must come;
And yet, I would that I were dumb.
Or you, or death, that stillest priest,
Must hear me.   Ah, I pray at least
You merely hear me.   If at ease,
In days to come, you coldly please
To wonder why a woman's soul,
Scourged past all modesty's control,
Sought speech or death, I shall not care."
" Nay, pause," I urged.   " Think well, beware."
" And I have thought!" she cried.   " If cheap
You held this instinct, could I leap
From silent guard to open wide
The secrets of a life ?   I bide
Your answer.   Is it life or death ? "

" Go on," I said, with bated breath.
" We cast our pearls to swine.　They know them
　　　not;
The pearl as ignorant: that my woman's lot.
I loved him.　Ah! but not as women love,
With reason, caution, something woven of
What 's left of old love-garments, odds and ends
From lavish likings, lovings,— sisters, friends.
I took one lonely life, and gave him all
My hoarded heart-wealth.　Like his billiard-ball
He used a soul : to win with, pass away
An idle hour,— base use and baser play.
'T is said that when to after life we go
The loved of earth we easily shall know.
Think you, if death consign to darker fate,
We shall as surely know the souls we hate ?
One night, in dreams, we stood a grave above,
Where lay at peace a meagre corpse of love.
Smiling and cold, he took a yellow skull,—
My own it seemed,— and mocked its sockets
　　　dull,
And bade it chatter of dead hopes.　Ah, well.
Twice, thrice I struck him; at my feet he fell
Dead.　Oh, the utter joy of that !　I laughed,
As one long prisoned, who at last has quaffed
The cup of sudden freedom,— heard a scream,
Sharp words I knew — ' You struck me.　Did
　　　you dream ? '
Alas ! I had but dreamed.　The days went by.
Ever red mists, that floated past my eye,
Blurred sight of him, and ever still in thought
I yearned to live my dream.　Think you that
　　　aught

Is sin for one who, slowly murdered, writhes,
Bound on the rack with custom's gnawing withes?
Was that a cry ? a boat ?   My husband !   Yes !
Well, you know surely life's too bitter stress
Brings strange confessions.   Should you chance
        to hear"—
" A pretty chase you 've led me !   Ah ! my dear !
I trust she has not troubled you.   I fear
At times she wanders."

1887.

THE HILL OF STONES:

WE two, my guide and I, through dusty ways
And formal avenues of well pruned trees,
Went past the village and thy dark gray walls,
Antique, deserted Fontainebleau; and still
With talk of him the shade of whose despair
Lies on thy court-yard yet, we loitering
Strolled through the deeper wood, and found at last
A barren space that crowned a hill's green slope,
Where, lonely as a king, a single oak,
Crippled in boisterous battle with the winds,
And gay with leafy flattery of the spring,
Seemed like an old man, cheated suddenly
With some gay dream of childhood's tender hours.
" Here let us rest," he said, and casting down
His woodman's staff, set out upon the grass
Twin flasks of Léoville and fair white loaves;
There as at ease we lay, and ate and drank,
My roving gaze in pleasant wanderings went
Down the green hill, along the valley's range.
The noonday sun hung half asleep in heaven,
And in the drowsied wood no leaflet's stir
Broke the still shadows slumbering on the ground.

Adown the hill, beside a brook that lay
A silver thread, heat-wasted,— far below,
Gaunt rocks in wild confusion tumbled lay,
Thick strewn along the narrowing vale, and barred
The distant thickets with their broken lines.
High on the further hill, twin mount to ours,
A single slab, time-worn, imperial, towered,
And all around it cumbering the sod
A time-worn host of barren rocks was cast
Each upon each,— as after battle lie
The dead upon the dead, to war no more,—
Whilst over them the hot and curdled air
Shook in uneasy whirls that broke the crests
Of distant trees and hilltops far away.
In musing wonder tranced I lay and gazed
Down the cleft valley o'er the waste of stones,—
The while my comrade, stretched upon the grass,
Lay whistling cheerily his ballad gay
Of good king Dagobert; or smiling told,
With frequent urging, in his rough patois,
Some broken bit of legendary lore,
And at the last a story of these stones.

A thousand noisy years ago, 't is said,
Along yon silent vale at eventide
A bearded king, grown weary of the chase,
Rode thoughtful home, but pausing here awhile,
Said: " When life palls, and I no more can ride
With lance in rest, or smite with gleaming blade,
When sorrows sweeten the near cup of death,
Then in this valley's quiet I will build
A palace, where the wise and old shall come,
And none shall talk of what has been, and all

Shall ponder, with clear vision looking on
To that which is to be."
                              Then pensive still
He turned away, and westward rode again,
Whilst after him an hundred barons came,
And riding swiftly, starred at intervals
The dark wood spaces with their robes of gold.
Next morn at Fontainebleau the bearded king
Held, 'neath the oaks, his court, when suddenly
A young knight, breaking through the outer
          guard,
Leapt featly from his jaded horse and cried,
Like one whom some dream-wonder spurs to
          speech :
" Good Sire, last night a lonely man I slept
Upon the hill you love; and where at eve
The bald brown summit lay a dreary waste,
And where the sun of yesterday looked down
On utter solitude, and sowed the ground
With wild-eyed violets — O my liege, to-day
There stands a castle fair with courts and towers
And turrets tall and fretted pinnacles
Upgrown by night, in one still summer night,
As if fay-builded, and around it leap
A thousand soaring fountains, and the air
Reluctant from its bowered garden floats
Sweet with strange odors.   Underneath a porch
Of leaf-carved masonry, I saw, my lord,
As peering through the thicket's fence I gazed,
The queen of women holding wondrous court
Of maidens only just less fair than she."
Then said the king : " The good knight's brain is
          crazed;

Or hath he dreamed? or do we live anew
An age of magic?
                    " Nay," the knight replied;
" I dreamed it not;" and smiled his bearded lord,
While merry laughter shook the mailed ring.
" Give me, good Sire, to seek again the hill,
And fill me with the beauty that doth glow
In her deep eyes, and either I will bring
This royal woman back again with me,
Or if there be delusion in my words,
The dream will break, and I ashamed shall come
To this fair court no more."   Then as the king
In silence bent, he took his palfrey's rein,
And downward gazing parted wide the crowd,
And passed the yielding wood.
                              Whereon the king:
" The test is fair; 't is chivalrous and just
That no man follow him;" and so with this
He went alone, and was no more with men.
Along the valley up the tufted sward
By cold-eyed statues underneath an arch
Of swaying fountains silently he went,
And half dismayed the rosy hedges broke,
And saw the lady and her maiden court.
Then there was sweet confusion, and a maze
Of white and shining arms in wonder raised,
And low, quick, modest cries from girls who fled
For shelter in the thickets, or took flight
Behind their queenly mistress.   She alone
Towered, red and angry, one foot forward set.
" O woman wonderful," he cried — and bent
Before the tempest of her stormy eyes, —
" Send me not forth alone for aye, to hold

Thy memory only like a dagger sharp
To my sad heart; more sweet by far were death."
" Go, sir," she cried; "what right hast thou in me?
Mine only is my beauty."   " Nay," he urged,
Save that God put them in the world with us,
What right have we in yonder wide estate
Of sun and sky and flower-haunted sod?"
" No man on earth is peer of mine," she said,—
And saying this her cold eyes fell on him.
Her cold eyes fell on him; and deadly pale,
Bereft of thought, as one who gropes along,
He turned and went, whilst scornful laughter rang
From briery thickets everywhere around,
And chased his quick uncertain steps, that brake
The garden paths, till on the lone hillside
A sudden coldness fettered limb and trunk,
And in his veins the liquid life grew still,
Whilst form and feature shrunk, and half-way down
On the drear mountain side, a weight of stone
The knight at evening lay, to love no more.
Then quoth the waiting king as days went by:
" He hath not as he promised brought us back
The stately mistress of his fairy hall.
Who is there here, of all my lords, will seek
Yon magic palace, and with winsome wiles
And all the pleasant archery of love,
Fetch me this woman, captive of the heart?"
" And I, and I, and I," an hundred said;
And the sharp clangor of their shaken mail
Rang through the forest ways, as up they leapt.
So, one by one, as the cast die decreed,
They laughing went, and were no more with men.
But as the golden days of summer fled,

Thick-clustered stones upon the hillside marked
Where slept the flower of all that kingly court,
And heard no more the tread of dainty feet
Hail footfalls round them, when the mellow tones
Of music floating from the terraced lawns
Struck echoes from their stony forms that lay
To wait their brothers when the curse should fall.
And so it chanced, that as the hillside grew
Aghast with stony death, all living things
Its deadly boundaries fled, and man and beast
Turned from it ever with unquiet steps.
Yet now and then, when from a distant steep
The shepherd gazed, he saw some fated man
Climb with quick strides the hill, and through the
    stones
Depart from view; and looking then again,
Or hours or days thereafter, scared he saw
The same man, cold and palsied, issue forth
And reel and die, and smite the summer grass
With stony weight. And yet while men amazed
Stared, wondering that God and this could be,
The palace towers, ivy-curtained, stood
Unmoved and stern, as if a century long
Their breadth of shade, with each day's march,
    had crossed
The garden moats, and seen the lily buds
Unbosom tenderly to wild wind wooing
Each wanton morning of a hundred Junes;
Still ever through the silence of the night
A thousand fountains trembled high in air,
And not a breeze but rich as laden bee
Sailed from the garden, heavy with the freight
Of endless music, and the tender chime

Of cadenced voices, echoed high or low
From porch and hall and windowed gallery.

Again came June to lordly Fontainebleau,
And once again on field and woodland fell
The lazy lull of noontide drowsiness,
Where in cool caves of shadow slept the winds,
Whilst warm and still the moveless forest lay.
Therein betimes, at fitful intervals,
The quiet mystery of this noonday trance,
Distant and grave, a solemn anthem filled,
And, soaring lark-like through the listening leaves
That trembled with its sorrow, died away;
But in its place a hymn rose, sweet and clear,
Such as at evening, coming from the wells,
With balanced water-jars upon their heads,
The maidens sing.

       And thus from leafy shades
A knight full armed rode, singing as he went:—

> In olden days did Christ decree
> Twelve knightly hearts with him to be,
> And bade them wear no armor bright
> Save charity and conscience white.
>
> And through all lands they went and came,
> Not covetous of earthly fame,
> And gave the alms of Christian cheer
> To lowly serf and haughty peer.
>
> For Christ they fought with word and prayer,
> For Christ they died,— oh, birthright fair!
> Sweet Mary Mother, grant to me
> That I, like them, pure-hearted be.

Then, as the knight rode on through sun to shade,
And sang how good deeds, mightier than kings,

Are as the holy accolade of God,
And bid the poorest rise a knight of Christ,
From branch and thicket came the birds, and
    sailed
Around his silver casque, and carolling
Awoke the sleeping breezes, till he rode
With tossing plumes upon the open hill.
There all day long in silence wrapt, the knight
Knelt on the green turf gathering faith and strength;
And all day long the same sweet retinue
Of summer songsters circled round his head.
When fell the night he rose, and, stern and calm,
Unlaced his armor slowly, piece by piece,
Laid down his helmet and his spurs of gold,
Ungirt his sword, and cast its jewelled weight
Beside his spear upon the burdened grass.
Then all unarmed and weaponless, he strode
Adown the hill, and sad and silent wound
Its cumbering stones among, till by the brook
Kneeling he crossed himself, and stayed no more,
But through the night, white robed and tranquil,
    went,
Passed in among the wood of founts that shook
Their silvery leafage in the moonlight gray,
Crossed with quick step the flower-beds, and passed
Where gleaming statues sentinelled the path;
Then, while the mirth rose wildest, and the sound
Of merry music shook the stems he touched,
He broke the rose-hedge, and untroubled stood
Amidst the wonder of the magic court.
Grave, glancing right and left, quoth he aloud:
"The peace of God, which passeth other peace,
Be on ye ever,"— and so trembling stood,

Dazed by the mystery of half-seen limbs
And rosy secrets, chastened by the moon.
Swift moving through her shrinking court, the
    queen,
A head above them towering, flushed with wrath,
Shook from white neck and arms the roses red
That, ere he came, a hundred laughing girls
Showered from quick hands, which on a sudden
    checked,
Drooped with their flowery loads,— and "Sir," she
    cried :
" Dost dream as others have to woo us home ? "
" Most near the holy love of God," he said,
" Is such deep worship as a knightly heart
Doth give in some one woman unto all ;
For whatsoever hath love's sweet disguise
Should in the tender eye of woman win
The gentle estimate of charity."
" A priest," she cried,— and smote the ground and
    shook
The lingering roses from her fallen hair ;
Upon the ground the good knight kneeling prayed :
" God grant," he murmured, " all my heart be pure ;
Such love I give thee, woman, as thou hadst
For yonder stones, my brothers, they who lie
Awaiting God upon the mountain side."
" Enough," she cried ; " go, fool, and share with
    them
Their folly and their fate."   And so on him
Her cold-eyed anger fell, and still and chill
In the white moonlight they two stood and gazed
Each on the other, steady, eye to eye,
And yet he went not, though through trunk and
    limb

The slow blood crept, and on his lip a prayer
Died in the saying.
                  "Thou shalt go," she cried;
And, bending, garnered from the flowery fence
A rosy handful.   Then in haste cast back
The snowy cloak that drifted from her neck,
And crying once a shrill and gnarled phrase,
Smote with the roses red his startled face.
On brow and cheek the flying roses struck,
And fell not down again, for suddenly
Twin petals flashed to wings; and they who looked
Saw bud and blossom turned to flitting birds,
Which through the broken moonlight went and
      came,
And sang sweet carols round the white-robed knight.
This while the lady stood amazed and still
And all her court of wonder-fettered maids
Like silence kept for fear, till at the last
The good knight, marvelling, put out his hand,
And took the lady's finger tips, and went
With knightly courtesy and whispered prayer
Along the garden paths. And as they passed,
Behind their steps the wind-tossed grasses shrunk,
The flowers drooped, the busy fountains ceased,
And vase and statue, fading into mist,
Went floating formless from the mountain top.
Still on they moved, she like a lily bent,
And all her women slowly followed her.
"Here pause," he said, and on the middle slope
Her trembling maids fell moaning round their
      queen,
A silver ring upon the dark green turf.
"Behold, morn waketh," said the knight; "no more,

No more for you shall any morning wake;
I charge you look along yon valley drear."
Thereon she silent raised her head and gazed
Adown the hillside thick with deathful stones,
And felt in heart and vein the pulsing blood
Stand still and curdle.   So the hand he held
Stayed pointing down the valley, and he leapt
Across the ring of cold and moveless forms,
And walked in wonder down the mountain side,
And she and they stayed waiting on the hill,
A tumbled heap of dreary rocks, that lay
About the statue of their stony queen.

1858.

THE CUP OF YOUTH

SCENE, A SEA BEACH NEAR RAVENNA. MOONLIGHT.

DRAMATIS PERSONÆ.

GASPAR.	GELOSA, his wife.
UBERTO.	EMILIA, his wife.
GALILEO.	

TIME, *circa* 1632.

SCENE I.   GASPAR *and* GELOSA.   GELOSA *playing with the sand.*

GELOSA (*letting the sand fall slowly through her fingers*).
See, Gaspar, how I hold the hours of love,
Or bid the merry minutes flit away.
  GASPAR.   Time should be captive in those pretty hands,
With none to ransom him, had I my way.
Yet must I break the spell and hustle in
The rough world's business.   Wherefore, little one,
This long delay?   You lacked not courage once.
  GELOSA.   Still am I in the bondage of my youth;
All my life long I feared that silent man
Who came across the garden from the tower,
Ate, slept, or to and fro athwart the grass
Trod one same path with bended head and back,
And shunned all company with this lower world.

153

She whose proud love and gold alike he spent,
She who did love him as the worst are loved
By those sad hearts who best know how to love,
Got but few words and bitter; but for her
I had not cared to see his face again.

GASPAR.   Men say his silence guards such fateful power
As makes yon stars the vassals of his will,
Turns baser metals into golden coin,
And wrings all secrets from the miser Time.

GELOSA.   And yet he knew not that one summer night
A little maid — Gelosa was her name —
Had stolen out beneath his starry slaves
To learn the subtle alchemy of love
That turns all fates to gold, nor lacks the power
To prophesy the sweetness of to-morrow.
Methinks he knew but little, knowing not
What love will dare; or haply knew too much
For all the gentler uses of the world
When, like a landlord with too full an inn,
He thrust out Love, that ever might have been
The fairest guest his learning entertained.

GASPAR.   Nor I more welcome.   I could laugh to think
How patiently I took the beggar's " Nay "
He cast in scorn.   " What! wed a landless squire,
Who spends in folly what he won in blood! —
None but a scholar wins my niece's lands."

GELOSA.   My lands indeed; if certain tales be true,
He married them these many years ago.

GASPAR.   Ay, and may keep them if he be but wise.
Fair over Arno tower my castle walls,
With vine-clad hillsides rolling to the plain.
Nothing I owe you save your own sweet self.
A scholar, I !   Not troubled will you be
By reason of my studies.   I shall learn
Love from your eyes; your lips shall be my law,
And if their ripe decisions please me not,
The fount of justice at its very source
I shall know how to bribe.   I brought you here
Because you willed it,— ay, and save for that
I care but little how this errand thrives.

GELOSA.   Kiss, kiss away the thoughts that trouble me;
The lapsing days will bring some pleasant chance.

GASPAR.   Who trusts that multitude of counsellors
Wins sad unrest.

GELOSA.   Oh, let my errand wait.
How very silent is the sea to-night !
The little waves climb up the shore and lay
Cool cheeks upon the ever-moving sands
That follow swift their whispering retreat.
I would I knew what things their busy tongues
Confess to earth.

GASPAR.   Let me confess you, sweet !
Tell me again you love me.

GELOSA.   Small my need.
'T is in my eyes; 't is on my lips; my heart
Beats to this music all the long day through.
A bird am I that have one single note
For song, for prayer, for thanks, for everything.

GASPAR.   You cannot know how passing sweet it is
To change the camp, the field, the storms of war,
For this and you; to watch the gray moon wane
And see the slumbrous sea leap here and there
To silver dreams.

GELOSA.   The hand of time seems stayed,
And joy to own the ever constant hours,
So full of still assurance is the night.
Love hath the quiet certainty of heaven,
Rich with the promise of unchanging years.

[Voices are heard near by.

GASPAR.   Hush, my Gelosa!   Who be these that come?

[Enter GALILEO *and* UBERTO, *who sit down among the
     dunes close by.*

GELOSA.   My uncle and his friend, the Florentine.
GASPAR.   Hark you, he speaks your name.   He said,
     " Gelosa."
He called you — was it Gelosetta, love?
Why, I shall call you Gelosetta too.

GELOSA.   Distance and absence leave him this one
     friend,
A scholar grave, and gentle as the gentlest.

GASPAR.   And that is Galileo!   I recall
One day in Florence walking with the Duke,
A man most studious of his fellow-men,
We saw this scholar wandering to and fro
Intent of gaze where Giotto's campanile

Athwart the plaza casts its length of shade.
The Duke had speech with him.   A serious face,
With eyes that seemed to search beyond the earth,
Large, open, steady, like Luini's saints.

GELOSA.   More sweet than mine?

GASPAR.   I 'll tell you when 't is day.
A mighty student of bright eyes am I;
Now there I 'll match my science with the best.
Those Florentines, who never want for wit
To label love or hate, say he 's moon-mad,
And hath for mistresses the starry host
That wink at him by night.
GELOSA.   Not Solomon
Had half so many.   Yet for earthly love
He lacks not time nor honest appetite;
He never starved his heart to feed his head.
Hush! now he speaks again.   The time may serve
To learn my uncle's mood.

GALILEO.   This niece of thine—

UBERTO.   Not ever greatly mine.   The wayward child
Grew to the wilful woman, ignorant,
Untrained, and wild, a dreamer by the sea,—
Nor hers the housewife's knowledge.   I have lived
Companionless of nobler intercourse,—
As to a friend I speak,— my wife wrapped up
In household cares and tendance of the poor,
Death busy with my manhood's friends.   I tread
An ever lonelier road.

GALILEO.   So seem all ways
To him who, yearning for too distant good,
Sees not the sweetness of the common path.
Life hath two hands for those who fitly live:
With one it gives, with one it takes away;
The willing palm still finds the touch of love,
And he alone has lost the art to live
Who cannot win new friends.   Unwise are they
Who scorn the large relationship of life.
Yon restless sea, the sky, the bird, the flower,
The laugh of folly, and the ways of men,
The woman's smile, the hours of idleness,
The court, the street, the busy market-place,—
All that the skies can teach, the earth reveal,—
Are wisdom's bread.   Alas! the common world
Hath lessons no philosophy can spare;
The tree that ever spreads its leaves to heaven
Casts equal anchors 'neath the soil below.
With man it is as with the world he treads:
No little stone of yonder pebbled beach
Could cease to be, and this great rolling orb
Feel not its loss.   Enough of this to-night.
Count me your gains a little.   Years have gone
Since last we met: what good things have they brought?

UBERTO.   To-morrow I will tell you all.   To-night
My mind is ill at ease; come, let us go,
But, as my love is valued by your own,
Speak not again of that unthankful child.

GALILEO.   And yet I loved her.   Have it as you will.
                    [*Exeunt* GALILEO *and* UBERTO.

GELOSA.   O Gaspar, said I not that age was hard?
Be but your youth as kind.

GASPAR.   Almost I thank
The misery that doubly sweetens love.
Strange seemed my life to him.   To me, as strange
This corner-pickled shrivel of a man,
That all things dreaming never waked enough
To win the sanity of open eyes.
One day in Rimini, before a mirror,
So near I stood my breath the image blurred.
Duke Francis, laughing, o'er my shoulder gazed;
Said I was like some men he knew, and went,
And would not read the riddle.   Now 't is clear.
The man that hath no mirror save himself
Blurs the clear image conscience shows us all.
Now for a schoolless, helmet-dinted head,
The guess is not so bad.— What, tears again?
Tears for this man who in your childhood scorned
Its glad prerogatives of love and trust?
A thoughtless falcon, bold and wild of wing,
Like to my lover-self, had better kept
God's pledge to childhood.

GELOSA.   Nay, no tears have I
For him who cost me many.   But for her,
The simple, kindly dame who had no will
That was not his,— I am more sad for her,
Because she never learned the woman's art
To traffic with her sadness.   Yet had she
A childless youth; the children of old age,
Love, solace, cheerful days of quietness,
Dead as the little ones she never knew.

Though sad at best the husbandry of years,
Time in the happy face no furrow cuts
That is not wholesome; but the loveless hours
Of uncompanioned sorrow and neglect
Make records sore with shame as are the scars
A master's whip leaves on the beaten slave.
Has life no answering scourge for them that sin?

GASPAR.   For less than this, ay, for a moment's wrong,
I have seen men die young.

GELOSA.   Come, let us go.
The night has lost its grace.   These memories
Serve but to stir dead hates.   To bed,— to bed.
Like his, my mind is very ill at ease;
I would his hurt were equal to my own.

SCENE II.   *Garden of a villa near the sea and border-
      ing on a road.   Enter* UBERTO, *who walks to and
      fro.   Night of the day after the last act.*

UBERTO.   For gold, for lands, for any bribe of power
The soldier wastes the substance of the poor,
Sets ravage free and spills the innocent blood,
Yet sleeps as soundly.   Shall I hesitate,
Checked by the memory of an outworn love,
A thoughtless woman and a foolish girl?
My friend — but he has won the laurel crown.
Dim continents of thought before me lie;
Their harvests wait the vigor of the scythe,
While in my heart the tardy blood of age
Unequal throbs.   The mind, as tremulous
As these thin hands, has lost its certain grasp;

Pass, ye weak phantasies that bar my way,—
Children of habit,— I will do this thing!

Enter EMILIA.

EMILIA (*aside*). Now help me, Mary Mother, in my
    need.
Perhaps some memory of our joyous youth —

UBERTO. What, not abed?

EMILIA. I cannot sleep of late.
As if life were not long enough, the days
Live through the night, and mock with time's excess.

UBERTO. Why vex my soul with that of which each
    hour
Tells the sad tale?

EMILIA. Let us forget, Uberto!
Just half a century gone, when you and I,
Just fifty years ago this very night,
Walked 'neath the flowering locust, how I blessed
The kindly shade that hid my blushing cheek.
Not redder was the moon that night of May.

UBERTO. Still shall it mock the cheek of other loves
When you and I are dead. Oh, cruel time!
You lost the plaything of a pretty face; —
What was your loss to mine? What comfort lies
In useless babble o'er a squandered past?
Lo, when the eager spirit, worn with toil,
Has gathered knowledge, won its lordliest growth,
This robber comes to plunder memory

And lash with needless anguish to the grave.
We scorn the miser who in death laments
The gold he cannot carry; let us jest
At him whose usury of knowledge stops.

EMILIA.   How know you that it doth? To me it
      seems
As if no office of our mortal frame
Has more the signet of immortal use
Than just this common gift of memory.
Forgive the thoughts that come I know not whence,—
I think our Galileo said it once,—
The ghosts that haunt the peaceful hours of night
Are not more unaccountable of man
Than the dead thoughts of life that, at a touch,
A taste, an odor, rise, we know not whence,
To scare us with the unforgotten past.
Your knowledge is not like the miser's gold,
For this world's usage only. Yet, perchance,
'T is like in this, that what it was on earth,
Self-ful, or helpful of another's pain,
May set what interest on that gathered hoard
The soul falls heir to in a world to come.

UBERTO. Alas, were I but sure that after death
I still should carry all life's nobler seed
To ripen largely under other skies,
I should not mourn at death.

EMILIA.   Why is it, friend,
That I, for whom this life so little holds,
Should in its cup of emptied sweetness find
The pearl content, and with calm vision see

The stir of angel wings 'neath death's black cloak?
And life, ah, life might still be sweet to me!
O husband, had you been as some have been,
We might have lived a length of tranquil days,
With love slow moving through its autumn-time
To merge in loving friendship, and at last
To find the cloistered peace of patient age,
Tranquil and passionless, and so have walked
Like little children through life's wintry ways
To meet what fate the kindly years decreed.

UBERTO.   Alas, the best is ever to be won!
There is no rose but might have been more red,
There is no fruit might not have been more sweet,
There is no sight so clear but sadly serves
To set the far horizon farther still.
            [*Voices are heard on the road back of them.*

EMILIA (*aside*).   Heart of my hearts!   It is the little one!
My Gelosetta!   Will he know the voice?

GELOSA (*on the road as she goes by with* GASPAR).
            Can the rosebud ever know
            Half how red the rose will grow?
            Can the May-day ever guess
            Half the summer's loveliness?

UBERTO.   What voice is that?

EMILIA.   Some wandering village girl.

UBERTO.   No, 't was Gelosa's.

EMILIA.   Would indeed it were!
Ah, that were joy!   Alas, 't is but the girl
I helped last winter, one the plague cast out
With other Florentines.   (*Aside.*) Would I could see!

UBERTO.   Come back again to drain our meagre purse
Ay, there 's the man,— a woman and a man.

A man's voice sings.
'T is better to guess than to see,
'T is better to dream than to be.
  The best of life's loving
  Is lost in the proving,
'T is better to dream than to be.
  The joy of love's sweetness
  Is lost with completeness,
'T is better to dream than to be.

EMILIA.   A pair of lovers!   She has found her mate.
UBERTO.   Already doth your cynic lover sing
The death and funeral of love and trust.
Thrice happy these with wingless instincts born.
Perhaps is best the woman's ordered life,
Market and house, the husband and the child.

EMILIA.   Mother of God! and I that have no child!

UBERTO.   St. Margaret! but you women-folk are tender.

Behind a hedge GASPAR *and* GELOSA, *while* UBERTO
continues.

Forget my haste, Emilia; all my mind
Dwells on the nearness of one fateful hour.

EMILIA.   Again the dream that through these weary
    years
Has turned your life from God, and home, and me,—
To win for you that doubtful cup of youth.
Think yet, Uberto, on the thing you do;
It cannot be that I, grown drear and old,
The very death-tide oozing round my feet,
Shall see you glad and young.   It cannot be
Earth holds for me that agonizing hour.
                    [UBERTO *remains silent.*

GASPAR (*to* GELOSA *apart*).   No answer hath he.   Now
    speak you to him.
It seems the wise man hath no wiser dreams
Than fools are heir to.

GELOSA.   Heard you all he said?

GASPAR.   Ay, all I cared to hear.   Come, let us go.
Seek you his wife alone.   Forget this fool.

GELOSA.   Didst hear, my Gaspar?   Can it be he owns
A cup which, drained, shall fetch his youth again?
Men say the thing has been in other days.
To leave her old and withered were to add
A crime, unthought of yet, to sin's dark list.

GASPAR.   Less base it were to stab her where she stands.
                    [*Exit* EMILIA *silently.*

GELOSA.   Hush! she has left him,—left him.   Were
    I she,
I would crawl out at midnight to his tower.
Deep would I drain the damnèd cup of life,
And wander back a maiden fair and young,

11*

To curse his age with jealous misery.
Or I would kill him as he lay asleep,
And keep him old forever,— that would I.

GASPAR.   Now here 's a wicked lady.   Should I chance
To fall in love with larger length of days,
I shall be very careful of my diet.
Comes now the Florentine.   The play were good,
Were you not in the plot.   They say in Florence
The Pope will have it that this man of stars
Shall spread no gossip as to worlds that roll,
Nor play at Joshua with the Emperor Sun.
To be so wise that all the world 's a fool
Might breed uneasy life.

GELOSA.   ,   Perhaps ; and yet,—
You know we little women will have thoughts,—
I was but thinking that for one to own
A soul for actions great beyond compare,
A mind for thoughts that have the native flight
Of eaglets rising from the parent nest,
To soar so high they cast no earthward shade,
Might bring a very childhood of content.

GASPAR.   There 's ever music in your Umbrian heart
That lived where Dante died.   Yet vain the thought ;
For me the world may skip, or stop, or turn
Back somersaults as likes the blessed Pope.
Where got you, love, these riddles of the brain,
These comments on a world you never knew ?

GELOSA.   A certain soldier taught me.   Ah, you
   smile !

To greatly love is to be greatly wise.
God were less wise were He not also love.
Ah, there 's a riddle only love can read !

Enter GALILEO.   *To* UBERTO, *still seated.*

GALILEO.   Far have I sought you through the ilex
   grove,
Among Emilia's roses, in your tower.

UBERTO.   My tower — you saw —

GALILEO.   Saw nothing. (*Aside.*) He distrusts me.

UBERTO.   Forgive me.   You shall see, shall hear, to-
   night.

GALILEO.   Those many years that I, a jocund lad,
To you, my elder, turned for counsel, help,
Came back to me to-day.   You were more kind
Than brothers are.   Ah, happy, studious hours !
What was the Pope to me, or I to him ?
A cardinal was as the farthest star,
Outside the orbit of my hopes and fears.
I came to you to share some idle days,
To get again within your life of thought,
To question and be questioned.

UBERTO.   Wherefore not ?

GALILEO.   A messenger who followed me with haste
Bids me to Rome to answer as I may.
My sin you know.

UBERTO.   What answer can you make ?

GALILEO.   Alas, it moves! This ever-patient globe
Moves, with the Pope and me; would move without.
Could I but summon God to answer them!
If He has whispered in my listening ear
This secret, guarded since the morn of time,
How shall I say I know not it nor Him?
A man may love or not, rejoice or not,
May hate or not, but what he thinks is sped
In word-winged arrows of eternal flight.

UBERTO.   And you, the archer, you who loosed the
        string,
What harm if you should say this was not yours?—
This troubling doctrine long ago was born;
Sages in Egypt knew it.   Or, at need,
Say that the world is stiller than a snail.
Say what you will, but live to draw anew
That bow of thought which you alone can draw.

GALILEO.   Death is more wise than any wisest thought
The living man can think; death is more great
Than any life; and as for that stern hour
I meet in Rome next week, I know not now
How I shall judge my judge.

UBERTO.   The fate I fear,
I fear for you, but would not for myself.
Ay, at this hour would I change lives with you;
For come what may, chains, prison, rack, or axe,
You will have lived so largely that no fate
Can pain your age with sense of unfulfilment.
But I have all things willed, yet nothing done.

Galileo. I cannot think your solitary years
Have won us nothing, as you seem to say.
My hours are few and I go hence to-morrow
Perhaps no more to hear a friendly voice,
Or guess the starry secrets of the night.

Uberto. Be patient with me. Many a year ago,
At twilight walking by the darkened sea,
The sudden glory of a broadening thought
Smote me with light as if through doors cast wide
To one in darkness prisoned. Then I saw
Dimly, as if at dusk, vast open space
Of things long guessed, but waiting fuller light.
What could I but despair? The hand and brain
No longer did my errands. There was set
A task for youth and vigor. Steadily
I gave my age to win the gift of youth,
That youth might help my quest.
                              That charm I sought
Which vexed the soul of old philosophy.
I won it, friend! To-night I drain this cup.
Like autumn leaves the withered years shall fall,
And sudden spring be mine. With wisdom clad,
With knowledge, not of youth, assured of time,
I shall speed swiftly to my certain goal.
The midnight calls my steps to yonder tower,
Where youth, the bride, awaits my joy's delay.
You have my secret. Oh, my God, if youth,
This second youth, should mock me like the first,
And bring no larger gain!

Galileo.   In this wild search
Great minds have perished. Where you think to win,—

In this the masters failed. Their wasted thoughts
Are in huge volumes scattered. It may be.
The strange is only what has never been,
And every century gives the last the lie.
But if 't is so, there 's that within your cup
Might stay the wiser hand. Ay, if 't is so!

UBERTO. If? if 't is so? It is! Not vain the work
That filled these longing years. For no base end
These wasting vigils and these anxious days.
The gains I win shall lessen human pain.
One re-created life to man shall bring
Uncounted centuries in the gathering sum.

GALILEO. I too am of that sacred guild whose creed,
Before Christ died or Luke the healer lived,
Taught temperance, honor, chastity, and love.
I neither doubt the harvest nor the power
To reap its glorious fruit. And yet — and yet —
If the strong river of your flowing life
You shall turn back to be again the brook,
Is 't natural to think 't will float great ships,
Or with its lessened vigor turn the wheel?
Enough of me. I go to meet my fate.
Would I could stay!

UBERTO.   Ah! when in Pisa's dome
You watched the lamp swing constant in its arc,
You gave to man another punctual slave,
And bade it time for us the throbbing pulse;
Joyful I guessed the gain for art and life.
Not that frail English boy Fabricius taught,
Not sad Servetus, nor that daring soul,

Our brave Vesalius, e'er had matched your power
To read the riddles of this mortal frame.
And then you left us. Would our strange machine
Had kept your toil, and cheated yon fair stars!

  GALILEO. We do but what we must. Some instinct
      guides.
To-night, when all the morrow world seems dim
And life itself a thing of numbered hours,
With clearing vision still for you I doubt.
Life hath its despot laws. You more than I
Know all their tyrant rigor. Tempt it not,
Lest failure, anguish, lurk within the cup.
Think sanely of this venture; let it pass.
Fill full, God helping, all the time He leaves.
Set 'gainst the darkness of death's nearing hour
In wholesome light all human action shines.
This dream is childlike; you will wake to tears.
Ask of your life if you have life deserved.
What did you with the gift? You had of it
All that another hath, or long or short.
Not time, but action, is the clock of man.
I should go happier hence if I could set
Your fatal cup aside. Nay, sorrow not;
Thank God for me. I have not vainly lived.
Truth have I served, and God, in serving her:
That heritage is deathless as Himself.
Something the thinker of the poet hath;
Our Dante was no mean philosopher:
With prophet eyes I see a freer day,
When thought shall mock at Kaiser and at Pope.
How can they think to chain the viewless mind,
Which is the very life within the life,

And in the irresponsible hours of sleep
Brings thought unto fruition?   Yea, ethereal!
Of all God's mysteries most near to Him;
Instinctively creative, like the woman,
Pledged by conception's joy to labor's toil.
Grieve not for me.   All that is best shall live.
There is no rack for thought; no axe, no block,
Can silence that.

UBERTO.   But what, dear friend, if I
Should bid you laugh at pope or cardinal?
Take you this cup of mine.   Take this and live.
In youth's disguise lie safety, freedom, life.
    GALILEO (*aside*).   Not stranger in its orbit moves my
        world
Than man, its habitant.   Why, here is one
Could squander years and cheat a woman's love,
Yet turn to offer this.   Not I, indeed!
(*Aloud.*) Life has been very dear to me, Uberto,
For that it has and that it has not been.
How many in their tender multitude
The cobweb ties of friendship, labor, love,
I knew not till this cruel storm of fate
Did thread them thick with jewels numberless.
And yet life owns no bribe would bid me back
To live it o'er anew.   I can but thank you.

UBERTO.   Is it only they who have no life of worth
Would live it o'er again?

GALILEO.   That is not all.
Vainly and long would we have talked of it
In other days.   No life is what it seems.

If thought were man's whole company in life,
Who would not live it o'er?   But from our side
Friends, comrades, fall and torture us with loss.
Who is there born would will to live again
Such anguish as the happiest have known?
This is the heart's. half only; more there is.
But the night wastes.   [*Rises.*

   UBERTO.   To-morrow you go hence?
Write me from Rome.   Before the day is spent
I shall have won or lost.   Good-night, good friend.
                                    [*Exeunt both.*

   GASPAR.   These learned folks are not more gay to hear
Than Lenten priests.   I gave their riddles up
This half hour since.   And you?

   GELOSA.   I heard it all.
Love, friendship, reason, all alike are vain.

   GASPAR.   Had I a moment in his secret den,
That draught of his should give eternal life
To weeds that rot around the moat below.
                              [GELOSA *whispers.*
The jest were good.   Is there no peril in it?

   GELOSA.   None, Gaspar. Wait for me beside the gate.
Quick, ere the chance be lost!   'T is past eleven.
Oh, he will like my jest.   Come, this way, come!

SCENE III.   *Stairway of the tower, where* EMILIA *sits weeping at the door of the astrologer's laboratory, a small lamp beside her.*

EMILIA.   Though he should kill me, I will wait for him.
To die were easy, if to die would stay
His hand from wrong.   Alas! too sure it is,
Alive or dead, I nothing am to him.
Who is it comes ?   Say, is it you, Uberto ?

GELOSA *comes up the stairs.*

GELOSA.   Oh, mother, it is I, your little one !
Friends, husband, wealth, all that life hath to give,
Are mine to-day.   Come to my Tuscan home.
The flowers you love watch for you on the hills.
My children shall be yours.   My good lord waits
Our coming at the gate.   Leave, leave this man.

EMILIA.   I cannot, child.

GELOSA.   Then will I talk with him.
For this we came from Florence.   Once again,
I would be sure his will is as of old.
Beside the tower my good lord waits for me.

EMILIA.   Vain is your errand, child.

GELOSA.   Yet must I try;
(*Aside.*) The equal years give me at last my turn.
(*Aloud.*) Is the door barred ?

EMILIA.   Nay, but I dare not enter.

GELOSA. Not long the thing you fear shall vex your
    soul.
Come with me. Spill the cursèd cup, or wreck
With wholesome fire this chamber of your fear.

EMILIA. Who has betrayed his secrets?

GELOSA.   He himself.
Hid by the ilex hedge I heard it all.
Wept with you, for you; heard your tender plea.
Of other make am I. Give me your ring.
You used to say I had your sister's voice,
Twin to your own.

EMILIA.   What would you say to him?
What do to him? You cannot mean him ill.

GELOSA. Not I, indeed. Hark! there's a voice
    without.
Trust me a little. Quick! the ring, the ring!
No other hope is left. Give me the ring!

EMILIA. You will not harm him? I shall have it
    back?
He gave it me the day we were betrothed.

GELOSA. A goodly half of this world's misery
Is born of woman's patience. Could you live
From that to this?

EMILIA.   What can a woman else?

GELOSA. What else? Naught now. The ring, and
    have no fear!
    [*Takes her hand and removes the emerald ring, which
      is yielded reluctantly.*

Alas, poor withered hand ! how dear thou art,
And sweet with use of bounty !
                              Quick, the lamp :
And wait for me upon the upper stair. [*Urges her hastily.*

EMILIA.   Nay, tell me more.   I am afraid, Gelosa.

GELOSA.   Of me who love you ?   There, a kiss ; good-
    by.
And stir not, if you love or him or me.
    [GELOSA *opens the door, and with the lamp in her hand*
        enters the room.   EMILIA *ascends the upper staircase.*

There may be too much sweetness in a woman.
A little soured on the shadowed side
My Tuscan peaches are.
                              Now what a den !
A winter wealth of kindling in old books.
Bones, and a skull — gray vipers, slimy things,
A crocodile that hath an evil eye.   [*Crosses herself.*
And dust, ye Saints ! but here's a long day's work.
    [*Lifts a bell glass from a small Venice goblet contain-*
        ing a transparent fluid.

Around the rim twin serpents writhe in coils.
                              [*Reads the inscription below them.*

Ex morte vitam.   Life is child of death.
Is this in truth the draught shall make man young ?
Now should I drink, it were a merry jest
To find myself a baby tumbling round,
Athirst for mother's milk.   Not I, indeed.
    [*Empties cup on the floor, and refills it with water.*
        Blows out the light and veils herself.

The moon is quite enough.   Will he be long ?
Now, kindly uncle, for this pretty play.

  [*She conceals herself in a corner.   Enter* Uberto.

Uberto.   At last, 't is near.   The stairs my constant
  feet   .
Have worn with many steps more toilsome grow.
The hounds of time are on their panting prey;
I wait no longer.   No man owns to-morrow.
To-morrow is the fool's to-day.   Ah, soon
I shall go gayly tripping down the hill,
Glad as a springtide swallow on the wing,
A man new born.— Nay, this is like to death.
Why should I falter here ?   We both are old.
Soon in the common way our steps would part.
And to be young; to feel the sinews strong,
Eye, ear, and motion quick, the brain all life,—
The visions of my manhood round me whirl,
White limbs, red lips, and love's delirious dream,
The passion kiss of wine, the idle hours
Unmissed from youth's abounding heritage.
Off, off, ye brutal years that gnaw our age !
Come, joy ! come, life !— life at the full of flood !

             [*Pauses.*

Birth is not ours.   We are, and that is all.
Death is not ours.   We die, and that is all.
This stranger birth that waits upon my will,
Ay, this is mine alone.   The herd of men
Are born and die.   One sole ignoble lot
Awaits them all.   This none can share with me.
Auspicious planets shine upon the hour.

          [*Takes the hour-glass.*

Swift waste the sands.   So much of age is left.
Uncounted memories of things long lost
Leap to my view, as if to one who stands
Beside the waif-thronged surges of the deep,
And sees its dead roll passive to his feet,
Its pearls, its weeds, its wrecks.

                              So let it end.

                    [*Fills up the glass with wine.*

Nor fear, nor friend, nor love shall hinder me.

                              [*Drinks.*

Will it be swift ? or will the change be like
The wonder work of spring ?

   [*Lights a small lamp, and examines his face in a mirror.*

                         A ghastly face !
Is this the earthquake agony of change ?

                    [GELOSA, *still veiled, advances.*

GELOSA.   Change that will never come.   You that
      would cheat
A life-worn love of company to death,
Take the stern answer of a tortured soul.
You drained my cup of life, and cast aside
The poor mean vessel.   I, Emilia, stole
Your cup of life.   Mine is the youth you craved,
Mine the gay dream of girlhood's rosy joy,
Mine once again the wooing lips you kissed
When you and I were young.   Ah, sweet is youth !
Go, thieving dotard, to a loveless grave !

      [UBERTO *staggers forward, with the lamp in his hand.*

UBERTO.   My wife, Emilia ?   No, not my Emilia.

GELOSA.   Nay, touch me not!   And is your memory
   dead?
Why, even I some dim remembrance keep.
Take back this ring, this pledge of endless love.

> [UBERTO *receives it.*

UBERTO.   Her ring — your ring — Emilia! — Lost,
   lost, lost!
Life, honor, fame, and youth.   Emilia, wife,
Speak kindlier to me.   Speak, oh, speak again!
Your voice is like an echo from the past.—
What devil taught you this?   [*Advances.*

GELOSA.   Off, off, old man!
What has a girl to do with palsied age?
I 'll be a daughter to your feebleness,
And fetch your crutch, and set you in the sun,
And get me lovers kin to me in years.

UBERTO.   Black Satan take your kindness!   Yet
   have I
The strength to kill you!   You shall die for this!

> [*Seizes her.*

GELOSA.   What? — feeble fool!
   [*Pushes him away; he falls and remains on the floor.*

UBERTO.   This is not my Emilia.
Help, help, without there!   Help!

GELOSA.   Come in,— come in!
Well have I paid a fool with folly's coin.

> EMILIA *enters and runs to lift her husband.*

EMILIA.   Ill have you done, and cruel I have been.
Oh, you have slain my love !

GELOSA.   Not I, in truth.

UBERTO.   Out, lying baggage !   Now I know you
    well.

GELOSA.   Come you with me, dear mother of my love.
Leave we this base old man.   My husband waits.

EMILIA.   Get hence ! I never loved you.   He knew
    best.
Pray God I see no more the wicked face
That cheated him and me.   Begone, I say !

                        [*Exit* GELOSA.

1888.

MY LADY OF THE ROSES

At Venice, while the twilight hour
　　Yet lit a gray-walled garden space,
　　I saw a woman fair of face
Pass, as in thought, from flower to flower.
　　The roses, haply, something said,
　　For here and there she bent her head,
Till, startled from their hidden nest
In the covert of her breast,
　　Blushes rose, like fluttered birds,
　　At those naughty rosy words.
One need not wise as Portia be
To guess love held her heart in fee.
　　Prudently a full-blown rose
　　For her confidence she chose:
Whispering, she took its breath,
And, for what its fragrance saith,
　　Smiling. knelt, and kissed it twice;
　　Caught it, held it, kissed it thrice.
Ah! her kiss the rose had killed;
　　Wrecked, in tender disarray
　　On the ground its petals lay,
All its autumn fate fulfilled.
　　Swiftly from her paling face
　　Fell the rosy flush apace.

Had her kiss recalled a bliss
Life for evermore should miss?
  Had there been a fatal hour
  When false lips had hurt the flower
Of love, and now its sad estate
She saw in that dead rose's fate?
  Who may know?   A little while
  She lingered with a doubtful smile;
Took then a younger rose, whose slips
The garden knew, and with her lips
  Its color matched. What gracious words
  It said might know the garden birds,—
Something, perchance, that liked her well;
But roses kiss, and never tell.

  What confession, what dear boon,
  Heard that ruddy priest of June?
Was it a mad gypsy-rose
Fortunes eager to disclose,
  Gravely whispering predictions
  Rich with love's unending fictions,
Saying nonsense good to hear,
Like a pleasant-mannered seer?
  Gypsy palms are crossed with gold,
  But my lady, gayly bold,
In the antique coin of kisses
Paid for prophecy of blisses;
  And, to make assurance sure,
  This conspirator demure
Murmured, in a pretty way,
What her prophet ought to say.
  Low she laughed, and then was gone;
  My pleasant little play was done.

Alone I sit and muse.   Below,
Black gondolas glide to and fro,
   Like shadows that have stolen away
   From centuried arch and palace gray.
Then, as if out of memory brought,
   The sequel of my garden masque
Comes silently, by fancy wrought,—
   A gift I had not cared to ask.

Lo! where the terraced marble ends,
   Barred by the sweetbrier's scented bound,
The lady of my dream descends,
   And day by day the garden ground
Her footsteps know; with lingering gait,
She wanders early, wanders late,
   Or, sadly patient, on the lawn
Each day renews her gentle trust,
   When, from the busy highway drawn,
Float high its curves of sunlit dust.
   The children of her garden greet
   With counsel innocent and sweet
   The coming of her constant feet.
She whispers, and their low replies
Bring gladness to her lips and eyes;
   She will no other company;
   For her the flowers have come to be
   All of life's dim reality.
Purple pansies, gold embossed,
That in love had once been crossed,
Murmur, We have loved and lost;
   And the cool blue violets
   Sigh, We wait for life's regrets.
Thistles gray, beyond the fence,

Mutter prickly common sense;
  While the lilies, pale and bent,
  Say, We too sinned, are penitent;
  Only that can bring content.
Red generations of the rose
Unheeded passed to death's repose;
  The peach upon the crumbling wall,
  With springtide bloom and autumn fall,
No proverb had to foster fear,
No time-worn. wisdom brought her near.
  The willows o'er two noisy brooks,
  In marriage come to sober mood,
Were but green slips, that eve of May;
Now, underneath their shade she looks,
  And smiling says, " Time must be rude,
To keep him thus so many a day."
They tell her he is dead! " Ah ! nay,"
She answers; " he but rode away,
And he will come again in May.
  And I can wait," she says, and stands
  With roses in her thin white hands.
Childlike, with innocent replies,
She meets the world. Wide open lies
  Her book of life; Time turns the leaves,
  Like each to each, because she grieves
Nor less nor more, save when in fear,
On one dark eve of all the year,
  Dismayed lest love's divine distress
  Be dulled by time's forgetfulness.

Venice, *June*, 1891.

HOW THE POET FOR AN HOUR
WAS KING

Once in a garden space, Saädi saith,
I came upon a tower, where within
There lay a king imprisoned until death
Should set him free; and thinking deep of sin,
And those who took its madness to and fro
Below the dead hope of these prison bars,
I saw the thoughtless stream of pleasure flow
Till evening, and the sad reproachful stars
Loosed a great sorrow on me for this king
To whom in other days I joyed to sing.
Himself had trained himself to noble use
Of that great instrument, a man ; abuse
Of power he knew not ; never one
So served victorious virtue.   Then there came
Defeat and ruin.   Now no more the sun
Shall see again his face who reckoned fame
As but an accident of righteous deeds.
Thus evening found me thinking how exceeds
Man's strangest dream, what Allah wills for him,
Till through the shadows of the twilight dim
I heard the gray muezzin call to prayer.
Upon the sands I knelt alone, and there
Entreated Allah till the middle hour.

Among the palms that were around the tower
Came, as if pitiful, the nightingale,
And sang and sang as if 't were sin to fail;
Whilst I who loved this great soul come to naught
Stayed wondering if any solace brought
The happy song that knows not pain of thought.
But then I heard above me, clear and strong,
The king's voice rising gather force of song,
Till from the prison wall its tameless power
Triumphant rang, as in some doubtful hour
Of angry battle or when from retreat
It called again the shame of flying feet.
Now like a war drum rolling far away
Its stormy rhythms died.   No voice may say
Its after sweetness, for, as falls a bird
That high in air hath on a sudden heard
Its little ones below, and surely guessed
The lonely sadness of the yearning nest,
Fell earthward pitiful the singer's verse,
Cradled the many griefs of man, the curse
Of pain, of sin, and in its soothing rhyme
Rocked into peace these petty woes of time,
Till I, who would have given a caliph's gold
For consolation, was myself consoled.
Musing, I said, " Lo! I will be this king,
Because a poet can be anything,
And may inhabit for a wilful hour
A maiden heart, or haunt a dewy flower,
Or be the murdered, or the murderer's hate."
I called to mind all knowledge, small or great,
Men had of him who sang, when his estate
Knew power and its danger.   How he ruled
A wayward race I knew; how sternly schooled

His gentleness to give large justice sway;
How helped the kindly arts of peace, and gay,
And masterful of all that makes life sweet,
The jewel love set in this crown complete.
These, and much other gathered up from thought,
I took — and lo, how strange!   A moment
     brought
The whole to oneness, as when on a glass
The sun-rays fall, and bent together pass,
And glowing, flash a point of burning light;
So, for a time I was the king that night.

A king was I,— a king of Allah's birth,
In one brief hour I lived long years of earth.
I broke the robber tribes who vexed with wrong
My peaceful folk.   Yea, as the simoon strong
That hurls the sands of death, in will and deed
A king I rode.   Then saw my regal state
Fall from me ruined, and a brutal fate
Wreck law and justice; with a tranquil face
Beheld die out of life its joy and grace,
And quick death busy with whate'er I loved.
All these I saw, but with a heart unmoved,
And marvelled at myself, as in a dream
A man hath wonder when his visions seem
Fitting and true to sense.   And so erelong,
Considering what fault had let the wrong
O'ercome the right, I lost myself in song.

Am I the potter ?   Am I the clay ?
Allah, Thou knowest !   Soft and gray
Fall the curling shreds away.
Lo, the noiseless feet of years

Swift the rhythmic treadle ply;
Hath the potter doubts and fears?
Is the clay kept soft with tears?
Still the busy wheel doth fly.
He is the potter, I am the clay;
Swiftly drop the ribands gray,
Flower and vine leaf silently grow,
Strong and gracious the vase doth show,
Firm and large,— the cup of a king.
Hither and thither wandering
The potter's fingers deftly smooth
Tangled tracery, and groove
Emblems, texts, the rose of love.
Suddenly his fingers slip,
Cracks the ever-thinning lip.
Was it the potter?   Was it the clay?
Allah! Allah! who can say?
And the king I was that night
Smiled, to see the potter's plight.

I am the potter, I am the clay,
Spinning fall the earth-threads gray,
Deftly moulded, strong and tall
Grows the vase, and over all
Bud and roses, vine and grape,
Twine around its comely shape.
Was it potter?   Was it clay?
Did the potter's hand betray
Indecision?   Who can say?
At his feet the fragments roll;
Lo, beside the wheel he stands
Wondering, with idle hands.

Let him gather up his soul
And make the clay a poor man's bowl!

Thus said the quiet king I was that night,
And o'er me grew the life of morning light,
While from the constant minaret above,
As drops a feather from the angel love,
Fell the first call to prayer, and overhead
A strong voice from the prison tower said,
" Allah il Allah ! God is ever great.
Time is his prophet for the souls who wait."

1890.

THE VIOLIN

TIME 1750

THE TYROL

JOHAN.

> Sing sweet, sing sweet, my violin, sing;
> Sing all thy best,— sing sweet, sing sweet;
> Gay welcomes fling more swift to bring
> The cadence of her loitering feet.
> Ring strong along thy bounding wires
> A song shall throng with youth's desires.
> Let the yearning joy-notes linger
> 'Neath the coy, caressing finger,
> Till the swift bow, flitting over,
> Dainty as a doubtful lover,
> Slyly, shyly, kisses dreaming,
> Falters o'er the trembling strings,
> And the love-tones, slower streaming,
> Fade to fitful murmurings.
>
> Another year!   Ah, fate is hard!
> Another year!   My hands are scarred
> With rugged toil.   The tender skill
> With which they wrought my music's will
> Fails as the days go by; and yet

No term to misery is set.
Thou gentle conjurer of sound,
The one fast friend my life has found,
Vain all thy art; though I can wing
The love-larks from each leaping string,
And heavenward send them carolling;
Bend at my will the soul in prayer,
Bid man or maid my sorrow share;
Can stir the ferns upon the rock,
And anguish all the air with pain;
Or, velvet-voiced, delight to mock
The fairy footfalls of the rain.
It helps me not, though I have force
To thrill the forest with remorse,
Or torture sound till every air
Dark murder hisses, and despair;
And, 'mid the harmonies that flow,
Strange discords riot 'neath the bow,
Like 'wildered fiends astray in heaven,—
Alas, alas, why was it given,
This useless power?   My wasted art
Serves but to wring a peasant's heart.

ELSA.

My Johan, have you waited long?
I heard your viol's happy song;
I heard it call, "Come quick, come fast!"
As o'er the stepping-stones I passed.
I heard it calling, "Sweet, come fleet!"
As up I came among the wheat.
The birds o'erhead called, "Soon,— come soon!"
I think they know its pretty tune.
What, sad again, and ever sad?

Play, Johan, play!   'T is eventide;
The bells ring out the story glad
How came her joy to Mary's side.

JOHAN.

I cannot.   Better had I stayed
In yonder convent's tranquil shade,
At hopeless peace.   They meant it well
Who bade me be a priest.   The cell,
The fast, dead prayers, a palsied life,
I fought or bent to, till the strife
O'ermastered patience.   None too late
I fled beyond their cursèd gate;
And free was I as birds are free
To fly, and yet at liberty,
Like them, to quench no single note
That trembles in the eager throat.
What slavery sweet to feel within
The song which not to sing is sin!
If He at whose divine decree
These hands interpret Him can be
So careless of the gift He gave,
What has He left me but the grave?
I plough, I dig; far through the years
I see myself the slave of tears,—
I, that have dreamed of love and fame,
A village boor, without a name.
Last week the young duke opened wide,
To please the poor, his garden's pride.
There, wandering, I saw withal
The nectarines rotting on the wall,
The tumbling grapes caught up with thread,
The dead-ripe figs hung overhead,

The fattening peaches swung in nets.
What woman's starving baby gets
One half the care that saves these pets?
Sharp, sharp the lesson.   Break, sad heart,
Or learn to know the poor man's art,—
The art to bear with patience meek
The blow upon the other cheek.
How shall I bear it?   I could steal,
Cheat, for this chance.   You only feel,
And you alone, how hard the toil
That bends me o'er the silent soil,
And you alone what wild desires
Await a larger life; what fires
Of wordless anguish burn unguessed,
To think,— be sure,— that unexpressed,—
A serf, a boor,— my soul has here
A gift the waiting world holds dear.
Old violin, comrade of the hours
That labour spares, what music-flowers,
What whispers wild, what visions bright,
Thy friendship brings the tired night!
And yet, like one who, sick with sin,
Would murder love he cannot win,
Twice on the bridge, at night, I stood,
To cast thee in the wrecking flood.
But when a last farewell I sung
Too stern a pang my bosom wrung;
I could not drown the dreams that crave
Expression's life.   Best were the grave.

ELSA.

Yet that were sin!   Could I but give
My life to help your art to live!

> The Alp-horn calls; I cannot stay.
> One kiss.   Ah, Johan, wait and pray.
> > [*She sees a purse in the road.*
> A purse!

JOHAN.   I pray it be not thin.

ELSA.

> Nay, touch it not.   It lies within
> The shadow of the cross.   'T is sin.
> Who taketh but a flower or stone
> Where that holy shade is thrown
> Is cursed to death.   His dearest prayer,
> Fluttering like a prisoned bird,
> Never wins the happy air,
> Beats against the painted saints,
> At the altar hopeless faints,
> Never, never to be heard.

JOHAN.

> The ban is off,— the sun is on.
> St. George! 't is full; my luck has won.
> Good thirty ducats, gold beside!
> Ho for my love, my art, my bride!

ELSA.

> What, take at will another's gold,
> For love, for greed?   Stay, Johan,— hold!
> The duke has guests!   You cannot soil
> Your soul with this.

JOHAN.   And did they toil
> To win this money?   Out of earth

Some swarthy bondsman wrought its birth.
His sweat, his pain, to be at last
A wanton's wage, a gambler's cast!
Mine is it now to better end.

ELSA.

You cannot keep it.   Johan, friend,
A curse is on it.   Curses stay.
For gain did one Lord Christ betray:
When Satan gives another's gold,
So much of the Christ is sold.
Blessings come and heavenward go,
Wing-clipped curses bide below.
Thirty ducats, broad and bright,—
Hide them, Johan, out of sight.
Silver white, it fetcheth blight!
Gold, gold, is wicked, bold!
Hear now the story mother told:
Since ever I was a little maid
Ghost-gray silver makes me afraid.

Zillah's son, great Tubal Cain,
Deep he diggèd in the earth,
Where strong iron hath its birth,
Till the hurt earth sobbed with pain.
Little recked he, Tubal Cain.
The sword and the ploughshare
Out of iron he forged with care;
Brass and copper red he found
In their coffins underground.
Then Lord Satan hired he
To dig to all eternity.
Tore he from the broken mould

Moon-white silver, sun-red gold.
On the blessèd Sabbath morn,
Tubal Cain, with laugh and scorn,
Tortured from the silver white
Thirty pieces, broad and bright.
Quick were they and sore to keep;
None who had them gathered sleep.
Little Joseph's brethren said
They would dye his garments red;
Thirty coins of Tubal Cain
Gat they for their brother's pain.
At the holy city's gate
Joseph and Mary long did wait;
Neither corn nor gold had they
The cruel Roman tax to pay.
Little babe Jesu spake aloud,—
Marvelled greatly all the crowd,—
Spake the child in Mary's ear,
" Dig in the sand, and have no fear."
Deep they delved, and brought to light
Thirty pieces, broad and bright.
Foul-faced Judas sold his Lord
For to have this devil-hoard;
Black-faced Judas had for gain
The thirty coins of Tubal Cain.
On the floor the coins he spent,
Brake his heart, and out he went.
All the way adown the hill
Rolled the ducats with him still;
Underneath his gallows tree
Danced the ducats for to see.
Now they pay for murder done,
Now by them the thief is won.

Mary, Mother, and every saint
Keep me from the silver taint!
My heart from wrong, my body from pain,
My soul from sin like Tubal Cain!

JOHAN.

The purse is mine! No old monk's tale
Shall stay my hand. If this should fail —
All men own death. How shall it be?

ELSA.

Give me the purse! The purse or me?
Am I so little worth?

JOHAN. Take care;
I hear a horse.

Enter HORSEMAN.

HORSEMAN. Ho, fellow, there!
Hast seen a purse? Just here it lay.

ELSA.

My Johan found it.

HORSEMAN (*takes it*). Thanks. Good-day.
[*Rides away as a gentleman comes behind them, hidden
by the hedge.*

JOHAN.

Now is life over.

13*

ELSA.   Never less.
        Your soul is saved.   Now, Johan, guess
        A secret.   No?   Well, at the fair
        Last week I sold, I pledged my hair.
        To-morrow I shall fetch the gold
        To win your way.   Ah, love is bold.
        My father?   Think you I shall care?
        A little hurt; less ill to bear
        Than that worse hurt you bade me share.

JOHAN.

        Forgive, forget!   Ah, not again
        Your trust shall fail.

ELSA.   Just one more kiss;
        And ere your sinless face I miss,
        Take up the viol.   Say not nay.
        The twilight song.   Play, Johan, play
        The song that in the stillness brings
        My troubled soul from earthly things,
        When the blown horns the cattle call
        Back to the shelter of the stall.

JOHAN.   Come home, come home.
                Not through the sallow wheat,
                Come home, come home,
                Though to grass-tangled feet
                The dewy ways be sweet.
                Come home, come home,
                Meek eyes and skins of silk,
                Come home, come home.
                Fetch the clover-scented milk,
                Come home, come home.

With their pails the maidens wait,
Ever singing at the gate,
Come home, come home.
Come ye home to Mary's wings,
Joy to earth the angel rings,
Come home, come home.
Bring your load of care and sin,
Lo, she waits to let you in,
Come home, come home.

Stay, stay awhile.   Though dear my art,
More dear your love.   The tears that start
I know are joy.   Lo, Seraph wings
Flutter o'er the praying strings.
Hark and hear your gladdened soul
All the raptured viol thrill;
Viewless hands my touch control,
Other force than earthly will.
Purer than the chant of saints
Rings the anthem of your heart;
Though upon your lip it faints,
Though the tears your eyelids part,
Angel voices, pure and strong,
Catch the sweetness of the song.
Hark! the silver crash of cymbals;
Hear the joyous clash of timbrels,
Pouring through the shadows dim;
All the air is music-riven,
And the organ's stately hymn
Thunders to the vault of heaven.
Murmurs, whispers, sad, mysterious,
Language of another sphere,

Faint and solemn, tender, serious,
Wander to my listening ear.

Enter GENTLEMAN.

GENTLEMAN.
A poet-lover!   Did you find my purse ?

JOHAN.
Ay; and had kept it, too,— or worse,—
Except for her.

GENTLEMAN.   Would Eve had stayed
As honest as your blushing maid!
I always thought the story queer,
Would like that poor snake's tale to hear.
Sometimes I fancy Madam Eve
Tempted the Tempter to deceive.
I heard you tell a pretty tale
About some yellow hair for sale.
Wilt sell it now ?   Say, gold for gold !
Let 's see the goods.   [*Pulls out the comb.*
                    'T is worth, when sold,
A hundred ducats.

JOHAN.   No, my lord,
'T is not for sale.   No miser's hoard
Could buy it.

GENTLEMAN.   Say two hundred, then ;
A kiss to boot.   I know of men
Would ask for six.

ELSA.   'T is yours,— 't was mine !

GENTLEMAN.
>The gold is thine.   Too proudly shine
>Those locks above a heart of gold
>For me to part them.   When you 're old,
>And you have babes and he has fame,
>Teach in their prayers the wild duke's name.
>And you who thought a purse to keep,
>Within that battered violin sleep —
>Ah, but I heard — all wealth and power
>Man craves on earth.   In some full hour,
>When heaven is nearest, make for me
>One golden fugue, to live and be
>Remembered when the morrow's light
>Is gone for us.   Good-night, good-night.

1887.

FRANÇOIS VILLON

THE COUNT DE LILLE.
THE SEIGNEUR DE LUCE.

Time, circa 1463

SCENE, *The Garden of an Inn.*

DE LUCE.
    OUR good Duke Charles, you tell me, fain would
        know
    Where bides this other rhymer.   Be it so.
    I might have said, I know not: for to lie
    Is easy, natural, and hath brevity
    To win its hearing favor, whilst the truth
    Spins out forever like a woman's youth,
    And lacks the world for ally.   But mere pride
    Would make me honest.   Let the duke decide
    'Twixt boor and noble.   Ah! 't was gay, I think,
    When we were lads together.   What! not drink?
    Then, by St. Bacchus, here 's to you, my lord!
    Men say that luck, a liberal jade, has poured
    Her favors on you : lordships half a score,
    Castles and lands, that vineyard on the Loire;
    Something too much for one who lightly leaves
    Such wine as this.   Alas! who has, receives.

202

DE LILLE.
> Come when you will and share it.   I have served
> God and the king.   What fortune I 've deserved
> The good saints know; through many a year I 've
>   played
> The games of war and peace.   My father's blade
> Has no stain on it.   That, it seemeth me,
> Were pleasant to the conscience, when, set free
> From war and council and grown old and gray,
> Fades in monastic peace one's life away.
> These war-filled years gone by since last we met
> Have had their griefs.   What of yourself?   Forget
> My fates and me.   I think the latter wars
> Have missed your helping.   As for me, my scars
> Count half these years.

DE LUCE.   Well, as chance willed, I fought
> In Spain, or Italy, or France, and brought
> Some pretty plunder back; have killed my share,
> Dutch, Don, or Switzer, any — everywhere
> That bones were to be broken and the fare
> And game were good; have taken soldier pay
> On this side and on that.   In wine or play
> Spent gayly; found life but a merry friend
> That lent, and then forgot the debt.   To end,
> Came home.   And now my tale.   On Easter day
> It lost its hero.
>   Silence, once 't is broke,
> Can no man mend.   'T was thus this fellow spoke
> Of whom I talk.   I never owned the thing
> Folks like to label conscience, which the king
> Packs wisely on his chancellor.   My device,
> " *Suivez le Roi*," suits well with life.   Not nice

Need one to be who Louis, or the rest,
Loyally follows,— taking what is best
Each good day offers; yet, sometimes, De Lille,
Woman or wine, or one's too ready steel,
•Lures one a trifle past the line of sport,
And then,— you see my point,— a friend at court
Perchance is needed.   Gossip, hereabout,
Which spreads like oil on water, leaves no doubt
That I should speak.   That wastrel had a way,
A trick of speech, as when he said, one day,
" The pot of Silence cracked, 't were best to break."
Strange how his words stay with me!   Half awake
Last night, I saw him, laughing too, and gay,
A grinning ghost, De Lille.   What priest could lay
A rhyming, jesting fiend?   I have killed men,
Ay, and some pretty fellows too, but then
None troubled sleep.   This dead man, like an owl,
Roosts, wide-eyed, on my breast,— a feeble fowl—
Mere barnyard fowl at morn,— a carrion ghost.
The devil has bad locks to keep his host
Of poets, thieves, and tipplers.

DE LILLE.   Think you so ?
No man can tell, De Luce, when some chance blow
Shall give him memories none may care to know.
Once, when we charged nigh Burgos, sorely pressed,
I drove my rapier through a youngster's breast
In wild fierce mellay when none think,— and yet
I see him,— see him reeling; never can forget
His large eyes' sudden change, that one long cry !
'T was but a moment, and the charge went by.
Some unknown woman curses me in sleep,
Mother or mistress; why does memory keep

These nettles, let the roses fall ?   Well! well!
What more, De Luce ?   The tale you have to tell
Is told a friend !

DE LUCE.   Three bitter years ago
A woman, every year more fair, one Isabeau,
A Demoiselle De Meilleraye, began
To twist this coil which later cost a man
A pleasant reckless life, and you my tale.
Maids I have loved a many, widows frail
Loved *par amour*, but this one gayly spun
A pretty net about me.   It was done
Before I fully knew, and once begun,
No fly more surely netted.   Ever still
The web is on me.   At her merry will
What pranks she played! — and I, a fettered slave,
Was black or white, was all things, blithe or grave,
As met her humor.   Many a suitor came
Because her lands were broad, and, too, the game
Worth any candle.   She but laughed.   Some flared,
Or sputtered, and went out.   My lady shared
Their woe but little.   As for me, I fought
A good half dozen lordlings, also caught
A hurt or two.   But then, ah ! thàt was worse,
A fellow came who wooed my dame in verse,
And did it neatly,— made her triolets
Rhyming her great blue eyes to violets;
Wrote chansons, villanelles, and rondelettes,
Sonnets and other stuff, and chansonnettes,
And jesting, rhymed the color of my nose
With something,— possibly an o'erblown rose.
No need to say we fought, but luck went hard :
I thrust in tierce ; he parried, broke my guard,

And then, I slipped,— St. Denis! but I lay
A good six weeks to ponder on the way
The rascal did the thing.   And he the while
Had to himself my lady's gracious smile;
Whereon we played the game again, and time
Was that to which my rhymer ceased to rhyme.
A pretty trick there is, De Lille, you see
I learned in Padua; this way, on one knee
To drop a sudden; then a thrust in quarte
Settles the business.   You shall learn the art.
T' is very simple.   Ah! before he died
He fumbled at his neck, and vainly tried
To snatch at something, till at last I took
A locket from him, for his own hand shook,
As well might be.   He had but only breath
To mutter feebly " Isabeau," then death
Had him, and I the locket — have it still,
And some day she shall have it — in my will,
For scourge of memory.   This same Isabeau
Wept as a woman does, whilst to and fro
I wandered, waiting till the mood should go,
Then came again and found my lady fair
Reading my dead man's chansons.   Little care
Had she for others.   I, a love-fool, spent
The summer days like any boy, intent
To fit my will to hers.   I laugh again
To think I vexed my battle-wildered brain
In search of rhymes.— You smile, my lord?   'T is
        so,
To find me gallant rhymes to Isabeau.
Pardie, De Lille, she rhymed it thrice to — No!
Swore none could love who lacked the joyous art
To love in song.

                         Now, really when the heart
Gives out, and knows no more, one asks the head
To help that idiot ass. Some one has said,—
Ah! that man said it,— said, " 'T is heads that win
In love's chuck-penny game." And I had been
The heart's fool quite too long.—
                              At last, one day,
Hunting by St. Rileaux, I lost my way,
And wandering, lit upon a man who lay
Drowsing, or drunk, or dreaming mid the fern.
Quite motionless he stayed, as in I turn,
And say, " Get up there, villein! Ho! in there,—
Get up, and pilot me the way to Claire!"
On this rose lazily a lean, long man;
Yawned, stretched himself,— with eyes as brown as
     tan,
And somewhat insolent, regarded me; a nose
Fine as my lady's; red, too, I suppose,
With sun, or just so much of sun as glows
Shut up in wine: and thus far not a word.
Till I, not over gay, or somewhat stirred
By this brute's careless fashions, wrathful said,
" Art dumb, thou dog?" But he untroubled laid
His elbow 'gainst a tree trunk, set his hand
To prop his head, and then,—
                              " I understand.
You lost the way to Claire, while I have lost
The gladdest thought that haply ever crossed
A poet's brain. Think what it is, fair sir,
To feel within your soul a gentle stir,
To see a vision forming as from mist,
And just then as your lips have almost kissed
This thing of heaven, to have a man insist

You show the way to Claire.   A man may die
And still the world go on, but songs that fly
From laughing lip to lip, and make folk glad,
Have more than mortal life.   'T is passing sad.
You 've killed a thing had outlived you and me,
Bishops and kings, and danced, a voice of glee,
On lovers' tongues."   Loudly I laughed and long.
" Mad ! mad ! " I cried; " the whole world 's mad in
        song.
Out-memory kings ?   What noble trade have you
That rate a king so low ?   Speak out, or rue
The hour we met.   Your name, your name, man, too,
Unless you like sore bones."   At this he stayed,
No more disturbed than I, and undismayed
Said, " François Villon de Montcorbier
Men call me; but I really cannot say
I have not other names to suit at need,
As certain great folks have; and sir, indeed
As to my trade, I am a spinner, and I spin,
As please my moods, gay songs of love or sin,
Sonnets or psalms — could make a verse on you.
Hast ever heard my ' Ballade des Pendus ' ?
I gave the verse a certain swing, you see,
That humors well the subject; you 'll agree
To read it really shakes one; many a thief
That verse has set a-praying.   To be brief —
Ah, you 'll not hear it ? — then, sir, by my sword, —
But that 's in pawn, — or better, by my word, —
I can't pawn that, — ye saints ! if I but could !
Now just to pay your patience, — leave the wood
At yonder turning; then the road to Claire
Lies to the left; but you must be aware
The day is somewhat warm, and pray you try

To think how very, how unnatural dry
I am inside of me; for outwardly,
Thanks to the dews, I 'm damp; but could I put
My outside inside, — Ah! your little ' but '
Is really quite a philosophic thing
For lords who lose their way, and men who sing.
The simple fact is, I am deadly dry —
And that mere text once out, the sole reply,
The sermon, lies within your purse."   I said,
" Had you not put a notion in my head,
I long ago had broken yours.   Instead,
Sell me its use awhile."   " If talk be dull,"
Cried he, " 'twixt one who fasts and one who 's full,
St. George! 't is duller than the dullest worst
When one of them is just corpse-dry with thirst.
Once, by great Noah! a certain bishop-beast
Kept me for three long summer months at least
On bread and water,— water!   Were wine rain,
I never, never could catch up again."
Well, to be brief, De Lille, just there and then
We drove an honest bargain.   He, his pen
Sold for so long as need was,— I, to get
Three times a week some joyful rondelette,
Sirventes satiric, competent to fit
The case of any wooing, versing wit,
Dizains, rondeaux, and haply pastourelles,
With any other rhyming devil-spells
A well-soaked brain might hatch, whilst I agreed
To house, clothe, wine the man, and feed.
That day we settled it at Claire.   A tun
Of Burgundy it took before 't was done.
And then, to ease him at his task, you know,
Smiling he queried of this Isabeau:

Her eyes, her lips, her hair; because, forsooth,
"The trap of lies were baited best with truth."
Quoth I, half vexed, "Brown-red, her hair." "I
    know,"
My poet says; "gold — darkened, like the glow
The sunset casts, to crown a brow of snow."
Then I, a love-sick fool! — "She has a way —
Of" — "Yes, I understand; as lilies sway
When south winds flatter, and the month is May,
And love words has the maiden rose to say."
Here pausing, suddenly he let his head
Rest on his hands, and, half in whisper, said,
"Alack! Full many a year the daisies grow
Where rests at peace another Isabeau."
"The devil take thy memories! Guard thy
    tongue!"
Said I. What chanced was droll, for quick tears,
    wrung
From some low love-past, tumbled in his wine:
Cried he, "The saints weep through us. Can these
    tears be mine?
The dead are kings and rule us" — drank the liquor
    up,
Laughed outright like a girl, and turned the cup,
With "Never yet before, since life was young,
Did I put water in my wine," then flung
The glass behind him, shouted, "Quick, a bottle! —
Another; grief is but a thief to throttle.
Ho! let the ancient hangman Time appear
And tuck it a neat tie beneath the ear.
    Many a trade has master Time.
    He sits in corners, and spinneth rhyme.
    He is a partner of master Death,

Puff's man's candle out with a breath,
Leaves the wick to sputter and tell
In a sort of odorous epitaph
How foul the thought of a man may smell
For the world that lives, and has its laugh.
Ha! but Time has many trades!
Something in me now persuades
Master Time, grown debonair,
Hath turned for me a potter rare,
And made him a vase beyond compare:
Here below, a rounded waist,
Fit with roses to be laced;
Rising, ripely curved above
Into flowing lines of love.
Thinking, too, how sweet 't would grow,
Time called the proud vase Isabeau."
" By every saint of rhyme," laughed I, " good fellow,
If this a man can do when rather mellow "—
" What shall he do ripe-drunk ? " he cried ; " erelong
The vine shall live again a flower of song."
How much he drank that six months who may
    know ?
He kept his word.   There came a noble flow,—
Rondels and sonnets, songs, gay fabliaux,
Tencils, and virelais, and chants royaux,
That turned at last the head of Isabeau.
For, by and by, he spun a languid lay
Set her a weeping for an April day.
And then a reverdie, I scarcely knew
Just what it meant; by times the damsel grew
Pensive and tender, till at last she said,—
You see the bait was very nicely spread,—
" How chances it, fair sir, this gift of song

Lay thus unused?   You did yourself a wrong:
But now I love you,— love as one well may
A heart that hides its treasures, yet can say
At last their sweetness out.   This simple lay!—
How could you know my thoughts?"

                              On this in haste
I cast an arm around her little waist,
And kissed her lips, and murmured tenderly
Some pretty lines my poet made for me
And this occasion's chance.

                              So there, the dame
Well wooed and married, ends this pleasant game.

De Lille.
I knew your poet once,— of knaves the chief,
A gallows-mocking brawler, guzzler, thief,—
This orphan of the devil won with song
Our good Duke Charles, who thinks of no man wrong,
And least of all a poet.   Once or twice
Duke Charles has saved his neck.   One can't be nice
With poet friends, nor leave them in the lurch
Because they stab a man, or rob a church.
Also, that hog-priest-doctor, Rabelais,
Kept him a while, then bade the vagrant go
For half a nightingale and half a crow.
So there he slips from sight.   Then comes a tale
That stirs our rhyming Duke.   I must not fail
To know the sequel.

De Luce.   Months went by.   My man
I had no need for; soon my dame began

To droop and wilt, and, too, I knew not why,
To watch me sidewise with attentive eye,
Or stay for silent hours cloaked with thought,
Laughing or weeping readily at naught.
What changes women?   A wife is just a wife.
The thing tormented me, for now her life
Faced from me ever, and, her head bent low,
She lived with some worn sonnet or rondeau
Had served its purpose.   Vexed at last, I took
The wretched stuff, the whole of it, and shook
The fragments to the winds.   Now, by St. George!
The thing stuck ever bitter in my gorge,
That such a peasant-slave's mere words should be
The one strong bond that held this love to me,
That was my life, and is.   Alas! in vain
I played the lover over, till in pain
Because she pined, poor fool, I sought again
My butt of verse and wine, and gayly said,
" Here, fellow, there 's for drink!   Set me your head
To verse me something honest, that shall speak
A strong man's love, and to my lady's cheek
Fetch back its rose again."   But as for him,
This hound, he studied me with red eyes, dim
And dulled with wine, and lightly laughing cried,
" Not I, my lord.   Not ever, if I tried
The longest day of June.   Your falcon caught,
Be sure no jesses by another wrought
Will hold a captive;" and with rambling talk
Put me aside, sang, hummed, took up the chalk
The landlord wont to score his drinks withal,
A moment paused, and scribbled on the wall,
   " If God love to a sexton gave,
    Surely he would dig it a grave;

14*

If God fitted an ass with wings,
    What would he do with the pretty things?"
I cursed him for a useless sot, but he,
Leering and heedless, scrawled unsteadily
Just "Wallow, wallow, wallow; this from me
To all wise pigs that on this mad earth be;"
Wrote "François Villon" underneath, and there,
Smitten with drink, dropped on the nearest chair
And slept as sleep the dead.   I in despair
Went on my way.
                    But she, my gentle dame,
Grew slowly feebler, like an oilless flame,
Until this cursed thing happened.   On a day
I chanced upon her singing, joyous, gay;
Glad leapt my hopes.   I kissed her, saw her start,
Grow sudden pale, a quick hand on her heart.—
'Fore God, I love her dearly, but I tore
A paper from her bosom, yet forbore
One darkened moment's time to read it, then
Saw the wild love verse, knew what drunken pen
Had dared.—
                    Fierce-eyed she stayed a little space,
Then struck me red with words, as if my face
A man had struck, said, "What can be more base
Than bribe a peasant soul to win with thought
Above your thinking what you vainly sought?
I love you?   No—I loved the man who knew
To tell the gladness of his love through you;
A thief, no doubt; and pray what was he who
Thus stole my love?   You lied! and he, a sot!
A sot, you say, could rise above his pot,—
You never!   Love me!   Could one like you know
In love's sweet climate truth and honor grow?"

But I, seeing my folly clear, said, " Isabeau,
What matters it if I but used the flow
Of this man's fantasies to word the praise
I would have said a hundred eager ways
And moved you never ?   Is it rare one pays
A man to sing ? "
                    " Henceforth, my lord," said she,
" We talk tongues strange to each, but ever he
Talked that my heart knows best.   Your wife am I,
That 's past earth's mending ; what is left but try
To weary on to death ?   What else ? "   I turned,
Cried, " But I loved you well !   This boor has
      earned
A traitor's fate."
                " And you," she moaned ; nor more,
Save, " Let *all* traitors die," and on the floor
Fell in a heap.
             Thenceforward half distraught
I sought my poet thief, but never caught
The cunning fiend, till as it chanced one night,
My horse fallen lame, I, walking, saw the light
Still in her window.   There below it stood
A man where fell the moonlight all aflood,
And suddenly a hand of mastery swept
The zittern, and — a whining love song leapt.
Ah ! but too well knew I the song he sang ;
I smiled to think it was his last.   It rang
Mad chimes within my head.   " Now then," I cried,
" A dog-life for a love-life ! "   Quick aside
My poet cast his zittern, drew his sword,
Tried as he stood his footing on the sward,
And laughed.   He ever laughed, and laughing said,
" Before we two cut throats, and one is dead,

And talk gets quite one-sided, let me speak,
Perchance it may be this rat's final squeak;
Even a cat grants that, my lord, you know.
Speak certain words I must of this dame Isabeau.
And if you will not, this have I to say,
These legs of mine have ofttimes won the day,
And may again if I have not my way.
My thanks.   You 're very good, and now,— what if
Full twenty dozen times a week a whiff
Of some sweet rose is given just to smell,
The rose unseen,— you catch my meaning ? — Well,
One haply gets rose-hungry, and erelong
Desires the rose.   You think I did you wrong
Who bade me see her as one sees in song,
Her neck, her face, the sun-gloss of her hair,
Eyes such as poets dream, the love-curves fair;
These have you seen; but as for me, they were,
Unseen of sense, more lovely.
                                        Mark, my lord,
How sweet to-night the lilies.   Pray afford
A moment yet to my life out of yours.   Believe
A thing so strange you may not, nor conceive:
This woman, on the beauty of whose face
I never looked, nor shall,— whose virgin grace
I sold to you,— is mine while time endures.
Yea, for thy malady earth has no cures;
A brute, a thief am I that caged this love.
A sodden poet!   Some one from above
Looks on us both to-night; you nobly born,
I in the sties of life.   I do repent
In that I wronged this lady innocent.
But if you live or I, where'er she bide,
One François Villon walketh at her side.

Kiss her!   Your kiss?   It will be I who kiss.
Yea, every dream of love your life shall miss
I shall be dreaming ever!
                                   Well, the cat,
Patient or not, has waited.   As for that,
Be comforted.   Hell never lacks reward
For them that serve it.   Thanks.— On guard.   On
     guard."
No word said I.   Long had I listened, dazed.
Now scorn broke out in hatred; crazed,
Fiercely I lunged.   He, laughing, scarce so rash,
Parried and touched my arm.   The rapier clash
Went wild a minute; then a woman's cry
Broke from the hedge behind him, and near by
Some moonlit whiteness gleamed.   He turned, and I,
By heaven! 't was none too soon, I drove my sword
Clean through the peasant dog from point to guard,
And held her as I watched him.   Better men
A many have I killed, but this man!— Then
He staggered, reeling, clutched at empty air
And at his breast, and pitching here and there,
Fell, shuddered, and was dead.
                                   By Mary's grace,
The woman kneeling kissed the dead dog's face!

Take you the Duke my tale.   The woman lives.
The man is dead.   None knows but she.   What
     gives
Such needless haste to go?   'T is not yet late.
Think you the story of this peasant's fate
Will vex Duke Charles?   How looks the thing to
     you?
No comment?   None?

DE LILLE.   None I could well afford
To speak.   The Duke must judge, not I.

DE LUCE.   My lord,
Your fashions like me not, and plainly, mine
Are somewhat franker.

DE LILLE.   I must ride.   The wine?

DE LUCE.
I pay for that.   The man who drinks must pay.
"The wine of friendship lasteth but a day,"
So said that pot-house Solomon.   I suppose
'T is easily thinned with time.   As this world goes,
A sorry vintage.

    1890.   ·

THE MISER

A MASQUE

MISER.

Come in.   *[Covers the jewels with a cloth.*

Enter a Woman, *who unmasks.*

What wouldst thou, wench ?   Hast aught to sell ?

WOMAN.

I've that to sell for which men give their souls.

MISER.

Alack ! their souls.   Go seek yon market-place,
And learn what usury a soul will fetch.
The body of a man may sweat you gold,
Plow, sow, and reap, yet at the end be apt
As other carrion to fatten grapes.
How came you in ?   They keep slack guard below.

WOMAN.

Good looks, like gold, pass anywhere on earth —
[*Sings.*

A man and a maid
The warder prayed.
Here is gold, said he,
But a look gave she;
Sweet eyes went in,
And the man was stayed.
For this is the way
The world to win,
The world to win.
Honey of kisses,
Honey of sin,—
This is the way
The world to win.

MISER.

Ay.   The fool's world, not mine.   The hour-glass
wastes.

WOMAN.

Forget to turn it, and the hour is thine.
That minds me what the priest said Easter eve:
The devil owns the minutes, God the years.
What think you that he meant?

MISER.   Nay, ask of him.
Age hath its secrets.   Time shall sow for thee
Betwixt thy grand-dame wrinkles answers meet.
Thy errand, girl!

WOMAN.   Look in my face, and learn.

MISER.

> By Venus!   I have read that scroll too oft.
> Eyes that say, Yes! and lips that murmur, No!
> The red cheeks' mock-surrender.   All the cheats
> That make to-morrow lie to yesterday.

WOMAN.

> Like a philosopher lies yesterday,
> To-morrow like a poet; but to-day
> Is true until to-morrow makes it lie.
> What if the minute's coin that buys thee joy
> Ring false the morrow morn!   How old you look!
> Kiss me, and live.   A ducat for a kiss!
> A ducat each for these two eyes of mine!

MISER.

> A ducat!   By St. Mercury! not I,—
> A thing unchanging for a thing that dies.
> I 've been the fool of women, wit, and wine;
> Have argued much with doctors; had my fill,
> Ay that was best, of battle's stormy fate,
> Have fooled and have been fooled, been loved and
> > loved.

WOMAN.

> Were any like to me?

MISER.   The lips I love
> Betray me not at each new gallant's suit.
> What are thy charms to these?
> > [*Walks across the room, and returns with a casket
> > of gold coins, while the Woman hastily looks under
> > the table-cover and replaces it.*
> > > > See, this and this!

[*Shows her gold medals.*

Hast thou the eyes of Egypt's haughty queen?
These eager lips that kissed a world away?
Lo, here Zenobia,— wisdom, beauty, grace.
Match me this warrior maid — this huntress lithe
Set in the changeless chastity of gold.

WOMAN.

Their lips are cold.   A ducat for a kiss!

MISER.

Nay, get thee gone.   Here 's something sweeter far
Than wanton vouches of a woman's lips.

WOMAN.

I would not kiss thee for a world of ducats.

[*Exit Woman, who whispers, as she goes, to a Gentleman who enters, clad in a red cloak, hat, and cock's feather.*

MISER.

Who let thee in?

GENTLEMAN.   A girl, fair sir,— a girl.
Quite often 't is a girl that lets me in!

MISER.

Who art thou?

GENTLEMAN.   Many people.   Part of all,
For well-bred gentlemen my Lord Duke Satan,
Here somewhat late to thank you.   Truly, sir,
To sum the seed of sin you 've sown for me
Would puzzle the arithmetic of — Well,

One speaks not lightly of his home.   My thanks.
Give me your hand, good friend.

MISER.   Art drunk!   Begone!

GENTLEMAN.
Alas!   How sad, not know me.   Gratitude
Is rare in either world.   Yet men, I note,
Know not themselves, and therefore know not me.

MISER.
The jest is good.

GENTLEMAN.   What, I — I, Satan, jest!
How hard to satisfy!   Unhelped by me,
What hadst thou been?   Lo, under this frail cloth
                              [*Touches the table-cover.*
There lie the pledges of a hundred souls:
That zone of pearls!   That ruby coronal!

MISER.
Thou liest, fool!

GENTLEMAN.   The ring,— the sapphire ring.

MISER.
The thing is strange.

GENTLEMAN.   Nay, gentle partner, nay.
Behold, I come to thee in sore distress,
A bankrupt devil.   Why?   It matters not.
Perhaps I gambled for the morning star,
Gambled with Lucifer; in want, perchance,

For reason good, of some less sin-worn world.
Brothers are we.   No need for us to pray
Deliverance from temptation — to do good.
Not equals quite.   A trifle thou dost lack
Thy master's joy in evil for itself.
Only the crack-brained sin for love of sin,
And crime is wretchedly alloyed with good.
Ho! for one honest sinner!

MISER.   Out, foul fiend!

GENTLEMAN.
To waste your hours were but to squander mine.
Ha!   Shall I take my own?
                              [*Pulls off the table-cover.*

MISER.   '   Without there!   Help!
Help — help — a thief!

GENTLEMAN.   Nay.   Let me choose my coins,
Let me confess them.   They have tales to tell.
I am a devil-poet, and can see
Beneath the skin of things.
[*Takes coins in turn.*]   On this is writ
A maiden's honor gone.   And here is one
Helped the black barter of a traitor's soul.
This 'gainst a priestly conscience turned the scale.
And this is red with murder.   See, gray hairs
Stick to it yet.   Alas for charity!
Not one,— not one.   The devil has no friend
                              [*A knock is heard.*
Save him that enters.
          [*Opens the door to the cowled figure, DEATH.*

                        Pray you, sir, come in.
Lo, my best friend! the scavenger of time,
Who picks from off this dust-heap called a world
The scared and hurried ants that come and go
Without a whence or whither worth a thought.
Be easy with this partner of my cares.
This greedy dotard drunk with guzzling gold
Spare me a little.   Take thou hence the good,
The fair, the young, the chaste, the innocent.
                              [*To the* MISER.
Good night, my friend.   I leave you one who owns
The only truth this stupid planet holds.
                              [*Exit Gentleman.*

MISER.
    What feast of folly hath broke loose to-night?
    Who art thou?

DEATH.   Death!

MISER.   The devil and then Death!
    You have the play the wrong end first, my friend.
                              [*Laughs.*
DEATH.
    Then laugh again.   Full many a year has fled
    Since sound of laughter crackled in mine ears.
    There are who face me smiling.   Men like thee,
    Who gather ducats as I reap the years,
    To add them to the gathered hoard of time;
    Yea, men like thee, who poison souls for gain,
    And love life for its baseness, mock not me.
    Only the noble and the wretched smile
    When these lean fingers summon to the grave.
    Thy day is near; even now the clogging blood

Chills stagnant at my touch, and soon for thee
Shall come the yellow hags to stretch thy limbs,
And put the coins upon thy staring eyes.

                    [MISER *falls into a chair.*

MISER.

What cruel jest is this ?   I pray thee go.
My heart beats riotous, my legs grow weak.

DEATH.

Give me a hundred ducats.

MISER.   I !   Not one.

DEATH.

A hundred ducats for a year of greed.

MISER.

Not one, I say.

DEATH.   Then, to that nether world.
Two days I grant thee, till upon the stair
Thy coffined weight shall creak, and other hands
Shall count thy ducats.

MISER.   Take thou ten, and go.

DEATH.

Ten ducats for a journey round the world !

MISER.

Nay, nay, not one.   Thou surely art not Death.

DEATH.

Already on thy sallow cheek I see
The set grim smile which hardens on the face

When death unriddles life; thy jaw hangs slack;
The sweat wherewith man labors unto death
Drops from thy brow.

MISER.   Take what thou wilt, and go.
  You said a hundred ducats.   Take but that.
  Take them and leave me.   Not a ducat more.
                    [*Death takes a bag.*
DEATH.
  For this I give thee many a lingering year.
  Without there, gentlemen! Come in, come in!
    [*Enter* PRINCE *masked, the Court Fool as Mephis-
    topheles, women and courtiers in fancy dresses.
    The* MISER *leaps up.*

MISER.
  What robber-band is this?

PRINCE.   A jest, my friend.

GENTLEMAN.
  The Prince has lost his wager.   Death has won.

DEATH.
  To supper, gentlemen.   Here 's that shall pay.

MISER.
  My gold!   Alas, my gold!

DEATH.   But yet you live.
                    [*Exeunt* maskers *singing.*
    1884.

MISCELLANEOUS POEMS

MISCELLANEOUS POEMS

THE MOTHER

" I will incline mine ear to the parable, and show my dark speech upon the harp."

CHRISTMAS ! Christmas ! merry Christmas ! rang the
    bells.   O God of grace !
In the stillness of the death-room motionless I kept my
    place,
While beneath my eyes a wanness came upon the little
    face,
And an empty smile that stung me, as the pallor grew
    apace.
Then, as if from some far distance, spake a voice : " The
    child is dead."
" Dead ? " I cried.   " Is God not good ?   What thing
    accursed is that you said ? "
Swift I searched their eyes of pity, swaying, bowed, and
    all my soul,
Shrunken as a hand had crushed it, crumpled like a use-
    less scroll
Read and done with, passed from sorrows : only with me
    lingered yet
Some dim sense of easeful comfort in the glad leave to
    forget.

But again life's scattered fragments, memories of joy and
    woe,
Tremulously came to oneness, as a storm-torn lake may
    grow
Quiet, winning back its pictures, when the wild winds
    cease to blow.
As if called for God's great audit came a vision of my
    years,
Broken gleams of youth and girlhood, all the woman's
    love and tears.
Marvelling, myself I saw as one another sees, and smiled,
Crooning o'er my baby dolls,— part a mother, part a
    child;
Then, half sorry, ceased to wonder why I eft my silent
    brood,
Till the lessoning years went by me, and the instinct,
    love-renewed,'
Stirred again life's stronger fibre, and were mine twain
    living things;
Bone of my bone! flesh of my flesh! Who on earth a
    title brings
Flawless as this mother-title, free from aught of mortal
    stain,
Innocent and pure possession, double-born of joy and
    pain?
Oh, what wonder these could help me, set me laughing,
    though I sobbed
As they drew my very heart out, and the laden breasts
    were robbed!
Tender buds of changeful pleasure came as come the
    buds of May,
Trivial, wondrous, unexpected, blossoming from day to
    day.

Ah! the clutch of tendril-fingers, that with nature's cun-
    ning knew
So to coil in sturdy grapple round the stem from which
    they grew.
Shall a man this joy discover? How the heart-wine to
    the brain .
Rushed with shock of bliss when, startled, first I won this
    simple gain!
How I mocked those seeking fingers, eager for their
    earliest toy,
Telling none my new-found treasure! Miser of the
    mother's joy,
Quick I caught the first faint ripple, answering me with
    lip and eyes,
As I stooped with mirthful purpose, keen to capture
    fresh replies;
Oh, the pretty wonder of it, when was born the art to smile,
Or the new, gay trick of laughter filled my eyes with tears
    the while,—
Helpful tears, love's final language, when the lips no more
    can say,
Tears, like kindly prophets, warning of another, darker
    day.
Thus my vision lost its gladness, and I stood on life's dim
    strand,
Watching where a little love-bark drifted slowly from the
    land;
For again the bells seemed ringing Christmas o'er the snow
    of dawn,
And my dreaming memory hurt me with a hot face, gray
    and drawn,
And with small hands locked in anguish. Ah! those days
    of helpless pain!

Mine the mother's wrathful sorrow. Ah! my child,
    hadst thou been Cain,
Father of the primal murder, black with every hideous
    thought,
Cruel were the retribution; for, alas! what good is
    wrought
When the very torture ruins all the fine machine of
    thought?
So with reeling brain I questioned, while the fevered cheek
    grew white,
And at last I seemed to pass with him, released, to death's
    dark night.
Seraph voices whispered round me. "God," they said,
    "hath set our task,—
Thou to question, we to answer: fear not; ask what thou
    wouldst ask."
Wildly beat my heart. Thought only, regnant, held its
    sober pace,
Whilst, a wingèd mind, I wandered in the bleak domain
    of space.
Then I sought and seeing marvelled at the mystery of
    time,
Where beneath me rolled the earth-star in its first cha-
    otic slime,
As bewildering ages passing with their cyclic changes
    came,
Heaving land and 'whelming waters, ice and fierce vol-
    canic flame,
Sway and shock of tireless atoms, pulsing with the throb
    of force,
Whilst the planet, rent and shaken, fled upon its mighty
    course.

Last, with calm of wonder hushed, I saw amid the surg-
  ing strife
Rise the first faint stir of being and the tardy morn of
  life,—
Life in countless generations. Speechless, mercilessly
  dumb,
Swept by ravage of disaster, tribe on tribe in silence
  come,
Till the yearning sense found voices, and on hill, and
  shore, and plain,
Dreary from the battling myriads rose the birthright wail
  of pain.
God of pity! Son of sorrows! Wherefore should a power
  unseen
Launch on years of needless anguish this great agonized
  machine?
Was Himself who willed this torment but a slave to law
  self-made?
Or had some mad angel-demon here, unchecked and undismayed,
Leave to make of earth a Job; until the cruel game was
  played
Free to whirl the spinning earth-toy where his despot
  forces wrought,
While he watched each sense grow keener as the lifted
  creature bought
With the love-gift added sorrow, and there came to man's
  estate
Will, the helpless, thought, the bootless, all the deathward
  war with fate?
Had this lord of trampled millions joy or grief, when first
  the mind,

Awful prize of contests endless, rose its giant foes to
    bind;
When his puppet tamed the forces that had helped its
    birth to breed,
And with growth of wisdom master, trained them to its
    growing need;
Last, upon the monster turning, on the serpent form of
    Pain,
Cried, " Bring forth no more in anguish; " with the ar-
    rows of the brain
Smote this brute thing that no use had save to teach him
    to refrain
When earth's baser instincts tempted, and the better
    thought was vain ?
Then my soul one harshly answered, " Thou hast seen
    the whole of earth,
All its boundless years of misery, yea, its gladness and its
    mirth,
Yet thou hast a life created!   Hadst thou not a choice ?
    Why cast
Purity to life's mad chances, where defeat is sure at last ? "
Low I moaned, " My tortured baby," and a gentler voice
    replied,
"One alone thy soul can answer,— this, this only, is
    denied.
Yet take counsel of thy sadness. Should God give thy
    will a star
Freighted with eternal pleasure, free from agony and
    war,
Wouldst thou wish it ? Think! Time is not for the
    souls who roam in space.
Speak! Thy will shall have its way. Be mother of one
    joyous race.

Choose! Yon time-worn world beneath thee thou shalt
    people free from guilt.
There nor pain nor death shall ruin, never there shall blood
    be spilt."
Then I trembled, hesitating, for I saw its beauty
    born,
Saw a Christ-like world of beings where no beast by beast
    was torn,
Where the morrows bred no sorrows, and the gentle knew
    not scorn.
"Yet," I said, "if life have meaning, and man must be,
    what shall lift
These but born for joy's inaction, these who crave no
    added gift?
Let the world you bid me people hurl forever through the
    gloom,
Tenantless, a blasted record of some huge funereal
    doom,
Sad with unremembered slaughter, but a cold and lonely
    tomb."

Deep and deeper grew the stillness, and I knew how vain
    my quest.
Not by God's supremest angel is that awful secret
    guessed.
Yet with dull reiteration, like the pendulum's dead
    throb,
Beat my heart; a moaning infant, all my body seemed to
    sob,
And a voice like to my baby's called to me across the
    night
As the darkness fell asunder, and I saw a wall of light

Barred with crucificial shadows, whence a weary wind did
blow
Shuddering. I felt it pass me heavy with its freight of
woe.
Said a voice, " Behold God's dearest; also these no answer know.
These be they who paid in sorrow for the right to bid thee
hear.
Had their lives in ease been cradled, had they never
known a tear,
Feebly had their psalms of warning fallen upon the listening ear.
God the sun is God the shadow; and where pain is, God
is near.
Take again thy life and use it with a sweetened sense of
fear ;
God is Father! God is Mother! Regent of a growing
soul,
Free art thou to grant mere pleasure, free to teach it un-
control.
Time is childhood! larger manhood bides beyond life's
sunset hour,
Where far other foes are waiting ; and with ever gladder
power,
Still the lord of awful choice, O striving creature of the
sod,
Thou shalt learn that imperfection is the noblest gift of
God!
For they mock his ample purpose who but dream, beyond
the sky,
Of a heaven where will may slumber, and the trained de-
cision die
In the competence of answer found in death's immense
reply."

Then my vision passed, and weeping, lo! I woke, of death
    bereft;
At my breast the baby brother, yonder there the dead I
    left.
For my heart two worlds divided: his, my lost one's; his,
    who pressed
Closer, waking all the mother, as he drew the aching
    breast,
While twain spirits, joy and sorrow, hovered o'er my
    plundered nest.

NEWPORT, *October*, 1891.

OF ONE WHO SEEMED TO HAVE FAILED

DEATH 's but one more to-morrow. Thou art gray
With many a death of many a yesterday.
O yearning heart that lacked the athlete's force
And, stumbling, fell upon the beaten course,
And looked, and saw with ever glazing eyes
Some lower soul that seemed to win the prize!
Lo, Death, the just, who comes to all alike,
Life's sorry scales of right anew shall strike.
Forth, through the night, on unknown shores to win
The peace of God unstirred by sense of sin!
There love without desire shall, like a mist
At evening precious to the drooping flower,
Possess thy soul in ownership, and kissed
By viewless lips, whose touch shall be a dower
Of genius and of winged serenity,

Thou shalt abide in realms of poesy.
There soul hath touch of soul, and there the great
Cast wide to welcome thee joy's golden gate.
Freeborn to untold thoughts that age on age
Caressed sweet singers in their sacred sleep,
Thy soul shall enter on its heritage
Of God's unuttered wisdom.   Thou shalt sweep
With hand assured the ringing lyre of life,
Till the fierce anguish of its bitter strife,
Its pain, death, discord, sorrow, and despair,
Break into rhythmic music.   Thou shalt share
The prophet-joy that kept forever glad
God's poet-souls when all a world was sad.
Enter and live!   Thou hast not lived before;
We were but soul-cast shadows.   Ah, no more
The heart shall bear the burdens of the brain;
Now shall the strong heart think, nor think in vain.
In the dear company of peace, and those
Who bore for man life's utmost agony,
Thy soul shall climb to cliffs of still repose,
And see before thee lie Time's mystery,
And that which is God's time, Eternity;
Whence sweeping over thee dim myriad things,
The awful centuries yet to be, in hosts
That stir the vast of heaven with formless wings,
Shall cast for thee their shrouds, and, like to ghosts,
Unriddle all the past, till, awed and still,
Thy soul the secret hath of good and ill.

1889.

OF THE REMEMBERED DEAD

THERE is no moment when our dead lose power;
Unsignalled, unannounced they visit us.
Who calleth them I know not.   Sorrowful,
They haunt reproachfully some venal hour
In days of joy, or when the world is near,
And for a moment scourge with memories
The money changers of the temple-soul.
In the dim space between two gulfs of sleep,
Or in the stillness of the lonely shore,
They rise for balm or torment, sweet or sad,
And most are mine where, in the kindly woods,
Beside the child-like joy of summer streams,
The stately sweetness of the pine hath power
To call their kindred comforting anew.
Use well thy dead.   They come to ask of thee
What thou hast done with all this buried love,
The seed of purer life ?   Or has it fallen unused
In stony ways and brought thy life no gain ?
Wilt thou with gladness in another world
Say it has grown to forms of duty done
And ruled thee with a conscience not thine own ?
Another world !   How shall we find our dead ?
What forceful law shall bring us face to face ?
Another world ! What yearnings there shall guide ?
Will love souls twinned of love bring near again ?
And that one common bond of duty held
This living and that dead, when life was theirs ?
Or shall some stronger soul, in life revered,
Bring both to touch, with nature's certainty,

As the pure crystal atoms of its kind
Draws into fellowship of loveliness?

1889.

E. D. M.

THERE is a heart I knew in other days,
Not ever far from any one day's thought;
One pure as are the purest.   All the years
Of battle or of peace, of joy or grief,
Take him no further from me.   Oftentimes,
When the sweet tenderness of some glad girl
Disturbs with tears, full suddenly I know
It is because one memory ever dear
Is matched a moment with its living kin.
Or when at hearing of some gallant deed
My throat fills, and I may not dare to say
The quick praise in me, then I know, alas!
'T is by this dear dead nobleness my soul is stirred.
He lived, he loved, he died.   Brief epitaph!
What hour of duty in the long grim wards
Poisoned his life, I know not.   Painfully
He sickened, yearning for the strife of War
That went its thunderous way unhelped of him;
And then he died.   A little duty done;
A little love for many, much for me,
And that was all beneath this earthly sun.

1889.

PAINED UNTO DEATH

E. K. M.

ONE life I knew was a psalm, a terrible psalm of pain,
Dark with disaster of torment, heart and brain
Racked as if God were not, and hope a dream
Some demon memory brought to bid blaspheme
All life's dismembered sweetness.   " Peace, be still,"
I hear her spirit whisper.   " His the will
That from some unseen bow of purpose sped
Thy sorrow and my torture."   God of dread !
The long sad years that justify the dead,
The long sad years at last interpreted :
Serene as clouds that over stormy seas
At sunset rise with mystery of increase,
One with the passionate deep that gave them birth,
Her gentled spirit rose on wings of peace,
And was and was not of this under earth.

1890.

THE WHOLE CREATION GROANETH

ART glad with the gladness of youth in thy veins,
In thy hands, for the spending, earth's joy and its gains ?
Lo ! winged with storm shadows the torturers come,
And to-night, or to-morrow, thy lips shall be dumb,
Thy hands wet with pain-thrills, thy nerves, that were
    strung
To fineness of sense by earth's pleasure, be wrung

With pangs the beast knows not, nor he who in tents
Lives lone in the desert, and knoweth not whence
The bread of the morrow.   Pain like to a mist
Goeth up from the earth, and is lost, and none wist
Why ever it cometh, why ever it waits
In the heart of our loves, like a foe in our gates.
Lo! summer and sunshine are over the land,—
Who marshalled yon billows? what wind of command
Drives ever their merciless march on the strand?
Thus, dateless, relentless, the children of strife
None have seen, on the sun-lighted beaches of life
March ever the ravening billows of pain.
O heart that is breaking, go ask of the brain
If aught of God's spending is squandered in vain?
Yea, where is the sunshine of centuries dead?
Yea, where are the raindrops of yesterday shed?
God findeth anew his lost light in the force
That holdeth the world on its resolute course,
And surely, as surely the madness of pain
Shall pass into wisdom, and come back again
An angel of courage if thou art the one
That knoweth to deal with the lightnings that stun
To blindness the many.   A thousand shall fall
By the waysides of life, and in helplessness call
For the death-alms which nature gives freely to all;
And one, like the jewel, shall break the fierce light
That blindeth thy vision, and flash through the night
The colors that read us its meaning aright.

1890.

IN THE VALLEY OF THE SHADOW

THE CENTURION

A dark cell of the Circus Maximus.   The Centurion and his child.

"FATHER! father; hold me closer.   Are they lions
    that I hear?
Once beside the Syrian desert where we camped I heard
    them near
While our servants made us music; and there 's music
    now.   'T was night,
And 't is very dark here, father.   There we had the stars
    for light.
Father, father! that was laughter, and the noise of many
    hands.
Why is it they make so merry?   Shall we laugh soon?
    On the sands
How you smiled to see my terror!   'What,' you said, 'A
    Roman maid
Tremble in the Legion's camp!   A Roman maiden and
    afraid!'

"Hush! Who called? Who called me? Mother! Surely
    that was mother's voice."
But the gray centurion, trembling, murmured, "Little one,
    rejoice!"
Yet a single moan of sorrow broke the guard his man-
    hood set,
While the sweetness of her forehead with a storm of tears
    was wet.

16*

And he answered, as she questioned, " That was but the
    rain God sends
To the flowers he loves,"—then lower,—" Death and I
    are friends."

" Father, father, now 't is quiet. Was it mother? I am
    cold.
Who, I wonder, feeds my carp? who, I wonder, at the
    fold
Combs my lambs? who prunes my roses? Think you
    they will keep us long
From the sunshine? Hark, the lions! Ah! they must
    be fierce and strong!"

" Peace, my daughter. Soon together we shall walk
    through gardens fair,
Where the lilies psálms are singing, and the roses whisper
    prayer."
" Who will bring us to the garden ? " " Christ! Thou wilt
    not hear him call;
Suddenly wide doors shall open; on thy eyes the sun shall
    fall;
Thou shalt see God's lions, waiting, and, above, a living
    wall.
Yea, ten thousand faces waiting, come to help our holiday,
Music, flowers, and the Cæsar.— Rest upon my shoulder,
    lay
One small hand in mine,— and peace. A moment I
    would think and pray.

" I am sore with shame and scourging, I, a Roman! I,
    a knight !
Yea, if nobly born, the nobler for the birth of higher light.

Was it pain, and was it shame ?   The lictor's rods fell on
    a man ;
On the God-man fell those scourges, and the bitter drops
    that ran
Flowed from eyes that wept for millions, came of pain
    none else can know,
An eternity of anguish, counted as the blood drops flow.
Mine is but an atom's torment ; mine shall bring eternal
    gain ;
His, the murder pangs of ages, paid with usury of pain.

" Art thou weary of the darkness ?   Art thou cold, my
    little maid ?
Hast thou sorrow of my sorrow ?   Kiss my cheek.   Be
    not dismayed.
Lo, the nearness of one moment setteth age to lonely
    thought,
Would his will but make us one ere yet his perfect will
    be wrought.
That may not be.   Once, once only Love must drop the
    hand of love."
" Father, father ! Hark, the lions ! "   " Peace, my little
    one, my dove ;
Soon thy darkened cage will open, soon the voice of
    Christ will say,
' Come and be among my lilies, where the golden foun-
    tains play,
And an angel legion watches, and forever it is day.'
So, my hand upon thy shoulder.   You, so little ! I, so
    tall !
Now, one kiss — earth's last !   My darling." — Back the
    iron gate bolts fall.
Lo, the gray arena 's quiet, and the faces waiting all,

Waiting, and the lions waiting, while the gray centurion
  smiled,
As, beneath the white velarium, fell God's sunlight on the
  child:
For a gentle voice above them murmured, " Forth, and
  have no fear,"
And the little maiden answered, " Lo, Christ Jesu, I am
  here ! "

1890.

A CANTICLE OF TIME

HOURS of grieving,
Hours of thought;
Hours of believing,
Hours of naught.
Hours when the thieving
Fingers of doubt steal
Heart riches, faith bought.
Hours of spirit dearth,
Earthy, and born of earth,
When the racked universe
Is as a hell, or worse.
Hours when the curtain, furled
Backward, revealed to us
Sorrowful sin gulfs
Self had concealed from us.
Hours of wretchedness;
Palsies that blind.
Hours none else can guess,
When the dumb mind

Faints, and heart wisdom
Is all that we find.
Hours when the cloud
That hides the unknown,
A cumbering shroud,
About us is thrown.
Hours that seem to part
Goodness and God.
Hours of fierce yearning,
When fruit of love's earning
Is shred from the heart.
Hours when no angel
Hovers o'er life.
Hours when no Christ-God
Pities our strife.
Yea, such is life!

Slowly the hours
Gather to years;
They deal with our tears
That grief be not vain,
Gently as flowers
Deal with the rain.
Slowly the hours
Gather to years,
Sowing with roses
The graves of our fears.
Lo! the dark crosses
Of torture's completeness
Mistily fade into
Symbols of sweetness,
And behold it is evening.
Swift through the grass

Shuttles of shadow
Silently pass,
Weaving at last
Tapestries sombre,
Solemn and vast,
And behold it is night!
Silence profound,
Solitude vacant
Of touch and of sound
Thy being doth bound.
This is death's loneliness,
Answerless, pitiless!
What of thee was king,
Let it crownless descend
From its tottering throne;
Lo! thou art alone,
And behold, 't is the end!

What sayeth the soul?
" God wasteth naught.
Think you in vain
He sowed in thy childhood
Thought-seed in the brain,
And the joy to create,
Like his own joy, and will,
Like a fragment of fate
For the godlike control
Of the heaven of thy angels,
The loves of thy soul?
Ay, strong for the rule
Of devils that tempt thee,
Of demons that fool?
Shall so much of Him

Merely perish in haste,
Just stumble, and die,
And Death be a jester's mad riddle
Without a reply?
And Life naught but waste?
Behold, it is day,"
Saith the soul.

1890.

LINCOLN

CHAINED by stern duty to the rock of state,
His spirit armed in mail of rugged mirth,
Ever above, though ever near to earth,
Yet felt his heart the cruel tongues that sate
Base appetites, and foul with slander, wait
Till the keen lightnings bring the awful hour
When wounds and suffering shall give them power.
Most was he like to Luther, gay and great,
Solemn and mirthful, strong of heart and limb.
Tender and simple too; he was so near
To all things human that he cast out fear,
And, ever simpler, like a little child,
Lived in unconscious nearness unto Him
Who always on earth's little ones hath smiled.

NEWPORT, *October*, 1891.

COLERIDGE AT CHAMOUNY

I WOULD I knew what ever happy stone
Of all these dateless records, gray and vast,
Keeps silent memory of that sunrise lone
When, lost to earth, the soul of Coleridge passed
From earthly time to one immortal hour:
There thought's faint stir woke echoes of the mind
That broke to thunder tones of mightier power
From depths and heights mysterious, undefined;
As when the soft snows, drifting from the rock,
Rouse the wild clamor of the avalanche shock.

Who may not envy him that awful morn
When marvelling at his risen self he trod,
And thoughts·intense as pain were fiercely born,
Till rose his soul in one great psalm to God.
A man to-morrow weak as are the worst,
A man to whom all depths, all heights belong,
Now with too bitter hours of weakness cursed,
Now winged with vigor, as a giant strong
To take our groping hearts with tender hand,
And set them surely where God's angels stand.

On peaks of lofty contemplation raised,
Such as shall never see earth's common son,
High as the snowy altar which he praised,
An hour's creative ecstasy he won.
Yet, in this frenzy of the lifted soul
Mocked him the nothingness of human speech,
When through his being visions past control
Swept, strong as mountain streams.— Alas! To reach

Words equal-winged as thought to none is given,
To none of earth to speak the tongue of heaven.

The eagle-flight of genius gladness hath,
And joy is ever with its victor swoop
Through sun and storm.   Companionless its path
In earthly realms, and, when its pinions droop,
Faint memories only of the heavenly sun,
Dim records of ethereal space it brings
To show how haughty was the height it won,
To prove what freedom had its airy wings.
This is the curse of genius, that earth's night
Dims the proud glory of its heavenward flight.

1888.

TENNYSON

THE larks of song that high o'erhead
   Sung joyous in my boyhood's sky,
Save one, are with the silent dead,
   Those larks that knew to soar so high.

But still with ever surer flight,
   One singer of unfailing trust
Chants at the gates of morn and night
   Great songs that lift us from the dust,

And heavenward call tired hearts that grieve,
   Beneath the vast horizon given
With larger breadth of morn and eve,
   To this one lark alone in heaven.

1890.

CERVANTES

THERE are who gather with decisive power
The mantle of contentment round their souls,
And face with strange serenity the hour
Of pain, or grief, or any storm that rolls
Destruction o'er the tender joys of life.

There are whom some great quest of heart or brain
Keeps even-poised, whatever fate the years
May fetch to mock with lesser loss or gain,
And find brief joy in smiles, small grief in tears,
And tranquil take the hurts of human strife.

A few there be who, spendthrift heirs of mirth
Immortal, mock the insolence of fate,
And with a breath of jesting round the earth
Ripple men's cheeks with smiles, and gay, elate,
Sit ever in the sunshine of their mood.

Oh, royal master of all merry chords,
Of every note in mirth's delightful scale,
To thee was spared no pang that earth affords,
Nor any woe of sorrow's endless tale,—
Want, prison, wounds, all that has man subdued;

But, light of soul, as if all life were joy,
Forever armed with humor's shining mail,
True-hearted, gallant, free from scorn's alloy,
When life was beggared of its best, and frail
Grew hope, 't is said thou still wert lord of smiles.

This could I wish; and yet it well may be
Thy heart smiled not, for wit, like fairy gold,
Mayhap won naught for him who scattered glee,
No help for him by whom the jest was told,—
The world's sad fool, whose ever-ready wiles

Rang the glad bells of laughter down the years,
And cheated pain with merry mysteries,
And from a prison cell, the twins of tears,
Sent forth his Don and Squire to win at ease
Such joy of mirth as his could never be.

Ah, who can say!   His latest day of pain
Took Shakespeare's kindred soul.   I trust they met
Where smiles are frequent, and the saddest gain
What earth denies, the privilege to forget
"The oppressor's wrong, the proud man's contumely."

But where he sleeps, the land which gave him birth,
And gave no more to him, its greatest child,
Knows not to-day.   Some levelled heap of earth,
Some nameless stone, lies o'er him who beguiled
So many a heart from thinking on its pain.

Yet I can fancy that at morning there
The birds sing gladder, and at evening still
The peasant, resting from his day of care,
Goes joyous thence with some mysterious thrill
Of lightsome mirth, whose cause he seeks in vain.

October, 1888.

OF A POET

WRITTEN FOR A CHILD

HE sang of brooks, and trees, and flowers,
Of mountain tarns, of wood-wild bowers,
The wisdom of the starry skies,
The mystery of childhood's eyes,
The violet's scent, the daisy's dress,
The timid breeze's shy caress.
Whilst England waged her fiery wars
He praised the silence of the stars,
And clear and sweet as upland rills
The gracious wisdom of her hills.
Save once when Clifford's fate he sang,
And bugle-like his lyric rang,
He prized the ways of lowly men,
And trod, with them, the moor and fen.
Fair Nature to this lover dear
Bent low to whisper or to hear
The secrets of her sky and earth,
In gentle Words of golden Worth.

1886.

HERNDON

Ay, shout and rave, thou cruel sea,
 In triumph o'er that fated deck,
Grown holy by another grave —
 Thou hast the captain of the wreck.

No prayer was said, no lesson read,
  O'er him, the soldier of the sea;
And yet for him, through all the land,
  A thousand thoughts to-night shall be.

And many an eye shall dim with tears,
  And many a cheek be flushed with pride;
And men shall say, There died a man,
  And boys shall learn how well he died.

Ay, weep for him, whose noble soul
  Is with the God who made it great;
But weep not for so proud a death,—
  We could not spare so grand a fate.

Nor could Humanity resign
  That hour which bade her heart beat high,
And blazoned Duty's stainless shield,
  And set a star in Honor's sky.

O dreary night!　O grave of hope!
  O sea, and dark, unpitying sky!
Full many a wreck these waves shall claim
  Ere such another heart shall die.

Alas, how can we help but mourn
  When hero bosoms yield their breath!
A century itself may bear
  But once the flower of such a death;

So full of manliness, so sweet
  With utmost duty nobly done;
So thronged with deeds, so filled with life,
  As though with death that life begun.

It *has* begun, true gentleman !
  No better life we ask for thee ;
Thy Viking soul and woman heart
  Forever shall a beacon be,—

A starry thought to veering souls,
  To teach it is not best to live ;
To show that life has naught to match
  Such knighthood as the grave can give.

1857.

THE TOMBS OF THE REGICIDES

LUDLOW AND BROUGHTON

ALONE on the vine-covered hillside,
Set gray 'gainst the ivy-clad walnuts,
Stands, sombre as Calvin, and barren
Of crucifix, altar, and picture,
The church of St. Martin.   A stranger,
I stood where the pride of its arches
Looks scorn on the Puritan's sadness.
Not prouder for Switzerland's annals
The glory of Morat or Sempach
Than these darkened tablets that tell us
How gladly for Ludlow and Broughton
She lifted the shield of protection,
How sternly she answered the summons
To render her guests to the headsman.
The parents that gave their true soul-life
Were England and Freedom.   Ah, surely
With courage and conscience they honored

That parentage costly of sorrow,
And did the just deed and abided.
Long, long were the days that God gave them
With friendships and peace in this refuge,
Where sadly they yearned for the home-land,
And saw their great Oliver's England
Bowed low in the dust of dishonor.

VEVAY, *August* 19, 1888.

KEARSARGE

SUNDAY in Old England:
  In gray churches everywhere
The calm of low responses,
  The sacred hush of prayer.

Sunday in Old England;
  And summer winds that went
O'er the pleasant fields of Sussex,
  The garden lands of Kent,

Stole into dim church windows
  And passed the oaken door,
And fluttered open prayer-books
  With the cannon's awful roar.

Sunday in New England:
  Upon a mountain gray
The wind-bent pines are swaying
  Like giants at their play;

Across the barren lowlands,
  Where men find scanty food,
The north wind brings its vigor
  To homesteads plain and rude.

Ho, land of pine and granite!
  Ho, hardy northland breeze!
Well have you trained the manhood
  That shook the Channel seas,

When o'er those storied waters
  The iron war-bolts flew,
And through Old England's churches
  The summer breezes blew;

While in our other England
  Stirred one gaunt rocky steep,
When rode her sons as victors,
  Lords of the lonely deep.

LONDON, *July* 20, 1864.

HOW THE CUMBERLAND WENT DOWN

GRAY swept the angry waves
  O'er the gallant and the true,
Rolled high in mounded graves
  O'er the stately frigate's crew —
Over cannon, over deck,
Over all that ghastly wreck,—
    When the Cumberland went down.

Such a roar the waters rent
  As though a giant died,
When the wailing billows went
  Above those heroes tried;
And the sheeted foam leaped high,
Like white ghosts against the sky,—
    As the Cumberland went down.

O shrieking waves that gushed
  Above that loyal band,
Your cold, cold burial rushed
  O'er many a heart on land!
And from all the startled North
A cry of pain broke forth,
    When the Cumberland went down.

And forests old, that gave
  A thousand years of power
To her lordship of the wave
  And her beauty's regal dower,
Bent, as though before a blast,
When plunged her pennoned mast,
    And the Cumberland went down.

And grimy mines that sent
  To her their virgin strength,
And iron vigor lent
  To knit her lordly length,
Wildly stirred with throbs of life,
Echoes of that fatal strife,
    As the Cumberland went down.

Beneath the ocean vast,
　　Full many a captain bold,
By many a rotting mast,
　　And admiral of old,
Rolled restless in his grave
As he felt the sobbing wave,
　　　When the Cumberland went down.

And stern Vikings that lay
　　A thousand years at rest,
In many a deep blue bay
　　Beneath the Baltic's breast,
Leaped on the silver sands,
And shook their rusty brands,
　　　As the Cumberland went down.

1862.

MY CASTLES IN SPAIN

Ho, joyous friend with beard of brown !
A half hour back 't was gray;
A half hour back you wore a frown,
But now the world looks gay.
For here the mirror's courtly grace
Cheats you with a youthful face,
And here the poet clock of time
Each happy minute counts in rhyme;
And here the roses never die,
And " Yes " is here Love's sole reply.
Gladder land can no man gain
Than my mystic realm of Spain.

Come with me, for I am one
Hidalgo-born of Aragon;
I will show you why I choose
Thus to live in Andalouse.
Across the terrace, up the stair,
Our steps shall wander to and fro
Where pensive stand the statues fair,
And murmur songs of long ago.
Or will you see my pictures old,
The landscapes hung for my delight
In window-frames of fretted gold,
Where, glowing, shines in color bright
That Claude of mine at full of noon,
When the ripe, eager blood of June
Stirs bird and leaf, and everywhere
The world is one gay love affair?
Or shall we linger, looking west,
Just when my Turner 's at its best,
To watch the cold stars, one by one,
Crawl to the embers of the sun,
Whilst all the gray sierra snows
Are ruddy with the twilight rose?
Believe me, artists there are none
Like those of mine in Aragon;
Nor painter would I care to choose
Beside the sun of Andalouse.
Or shall we part the shining leaves
Down drooping from the vine-clad eaves,
And see, amidst the sombre pines,
The maiden take a shameless kiss?
Around his neck her white arm twines,
And still is sweet their changeless bliss.
I know she cannot aught refuse,

For that 's the law in Andalouse,
And ever 'neath this happy sun
There is no sin in Aragon.
Or shall we cast yon casement wide,
And see the knights before us ride,
The charging Cid, the Moors that flee?
Grim although the battles be
That through my window-frames I see,
No death is there, nor any pain,
Because on my estates in Spain
All passions gaily run their course,
But lack the shadow-fiend remorse.
Something 't is to make one vain
Thus to be grandee of Spain;
For the wine of Andalouse
All the world a man might lose,
Could he see what rosy shapes
Trample out my Spanish grapes,
Know how pink the feet that bruise
My gold-green grapes of Andalouse.
Ah, but if you 're not a don,
Drink no wine of Aragon.
Dreamland loves and elfin flavors,
Gay romances, fairy favors,
Moonlit mists and glad confusions,
Youth's brief mystery of delusions,
Racing, chasing, haunt the brain
Of him who drinks this wine of Spain.
Where the quarterings were won
That make of me a Spanish don
No one asks in Aragon.
Never blood of Bourbon grew
So magnificently blue;

Blood have I that once was Dante's;
Kinsman am I of Cervantes.
Come and see what nobles fine
Make my proud ancestral line:
In my gallery set apart,
Lo where art interprets art.
Yes, you needs must like it well,—
Shakespeare's face by Raphael.
Ah, 't is very nobly done,
But that 's the air of Aragon.
He left me that which till life ends
Is surely mine,— the best of friends;
And chiefly one, if you would know,
I love of all, Mercutio.
Velasquez?   Ay, he knew a man,
And well he drew my Puritan,
With eyes too full of heaven's light
To dream our day as aught but night.
If my soul stirs swift at wrong,
This sire made that instinct strong.
Da Vinci touched with love the face
That keeps for me young Surrey's grace.
And that,— ah, that is one to like,
My kinsman Sidney, by Vandyke.
Some words he gave, of which bereft
My life were poorer.   There, to left
Are they whose rills of English song
Unto my royal blood belong.
For poet, painter, priest, and lay
Went to make my Spanish clay;
And here away in Andalouse,
Whatever mood my soul may choose,
The poet's joy, the soldier's force,

Finds for me its parent source
Where, along the pictured wall,
Hero voices on me call,
With the falling of the dews,
In Aragon or Andalouse,
When the mystic shadows troop,
When my fairy flowers droop,
And the joyous day is done
In Andalouse or Aragon.

GRANADA, *May* 27, 1888.

DREAMLAND

Up anchor !   Up anchor !
  Set sail and away !
The ventures of dreamland
  Are thine for a day.
Yo, heave ho !
  Aloft and alow
Elf sailors are singing,
  Yo, heave ho !
The breeze that is blowing
  So sturdily strong
Shall fill up thy sail
  With the breath of a song.
A fay at the mast-head
  Keeps watch o'er the sea ;
Blown amber of tresses
  Thy banner shall be ;
Thy freight the lost laughter

That sad souls have missed,
Thy cargo the kisses
    That never were kissed.
And ho, for a fay maid
    Born merry in June,
Of dainty red roses
    Beneath a red moon.
The star-pearls that midnight
    Casts down on the sea,
Dark gold of the sunset
    Her fortune shall be.
And ever she whispers,
    More tenderly sweet,
" Love am I, love only,
    Love perfect, complete.
The world is my lordship,
    The heart is my slave ;
I mock at the ages,
    I laugh at the grave.
Wilt sail with me ever
    A dream-haunted sea,
Whose whispering waters
    Shall murmur to thee
The love-haunted lyrics
    Dead poets have made
Ere life had a fetter,
    Ere love was afraid ? "
Then up with the anchor !
    Set sail and away !
The ventures of loveland
    Are thine for a day.

NEWPORT, 1890.

FORGET-ME-NOTS

ON THE ALBULA PASS

THEY peep above the boulders gray,
   Stand dark against the snows,
Leap modest from the billow's kiss
   Gray Albula bestows.

They bend beneath the cloaking mist,
   Crowd every open spot,
And murmur with assurance gay
   One phrase, " *Forget me not.*"

The gentle chorus rises still
   Unanimously sweet;
They seem to leave their quiet nooks,
   And cluster round my feet.

Forget thee not ?   Yet how to learn
   The very ample art
To love an army corps of maids,
   All bidding for my heart !

There may be who would think those eyes,
   So constant and so true,
To be — forgive the daring thought —
   Monotonously blue.

And then, if all these myriad lips
   To but one song are set,
There might be luxury in the power
   A little to forget.

No gay arithmetic of love
  Could solve this puzzling sum,
Nor leave a Mormon lover aught
  But resolutely dumb;

For all historic cases fail
  Before my hopeless lot,
When fifty thousand viewless tongues
  Say just " *Forget me not.*"

Nor yet am I the first or last
  By whom their cry is heard;
They breathe it to the careless wind,
  They cast it to the bird.

Who gave these mountain-maids their song?
  What lover's murmured thought
Unnumbered centuries ago
  Their tender legend taught?

Or was it from some wounded soul
  In torture and despair
They learned these faint, appealing words,—
  The wail of human prayer?

I know not.   Love is boundless large;
  Past Albula's cloud-towers
A joyous shaft of sunshine falls
  On me and on the flowers.

Mysterious vestals of the hill,
  In pretty council met,
Pray teach me now that wiser art,
  How easiest to forget.

The song is hushed, the drooping mist
  Shrouds every silent form,
And thoughtful down the lonely pass
  I move amid the storm.

July 8, 1888.

THE QUAKER LADY

'MID drab and gray of mouldered leaves,
  The spoil of last October,
I see the Quaker lady stand
  In dainty garb and sober.

No speech has she for praise or prayer,
  No blushes, as I claim
To know what gentle whisper gave
  Her prettiness a name.

The wizard stillness of the hour
  My fancy aids: again
Return the days of hoop and hood
  And tranquil William Penn.

I see a maid amid the wood
  Demurely calm and meek,
Or troubled by the mob of curls
  That riots on her cheek.

Her eyes are blue, her cheeks are red,—
  Gay colors for a Friend,—
And Nature with her mocking rouge
  Stands by a blush to lend.

'The gown that holds her rosy grace
  Is truly of the oddest;
And wildly leaps her tender heart
  Beneath the kerchief modest.

It must have been the poet Love
  Who, while she slyly listened,
Divined the maiden in the flower,
  And thus her semblance christened.

Was he a proper Quaker lad
  In suit of simple gray?
What fortune had his venturous speech,
  And was it " yea " or " nay "?

And if indeed she murmured " yea,"
  And throbbed with worldly bliss,
I wonder if in such a case
  Do Quakers really kiss?

Or was it some love-wildered beau
  Of old colonial days,
With clouded cane and broidered coat,
  And very artful ways?

And did he whisper through her curls
  Some wicked, pleasant vow,
And swear no courtly dame had words
  As sweet as " thee " and " thou "?

Or did he praise her dimpled chin
  In eager song or sonnet,
And find a merry way to cheat
  Her kiss-defying bonnet?

And sang he then in verses gay,
  Amid this forest shady,
The dainty flower at her feet
  Was like his Quaker lady ?

And did she pine in English fogs,
  Or was his love enough ?
And did she learn to sport the fan,
  And use the patch and puff ?

Alas ! perhaps she played quadrille,
  And, naughty grown and older,
Was pleased to show a dainty neck
  Above a snowy shoulder.

But sometimes in the spring, I think,
  She saw, as in a dream,
The meeting-house, the home sedate,
  The Schuylkill's quiet stream ;

And sometimes in the minuet's pause
  Her heart went wide afield
To where, amid the woods of May,
  A blush its love revealed.

Till far away from court and king
  And powder and brocade,
The Quaker ladies at her feet
  Their quaint obeisance made.

NEWPORT, 1889.

THE QUAKER GRAVEYARD

Four straight brick walls, severely plain,
  A quiet city square surround;
A level space of nameless graves,—
  The Quakers' burial-ground.

In gown of gray, or coat of drab,
  They trod the common ways of life,
With passions held in sternest leash,
  And hearts that knew not strife.

To yon grim meeting-house they fared,
  With thoughts as sober as their speech,
To voiceless prayer, to songless praise,
  To hear the elders preach.

Through quiet lengths of days they came,
  With scarce a change to this repose;
Of all life's loveliness they took
  The thorn without the rose.

But in the porch and o'er the graves,
  Glad rings the southward robin's glee,
And sparrows fill the autumn air
  With merry mutiny;

While on the graves of drab and gray
  The red and gold of autumn lie,
And wilful Nature decks the sod
  In gentlest mockery.

1879.

DOMINIQUE DE GOURGUES

In his cheerful Norman orchard
　　Lay De Gourgues of Mont Marsan,
Gascon to the core, and merry,
　　Just a well-contented man,

With his pipe, that comrade constant,
　　Won in sorrowful Algiers,
In the slave's brief rest at evening
　　Left for curses and for tears.

Peacefully he pondered, gazing
　　Where his plough-ribbed cornfields lay,
With their touch of hopeful verdure,
　　Waiting patient for the May.

Joyous from the terrace o'er him
　　Came the voice of wife and child,
And the sunlit smoke curled upward
　　As the gaunt old trooper smiled.

" St. Denis," quoth the stout De Gourgues,
　　" Yon beehive's ever busy hum
Doth like me better than the noise
　　Of the musketoon and drum.

" Tough am I, though this skin of mine
　　By steel and bullet well is scarred,
Like those round pippins overhead
　　By the thrushes pecked and marred.

" Forsooth I 'm somewhat autumn-ripe,
    Yet like my apples sound and red.
And life is sweet," said stout De Gourgues,
    " Yea, verily sweet," he said.

" Three things there were I once did love —
    One that gay jester of Navarre,
And one to sack a Spanish town,
    And one the wild wrath of war.

" And two there were I hated well —
    One that carrion beast, a Moor,
And one that passeth him for spite,
    That 's a Spaniard, rest you sure."

Still he smoked, and musing murmured,
    " There be three things well I like,
My pipe, my ease, this quiet life,
    Better far than push of pike.

" And to-day there be two I love
    Who lured me out of the strife,
The lad who plays with my rusty blade,
    And the little Gascon wife.

" Parbleu ! parbleu ! " cried gray De Gourgues,
    For at his side there stood
A soldier, scarred and worn and white,
    In a cuirass dark with blood.

" Ventre Saint Gris ! good friend, halloa !
    Art sorely hurt, and how ? and why ?
Art Huguenot ?   Here 's help at need ;
    Or Catholic ?   What care I ! "

No motion had the white wan lips,
  The mail-clad chest no breathing stirred,
Though clear as rings a vengeful blade
  Fell every whispered word.

"That Jean Ribaut am I
  Who sailed for the land of flowers;
Fore God our tryst is surely set;
  I wearily count the hours."

And slowly rose the steel-clad hand,
  And westward pointing stayed as set:
"Thy peace is gone!   No morn shall dawn
  Will let thee e'er forget.

"Thy brothers, the dead, lie there,
  Where only, the winds complain,
And under their gallows walk
  The mocking lords of Spain.

"If ever this France be dear,
  And honor as life to thee,
Thy wife, thy child are naught to-day,
  Thy errand 's on the sea."

"St. Denis to save!" cried stout De Gourgues,
  "One may dream, it seems, by day."
The man was gone! — but where he stood
  A rusted steel glove lay.

"I 've heard — yea twice — this troublous tale,
  It groweth full old indeed;
But old or new, my sword is sheathed
  For ghost or king or creed."

Full slow he turned and climbed the hill,
  And thrice looked back to see:
"The dream! The glove!— How came it
    there ?—
  What matters a glove to me ?"

But day by day as one distraught
  He stood, or gazed upon the board;
Nor heard the voice of wife or boy,
  Nor took of the wine they poured.

He saw his bannerol flutter forth,
  As tossed by the wind of fight,
And watched his sword above the hearth
  Leap flashing to the light.

He told her all. "Now God be praised!"
  She cried, while the hot tears ran;
"She little loves who loves not more
  His honor than the man."

His lands are sold. A stranger's hand
  The juice of his grapes shall strain;
Another, too, shall reap the hopes
  He sowed with the winter grain.

His way was o'er the windy seas,
  But, sailed he fast or sailed he slow,
He saw by day, he saw by night,
  The face of Jean Ribaut.

The sun rose crimson with the morn,
  Or set at eve a ghastly red,
While over blue Bahama seas
  Beckoned him ever the dead.

Till spoke, sore set at last, De Gourgues:
  " Ho, brothers brave, and have ye sailed
For gain of gold this weary way ?
  Heaven's grace ! but ye have failed !

" A sterner task our God hath set ;
  In yon wild land of flowers
Our dead await the trusty blades
  Shall cleanse their fame and ours.

" Ye know the tale."   Few words they said :
  " We are thine for France to-day ! "
By cape and beach and palmy isles
  The avengers held their way.

The deed was done, the honor won,
  Nor land nor gain of gold got they,
Where 'neath the broad palmetto leaves
  Their dead at evening lay.

The deed was done, the honor won,
  And o'er the gibbet-loads was set
This legend grim for priests to read,
  And, if they could, forget :

" Not as to Spaniards : murderers these.
  Ladrones, robbers, hanged I here,
Ransom base for the costly souls
  Whom God and France hold dear."

How welcomed him that brave Rochelle,
  With cannon thunder and clash of bell,
What bitter fate his courage won,
  Some slender annals tell.

No legend tells what signal sweet
  Looked gladness from a woman's eyes,
Or how she welcomed him who brought
  Alas! one only prize,—

A noble deed in honor done
  And the wreck of a ruined life.
Ah, well if I knew what said the lips
  Of the little Gascon wife!

1890.

THE WRECK OF THE EMMELINE

This tack might fetch Absecom bar,
  The wind lies fair for the Dancin' Jane;
She's good on a wind.   If we keep this way,
  You might talk with folk in the land of Spain.

A tidy smack of a breeze it be;
  Just hear it whistle 'mong them dunes!
It ain't no more nor a gal for strong,—
  Sakes! but it hollers a lot of toones.

Ye 'd ought to hear it October-time
  A-fiddlin' 'mong them cat-tails tall;
Our Bill can fiddle, but 'gainst that wind
  He ain't no kind of a show at all.

Respectin' the wrack you want to see,
  It 's yon away, set hard and fast
On the outer bar.   When tides is low
  You kin see a mawsel of rib and mast.

Four there was on us, wrackers all,
  Born and bred to foller the sea,
And Dad beside; that 's him you seed
  Las' night a-mendin' them nets with me.

Waal, sir, it was n't no night for talk ;
  The pipes went out, an' we stood, we four,
A-starin' dumb through the rattlin' panes,
  And says Tom, " I 'd as lief be here ashore."

The wust wind ever I knowed
  Was swoopin' across the deep,
An' the waves was humpin' as white as snow,
  An' gallopin' in like frighted sheep.

Lord! sich a wind !　It tuk that sand
  An' flung it squar' on the winder-sash,
An' howled and mumbled 'mong the scrub,
  An' yelled like a hurt thing 'cross the ma'sh.

Old Dad as was sittin' side the fire,
  Jus' now an' agin he riz his head,
An' says he, " God help all folks at sea,—
  God help 'em livin', and bury 'em dead.

" God help them in smacks as sail,
  An' men as v'yage in cruisers tall ;
God help all as goes by water,
  Big ship and little,— help 'em all."

" Amen !" says Bill, jus' like it was church ;
  An' all of a sudden says Joe to me,
" Hallo !" an' thar was a flash of light,
  An' the roar of a gun away to sea.

"' An' it 's each for all!" cries Dad to me;
    "The night ain't much of a choice for sweet."
So up he jumps an' stamps aroun',
    Jus' for to waken his sleepy feet.

" An' it 's into ilers and on with boots,"
    Sings Dad; " thar be n't no time to spar'.
Pull in y'r waist-straps.   Hurry a bit;
    The shortest time 'll be long out thar."

I did n't like it, nor them no more,
    But roun' we scuttles for oar and ropes,
An' out we plunged in the old man's wake,
    For we knowed as we was thar only hopes.

The door druv' in; the cinders flew;
    The house, it shook; out went the light;
The air was thick with squandered sand,
    As nipt like the sting of a bluefly bite.

We passed yon belt of holly and pine,
    An' in among them cedar an' oak
We stood a bit on the upper shore,
    An' stared an' listened, but no man spoke.

" Whar lies she, Bill?" roars Dad to me,
    As down we bended.   Then bruk' a roar
As follered a lane of dancin' light
    That flashed and fluttered along the shore.

"She 's thar," says Joe; " I 'd sight of her then;
    She 's hard and high on the outer bar.
Nary a light, and fast enough,
    And nary a mawsel of mast or spar."

Groans Dad, " Good Lord, it 's got to be ! "
  Says Tom, "It ain't to be done, I fear."
Shouts Joe, a-laffin' (he allus laffed),
  " It ain't to be done by standin' here."

Waal, in she went, third time of tryin'—
  " In with a will," laffs Joe, in a roar,
Tom a-cussin' and Dad a-prayin',
  But spry enough with the steerin' oar.

Five hours — an' cold.   I was clean played out.
  " Give way," shouts Dad, " give way thar
        now ! "
" Hurray ! " laffs Joe.   An' we slung her along,
  With a prayer to aft an' a laff in the bow.

There was five men glad when we swep' her in
  Under the lee, an' none too soon.
" Aboard thar, mates ! " shouts Dad, an' the wind
  Just howled like a dog at full of moon.

" Up with you, Bill ! " sung Dad.   So I —
  I grabbed for a broken rope as hung.
Gosh ! it was stiff as an anchor-stock,
  But up I swarmed, and over I swung.

Ice ?   She was ice from stem to starn.
  I gripped the rail an' sarched the wrack,
An' cleared my eyes, an' sarched agin'
  For livin' sign on that slidin' deck.

Four dead men in the scuppers lay.
  Stiff as steel, they was froze that fast ;
An' one old man was hangin' awry,
  Tied to the stump of the broken mast.

Ice-bound he were.   But he kinder smiled,
  A-lookin' up.   I was sort of skeered.
Lord! thinks I, thar was many a prayer
  Froze in the snow of that orful beard.

Thar was one man lashed to the wheel,
  An' his eyes was a-starin' wild,
An' thar, close-snuggled up in his arms,—
  O Lord, sir, the pity! — a little child.

" Dead all," says I, as I lep to the boat.
  " Give way," an' we bent to the springin' oar;
An' never no word says boy or Dad,
  Till we crashed full high on the upper shore.

Then Dad, he dropped for to pray,
  But I stood all a-shake on the sand;
An' the old man says, " I could wish them souls
  Was fetched ashore to the joyful land."

But Joe, he laffs.   Says Dad, right mad,
  " Shut up.   Ye 'd grin if ye went to heaven."
"Why not?" says Joe.   "As for this here earth,
  It takes lots of laffin' to keep things even."

Ready about, an' mind for the boom;
  Ef ye keer for to hold that far,
You may see the Emmeline, keel and rib,
  Stuck fast an' firm on the outer bar.

Newport, *October*, 1891.

A PSALM OF THE WATERS

Lo! this is a psalm of the waters,—
The wavering, wandering waters:
With languages learned in the forest,
With secrets of earth's lonely caverns,
The mystical waters go by me
On errands of love and of beauty,
On embassies friendly and gentle,
With shimmer of brown and of silver.
In pools of dark quiet they ponder,
Where the birch, and the elm, and the maple
Are dreams in the soul of their stillness.
In eddying spirals they loiter,
For touch of the fern-plumes they linger,
Caress the red mesh of the pine roots,
And quench the strong thirst of the leafage
That high overhead with its shadows
Requites the soft touch of their giving
Like him whose supreme benediction
Made glad for love's service instinctive
The heart of the Syrian woman.
O company, stately and gracious,
That wait the sad axe on the hillside!
My kinsmen since far in the ages,
We tossed, you and I, as dull atoms,
The sport of the wind and the water.
We are as a greater has made us,
You less and I more; yet forever
The less is the giver, and thankful,
The guest of your quivering shadows,

I welcome the counselling voices
That haunt the dim aisles of the forest.

Lo, this is a psalm of the waters
That wake in us yearnings prophetic,
That cry in the wilderness lonely
With meanings for none but the tender.
I hear in the rapids below me
Gay voices of little ones playing,
And echoes of boisterous laughter
From grim walls of resonant granite.
'T is gone — it is here — this wild music!
Untamed by the ages, as gladsome
As when, from the hands of their Maker,
In wild unrestraint the swift waters
Leapt forth to the bountiful making
Of brook and of river and ocean.
I linger, I wonder, I listen.
Alas! is it I who interpret
The cry of the masterful north wind,
The hum of the rain in the hemlock,
As chorals of joy or of sadness,
To match the mere moods of my being?
Alas for the doubt and the wonder!
Alas for the strange incompleteness
That limits with boundaries solemn
The questioning soul!   Yet forever
I know that these choristers ancient
Have touch of my heart; and alas, too,
That never was love in its fulness
Told all the great soul of its loving!
I know, too, the years, that remorseless
Have hurt me with sorrow, bring ever

More near for my help the quick-healing,
The infinite comfort of nature;
For surely the childhood that enters
This heaven of wood and of water
Is won with gray hairs, in the nearing
That home ever open to childhood.

And you, you my brothers, who suffer
In serfdom of labor and sorrow,
What gain have your wounds, that forever
Man bridges with semblance of knowledge
The depths he can never illumine?
Or binds for his service the lightning,
Or prisons the steam of the waters?
What help has it brought to the weeper?
How lessened the toil of the weary?
Alas! since at evening, deserted,
Job sat in his desolate anguish,
The world has grown wise; but the mourner
Still weeps and will weep; and what helping
He hath from his God or his fellow
Eludes the grave sentinel reason,
Steals in at the heart's lowly portal,
And helps, but will never be questioned.
Yea, then, let us take what they give us,
And ask not to know why the murmur
Of winds in the pine-tree has power
To comfort the hurt of life's battle,
To help when our dearest are helpless.
Lo, here stands the mother. She speaketh
As when at his tent door the Arab
Calls, Welcome! in language we know not!
Cries, Enter, and share with thy servant!

1890.

EVENING, AFTER A STORM ON THE RISTIGOUCHE RIVER

A MOOD

THE air is cool; a mist hangs low
Above the wild waves' gleaming flow,
An earth-born cloud, a prisoner fair
Held captive from the upper air.
Its life is brief; 't is gone, unseen
As souls set free.   The blue serene
Shall claim it, as, of heaven's race,
It speeds a viewless way through space.
As souls set free!   Oh, memories fair
That substance of my boyhood were;
What subtle process of the brain
Called that dear company again:
Those honest eyes of tranquil gray,
That heart which knew but honor's way,
And one, the strong, the saint of pain,—
That visage smiles for me again,
Laughs as it laughed when life was here,
Smiles as it smiled when death was near.
What thought-linked sweetness of the hour
Bade memory's folded buds to flower?
The dim horizons of the mind
In vain I search, nor answer find.
The sombre woods make no reply;
The busy river, rambling by,
Is silent; silent is the sky.
And yet to-day this nature dear
Than human help seems far more near;

And closer to my listening soul
The rhythms of the rapid roll
Than any words of human tongue,
Than any song of poet sung.
Alas, the bounding walls of time
Still hem us in; the poet's rhyme,
The brain, the air, the river's flow,
The frank blue sky, the waves below,
Refuse to tell us half they know.
In vain our search, in vain our cries,
Our dearest loves lack some replies;
And thought as infinite as space
May never tell us face to face,
Though sought beneath death's awful shroud,
The secrets of one flitting cloud,
All of a monad's story brief,
The history of a single leaf.
Ah, mystery of mysteries,
To know if under other skies
Shall Nature wait with open hand,
To hold her secrets at command.

O'er other hills and far away
The red scourge of the lightning flies;
The thunder roar of smitten clouds
Reverberant in distance dies;
The western sky, an arch of green,
Fades o'er me, and my still canoe
Floats on a mystic sea of gold
Flecked thick with waves of sapphire blue;
The silent counsels of the night
Float downward with the failing light;

Strange whispers from the darkened stream
Rise like the voices of a dream;
The joy of mystery gathers near,
The joy that is almost a fear.
Speechless the infinite of space,
Star-peopled, looks upon my face,
The patience of heaven's planet gaze,
That bids me wait for death's amaze,
Or for the death of deaths to tell
The secrets Nature guards so well.
Lo, darkness that is substance falls
Between the mountains' nearing walls,
The sky drops down, and to my eye
The watery levels closer lie,
Till wood and wave and mountain fade
'Neath the dear mother's cloak of shade.
She brings for me the scented balm
Her spruce-trees yield; a sacred calm
Falls softly on my kneeling heart.
" Peace, child," she whispers, " mine thou art.
Lo, in my darkness thou hast found
Content my daylight does not bound;
My silence to thy soul doth preach;
Night unto night still uttereth speech,
And the black night of death shall be
As eloquent of truth to thee."

1886.

RAIN IN CAMP

THE camp-fire smoulders and will not burn,
And a sulky smoke from the blackened logs
Lazily swirls through the dank wood caves;
And the laden leaves with a quick relief
Let fall their loads, as the pool beyond
Leaps 'neath the thin gray lash of the rain,
And is builded thick with silver bells.
But I lie on my back in vague despair,
Trying it over thrice and again,
To see if my words will say the thing.
But the sodden moss, and the wet black wood,
And the shining curves of the dancing leaves,
The drip and drop, and tumble and patter,
The humming roar in the sturdy pines,
Alas, shall there no man paint or tell.

1870.

ELK COUNTY

FROM lands of the elk and the pine-tree,
Of hemlock and whitewood and maple,
You ask me to write you a lyric
Shall thrill with the cries of the forest,
And flow like the sap of the maple,—
The rich yellow blood of the maple,
That hath such a wild, lusty sweetness,
Such a taste of the wilderness in it.
And surely 't were pleasant to summon

The days which so lately have vanished,
The friends who were part of their pleasure.
Right cheery for me, in the city,
To think once again of the sunsets
We watched from the crest of the hill-top,
Alone on the stumps in the clearing;
When slowly the forms of the mountains,
Our own hills, our loved Alleghanies,
Grew hazy and distant and solemn,
Cloaked each with the shade of his neighbor;
Like rigid old Puritans scorning
The passion and riot of color,
Of yellow and purple and scarlet,
Which haunt the gay court of the sunset,
Where Eve, like a wild Cinderella,
Awaits the gray fairy of twilight.
Sweet, ever, to think of the forests,
Their cool, woody fragrance delicious;
To think of the camp-fires we builded
To baffle those terrible pungies;
To think how we wandered, bewildered
With wood-dreams and delicate fancies
Unknown to the life of the city.
To tread but those cushioning mosses;
To lie, almost float, on the fern-beds;
To feel the crisp crush of the foot on
The mouldering logs of the windfall,
Were things to be held in remembrance.
Dost recall how we lingered to listen
The sound of the wood-robin's bugle,
Or bent the witch-hopple to guide us,
As one folds the page he is reading,
And felt, as we peered through the stillness,

Through armies and legions of tree-trunks,
Such solemn and brooding sensations
As told of the birth of religions,
As whispered how men grow to Druids
When the fly-wheel of work is arrested,
And they live the still life of the forest ?
Ay, here in the face of the woodman,
You see how the woods have been preaching,
As he leans on the logs of his cabin
To watch the prim city-folk coming
O'er the chips, and the twigs, and the stubble,
Through the fire-scarred stumps, and the hem-
    locks
His axe hath so ruthlessly girdled.
Ay, he too has learned in the forest,
One half of him Nimrod and slayer,
Unsparing, enduring, and tireless,
In wait for the deer at the salt lick ;
Yet one stronger half of his nature —
This rough and bold out-of-door nature,
Hath touches of sadness upon it,
And is grown to the ways of the forest,
Till wildness and softness together
Are one in the sap of his being.

Right pleasant it were, friend and lady,
To tell you some tale of the woodland ;
To hear the faint voice of tradition,
Of childish and simple conceptions,
And find in their half-spoken meanings
Some thought all the nations have muttered
In the parable tongues of their childhood.
Alas for the tale and the writer !

The land has no story to tell us,—
No voice save the Clarion's waters,
No song save the murm'rous confusion
Of winds gone astray in the pine-tops,
Or the roar of the rain on the hemlocks;—
No record, no sign, not a word of
The lords of the axe and the rifle,
Who camped by the smooth Alleghany,
And blazed the first tree on the mountain.
Yet here, even here in the forest,—
The soul-calming deep of the forest,
Where cat-birds are noisy and dauntless,
And deft little miserly squirrels
Are hoarding the beech-nuts for winter;
Where rattlesnakes charm, and the hoot-owl
By night sounds his murderous war-pipe,—
Yes, here in the last home of Nature,
Where the greenness that swells o'er the hillock
Is pink with the blossoming laurel,
The wants of the city still haunt us,
When busy blue axes are ringing,
And totter the kings of the mountain.
Ah, well you recall, I can fancy,
The morn we looked down on the valley
That bears the proud name of the battle,
Itself a fair field for the winning;
Recall, too, the frank speech which told us
Who felled the first tree in the valley
Where now the red heifers are browsing,
And reapers are swinging their cradles,
And fat grow the stacks with the harvest.
Canst see, too, the dam and the mill-pond,
The trees in the dark amber water,

Where thousands of pine logs are tethered,
With maple and black birch and cherry?
Canst hear, as I hear, the gay hum of
The bright, whizzing saw in the steam-mill,
Its up-and-down old-fashioned neighbor
Singing, "Go it!" and "Go it!" and "Go it!"
As it whirrs through the heart of the pine-tree,
And spouts out the saw-dust, and filleth
The air with its resinous odors?
Ay, gnaw at them morning and evening,
Thou hungry old dog of a saw-mill!
The planks thou art shaping so deftly
Shall ring with the tramp of the raftsmen,
Shall drift on the shallow Ohio,
Shall build thy fair homes, Cincinnati,
Shall see the gay steamers go by them,
Shall float on the broad Mississippi,
Shall floor the rough cabins of Kansas.

And here is a tale for the poet,—
A story of Saxon endurance,
A story of work and completion,
A legend of rough-handed labor
As wild as the runes of the fiords.

1858.

A CAMP IN THREE LIGHTS

AGAINST the darkness sharply lined
 Our still white tents gleamed overhead,
And dancing cones of shadow cast
 When sudden flashed the camp-fire red,

Where fragrant hummed the moist swamp-spruce,
    And tongues unknown the cedar spoke,
While half a century's silent growth
    Went up in cheery flame and smoke.

Pile on the logs!   A flickering spire
    Of ruby flame the birch-bark gives,
And as we track its leaping sparks,
    Behold in heaven the North-light lives!

An arch of deep, supremest blue,
    A band above of silver shade,
Where, like the frost-work's crystal spears,
    A thousand lances grow and fade,

Or shiver, touched with palest tints
    Of pink and blue, and changing die,
Or toss in one triumphant blaze
    Their golden banners up the sky,

With faint, quick, silken murmurings,
    A noise as of an angel's flight,
Heard like the whispers of a dream
    Across the cool, clear northern night.

Our pipes are out, the camp-fire fades,
    The wild auroral ghost-lights die,
And stealing up the distant wood
    The moon's white spectre floats on high,

And, lingering, sets in awful light
    A blackened pine-tree's ghastly cross,
Then swiftly pays in silver white
    The faded fire, the aurora's loss.

1870.

LAKE HELEN

I LIE in my red canoe
  On the waters still and deep,
And o'er me darkens the sky,
  And beneath the billows sleep ;

Till, between the stars above
  And those in the lake's embrace,
I seem to float like the dead
  In the noiselessness of space.

Betwixt two worlds I drift,
  A bodiless soul again,—
Between the still thoughts of God
  And those which belong to men ;

And out of the height above,
  And out of the deep below,
A thought that is like a ghost
  Doth gather and gain and grow,

That now and forevermore
  This silence of death shall hold,
While the nations fade and die,
  And the countless years are rolled.

But I turn the light canoe,
  And, darting across the night,
Am glad of the paddle's noise
  And the camp-fire's honest light.

1870.

NIPIGON LAKE

HIGH-SHOULDERED and ruddy and sturdy,
Like droves of pre-Adamite monsters,
The vast mounded rocks of red basalt
Lie basking round Nipigon's waters;
And still lies the lake, as if fearing
To trouble their centuried slumber;
And heavy o'er lake and in heaven
A dim veil of smoke tells of forests
Ablaze in the far lonely Northland:
And over us, blood-red and sullen,
The sun shines on gray-shrouded islands,
And under us, blood-red and sullen,
The sun in the dark umber water
Looks up at the gray, murky heaven,
While one lonely loon on the water
Is wailing his mate, and beside us
Two shaggy-haired Chippewa children
In silence watch sadly the white man.

1871.

EVENING STORM — NIPIGON

UPON the beach, with low, quick, mournful sob,
The weary waters shudder to our feet;
And far beyond the sunset's golden light,
Forever brighter in its lessening span,
Shares not the sadness of yon dark wood-wall,

Where green and noiseless deeps of shadow rest
In growing gloom 'twixt golden lake and sky.
Fast fades the lessening day, and far beneath
The tamarack shivers and the cedar's cone
Uneasy sways, while fitful tremors stir
The tattered livery of the ragged birch ;
And over all the arch of heaven is wild
With tumbled clouds, where swift the lightning's lance
Gleams ruby red and thunder-echoes roll ;
Far, far below —sweet as the dream of hope
What time despair is nearest—lies the lake.
Fast comes the storm ; spiked black with pattering rain,
The darkened water gleams with bells of foam.
Fast comes the storm, till over lake and sky,
O'er yellow lake and ever-yellowing sky,
Cruel and cold, the gray storm-twilights rest ;
And so the day before its time is dead.

1870.

NOONDAY WOODS—NIPIGON

BETWEEN thin fingers of the pine
   The fluid gold of sunlight slips,
And through the tamarack's gray-green fringe
   Upon the level birch leaves drips.

Through all the still, moist forest air
   Slow trickles down the soft, warm sheen,
And flecks the branching wood of ferns
   With tender tints of pallid green,

To rest where close to mouldered trunks
  The red and purple berries lie,
Where tiny jungles of the moss
  Their tropic forests rear on high.

Fast, fast asleep the woodland rests,
  Stirs not the tamarack's topmost sheaf,
And slow the subtle sunlight glides
  With noiseless step from leaf to leaf.

And lo, he comes! the fairy prince,
  The heir of richer, softer strands:
A summer guest of sterner climes,
  He moves across the vassal lands.

And lo, he comes! the fairy prince,
  The joyous sweet southwestern breeze:
He bounds across the dreaming lake,
  And bends to kiss the startled trees,

Till all the woodland wakes to life,
  The pheasant chirps, the chipmunks cry,
And scattered flakes of golden light
  Athwart the dark wood-spaces fly.

Ah, but a moment, and away!
  The fair, false prince has kissed and fled:
No more the wood shall feel his touch,
  No more shall know his joyous tread.

1872.

A PADDLE-SONG OF CANADIAN VOYAGEURS

FROM THE FRENCH

THE mist is thick, the waters quick,
  And fast we flit along;
The foam-bells flash, the paddles splash,—
  Sing us a merry song.

What 's this I see come swift to me
  Across the rapids dark?
A princess fair, with yellow hair,
  A red canoe of bark.

Her golden hair floats thick and fair
  Far, far behind her lee,
And pike and trout come leaping out,
  Her merry locks to see.

With a silver gun, a silver gun,
  The tall white swan she slew:
He moaned a hymn, his sight grew dim,
  It might have been I or you.

The feathers, white as the still moonlight,
  Toss red on the waters free,
And gay trout break the silent lake,
  The small white boats to see.

The silver ball has found his heart:
  It might have hit you or me.
The round white ball has found his heart:
  Ah sad! ah sad to see!

Quick is the flash of her paddle's dash,
  And far and free behind,
In the roar and splash of the rapids' crash,
  Her hair floats on the wind.

Turn not to view her swift canoe;
  Ave' Maria! beware! beware!
Look not behind, where wave and wind
  Roll out her rippled hair.

1871.

AFTER SUNSET — LAKE WEELOKENE-
BAKOK

At twilight Azescohos standeth
With domes that are builded of color:
Its deep-wrinkled strata and boulders,
Its sombre-leaved greenness of noonday,
Fade, lost in the blue misty splendor
That seems like the soul of a color;
While far, far away to the eastward
One vast fading glory of scarlet —
A color that seems as if living —
Possesses the sky like a passion,
And higher and higher in heaven
Fades out in the soft bluish greenness
That climbs to the zenith above us.
Below, far below, as if thinking,
At rest lies the sensitive lake; and
Like one who sings but to her own heart
Such thoughts as a loving lip whispers,

Thus deep in the waters are pictured
The beauty of sunset and hill-side.
For the blue that was blue on the mountain,
Seen deep in the heart of the water,
Hath the touch of some blessing upon it,—
Some strangeness of purity in it,
Like color that shall be in heaven.
This water-held vision of sunset,
Ablaze in the depths of the darkness,
Is it but for the sight ?   Canst not hear it,
This prophet of color, to tell us
Of what may be yet, when the senses
Awaken to lordlier being,
And the thought of the blind man is ours:
When colors unearthly men know not
Shall float from the trumpets of angels,
And tints of the glory of heaven
Shall be for us color and music ?

1871.

FRAGMENT OF A CHIPPEWA LEGEND

DESPAIRING and sunburnt and thirsty,
The forest-trees bend o'er the lake-brink,
Where, mocking them, chatter the squirrels
At play on the mouldering mosses;
While over them, blue and relentless,
Rise, cloudless and sultry, the heavens.
And where, cried the pine-tree in anger,
Ah, where is my warrior North Wind ?

Asleep, quoth the gossiping chipmunk,
On white-bosomed snows of the Northland.
And where, moaned the glossy-limbed beeches,
Where hide our sweet chiefs of the summer,
The rose-breathing South and the West Wind?
Shrilled sharply the loon, from the water,
In gardens of jasmine they wander,
In tents of the lily they linger.
Spake sadly the tamarack stately:
O'er forest and mountain top vainly
A-weary I watch for the East Wind,—
My wild warring rover, the East Wind,
Who smites the dark sea in his fury,
And comes to me eager and angry.
Forgotten, forgotten, forgotten,
The nightingale sings from the alders.

1870.

A CONCEIT

LOITERING scents from the garden come,
  Blown from shelter of wind-stirred trees;
Like bits of song from the lips we love,
  They rise and fade on the evening breeze.

And shall we marry in wedlock sweet
  The poet's soul and the floweret's breath,
And, musing, wonder what many tongues
  The yearning singer may gain in death?

Whom wilt thou hear in the rich wild scents
  Of the ancient gardens' well-trimmed shade?
Who shall the jessamine's laureate be,
  And who for the summer's noble maid,

The great red rose, shall tell us in song
   Her tender passion of sweet perfume?
And whose shall the frail clematis be,
   With its faint aroma and fringe of bloom?

Wilt give unto Keats the waiting rose?
   To Shelley's voice the violet's scent;
And Spenser's measure of stately song
   To haunt the lily's silvery tent?

1864.

THE ROMAN CAMPAGNA

How gentle here is Nature's mood!   She lays
   A woman-hand upon the troubled heart,
   Bidding the world away and time depart,
While the brief minutes swoon to endless days
Filled full of sad, inconstant thoughtfulness.

Behold 't is eventide.   Dun cattle stand
   Drowsed in the misted grasses.   From the hollows
      deep,
   Dim veils, adrift, o'er arch and tower sweep,
Casting a dreary doubt along the land,
Weighting the twilight with some vague distress.

Transient and subtle, not to thought more near
   Than spirit is to flesh, about me rise
   Dim memories, long lost to love's sad eyes;
Now are they wandering shadows, strange and drear,
That from their natal substance far have strayed.

The witches of the mind possess the time,
  And cry, " Behold thy dead!" They come, they
    pass;
  We yearn to give them feature, face. Alas!
Love hath no morn for memory's failing prime;
What once was sweet with truth is but a shade.

The ghosts of nameless sorrow, joy, despair,
  Emotions that have no remembered source,
  Love-waifs from other worlds, hope, fear, remorse
Born of some vision's crime, wail through the air,
Crying, We were and are not,—that is all.

Yet sweet the indecisive evening hour
  That hath of earth the least. Unreal as dreams
  Dreamed within dreams, and ever further, seems
The sound of human toil, while grass and flower
Bend where the mercy of the dew doth fall.

Strange mysteries of expectation wait
  Above the grave-mounds of the storied space,
  Where, buried, lie a nation's strength and grace,
And the sad joys of Rome's imperious state
That perished of its insolent excess.

A dull, gray shroud o'er this vast burial rests,
  Is deathly still, or seems to rise and fall,
  As on a dear one, dead, the moveless pall
Doth cheat the heart with stir of her white breasts,
Mocking the troubled hour with worse distress.

A deathful languor holds the twilight mist,
  Unearthly colors drape the Alban hills,
  A dull malaria the spirit fills;
Death and decay all beauty here have kissed,
Pledging the land to sorrowing loveliness.

ROME, *May*, 1891.

THE GRAVE OF KEATS

THE PROTESTANT CEMETERY AT ROME

" Here lies one whose name was writ in water."

FAIR little city of the pilgrim dead,
Dear are thy marble streets, thy rosy lanes:
Easy it seems and natural here to die,
And death a mother, who with tender care
Doth lay to sleep her ailing little ones.
Old are these graves, and they who, mournfully,
Saw dust to dust return, themselves are mourned;
Yet, in green cloisters of the cypress shade,
Full-choired chants the fearless nightingale
Ancestral songs learned when the world was young.
Sing on, sing ever in thy breezy homes;
Toss earthward from the white acacia bloom
The mingled joy of fragrance and of song;
Sing in the pure security of bliss.
These dead concern thee not, nor thee the fear
That is the shadow of our earthly loves.
And me thou canst not comfort; tender hearts
Inherit here the anguish of the doubt

Writ on this gravestone.   He, at last, I trust,
Serenity of sure attainment knows.
The night falls, and the darkened verdure starred
With pallid roses shuts the world away.
Sad wandering souls of song, frail ghosts of thought
That voiceless died, the massing shadows haunt,
Troubling the heart with unfulfilled delight.
The moon is listening in the vault of heaven,
And, like the airy march of mighty wings,
The rhythmic throb of stately cadences
Inthralls the ear with some high-measured verse,
Where ecstasies of passion-nurtured words
For great thoughts find a home, and fill the mind
With echoes of divinely purposed hopes
That wore on earth the death-pall of despair.
Night darkens round me.   Never more in life
May I, companioned by the friendly dead,
Walk in this sacred fellowship again;
Therefore, thou silent singer 'neath the grass,
Still sing to me those sweeter songs unsung,
" Pipe to the spirit ditties of no tone,"
Caressing thought with wonderments of phrase
Such as thy springtide rapture knew to win.
Ay, sing to me thy unborn summer songs,
And the ripe autumn lays that might have been;
Strong wine of fruit mature, whose flowers alone we
   know.

ROME, *May*, 1891.

ROMA

Ripe hours there be that do anticipate
    The heritage of death, and bid us see,
    As from the vantage of eternity,
The shadow-symbols of historic fate.

As o'er some Alpine summit's lonely steep,
    Blinding and terrible with spears of light,
    Hurling the snows from many a shaken height,
The storm-clad spirits of the mountain sweep,—

Thus, in the solitude where broodeth thought,
    Torn from rent chasms of the soundless past,
    Go by me, as if borne upon the blast,
The awful forms which time and man have wrought.

Swift through the gloom each mournful chariot rolls,
    Dim shapes of empire urge the flying steeds,
    Featured with man's irrevocable deeds,
Robed with the changeful passions of men's souls.

Ethereal visions pass serene in prayer,
    Their eyes aglow with sacrificial light;
    Phantoms of creeds long dead, their garments
        bright,
Drip red with blood of torture and despair.

In such an hour my spirit did behold
    A woman wonderful.　Unnumbered years
    Left in her eyes the beauty born of tears,
And full they were of fatal stories old.

The trophies of her immemorial reign
  The shadowy great of eld beside her bore;
  A broidery of ancient song she wore,
And the glad muses held her regal train.

Still hath she kingdom o'er the souls of men;
  Dear is she always in her less estate.
  The sad, the gay, the thoughtful, on her wait,
Praising her evermore with tongue and pen.

Stately her ways and sweet, and all her own;
  As one who has forgotten time she lives,
  Loves, loses, lures anew, and ever gives,—
She who all misery and all joy hath known.

If thou wouldst see her, as the twilight fails,
  Go forth along the ancient street of tombs,
  And when the purple shade divinely glooms
High o'er the Alban hills, and night prevails,

If then she is not with thee while the light
  Glows over roof and column, tower and dome,
  And the dead stir beneath thy feet, and Rome
Lies in the solemn keeping of the night,—

If then she be not thine, not thine the lot
  Of those some angel rescues for an hour
  From earth's mean limitations, granting power
To see as man may see when time is not.

ROME, *May*, 1891.

VENICE

I AM Venezia, that sad Magdalen,
  Who with her lovers' arms the turbaned East
Smote, and through lusty centuries of gain
  Lived a wild queen of battle and of feast.
I netted, in gold meshes of my hair,
  The great of soul; painter and poet, priest,
Bent at my will with picture, song, and prayer,
And ever love of me their fame increased,
  Till I, a queen, became the slave of slaves,
    And, like the ghost-kings of the Umbrian plain,
  Saw from my centuries torn, as from their graves,
The priceless jewels of my haughty reign.
    Gone are my days of gladness; now in vain
I hurt the tender with my speechless pain.

VENICE, *June*, 1891.

VENICE TO ITALY

O ITALY, my fateful mistress-land,
  That, like Delilah, won with deathful bliss
  Each conquering foe who wooed thy wanton kiss,
And sheared thy lovers' strength with certain hand,
And gave them to Philistia's bonds of vice;
  Smiling to see the strong limbs waste away,
  The manly vigor crippled by decay,
Usurious years exact the minute's price.

Ah! when *my* great were greatest, ever glad,
    I thanked them with the hope of nobler deeds.
  Statesman and poet, painter, sculptor, knight,—
These my dear lovers were ere days grew sad,
    And them I taught how mightily exceeds
All other love the love that holds God's light.

    Venice, *June*, 1891.

THE DECAY OF VENICE

The glowing pageant of my story lies,
  A shaft of light, across the stormy years,
  When, 'mid the agony of blood and tears,
Or pope or kaiser won the mournful prize,
Till I, the fearless child of ocean, heard
  The step of doom, and trembling to my fall,
Remorseful knew that I had seen unstirred
    Proud Freedom's death, the tyrant's festival;
    Whilst that Italia which was yet to be,
  And is, and shall be, sat, a virgin pure,
High over Umbria on the mountain slopes,
    And saw the failing fires of liberty
    Fade on the chosen shrine she deemed secure,
When died for many a year man's noblest hopes.

    Venice, *June*, 1891.

PISA: THE DUOMO

Lo, this is like a song writ long ago,
  Born of the easy strength of simpler days,
  Filled with the life of man, his joy, his praise,
Marriage and childhood, love, and sin, and woe,
Defeat and victory, and all men know
  Of passionate remorses, and the stays
  That help the weary on life's rugged ways.
A dreaming seraph felt this beauty grow
    In sleep's pure hour, and with joy grown bold
Set the fair crystal in the thought of man;
And Time, with antique tints of ivory wan,
  And gentle industries of rain and light,
    Its stones rejoiced, and o'er them crumbled gold
Won from the boundaries of day and night.

    PISA, *May*, 1891.

THE VESTAL'S DREAM

AH, Venus, white-limbed mother of delight,
  Why shouldst thou tease her with a dream so dear ?
  Winged tenderness of kisses, hovering near,
Her gentle longings cheat.   Forbidden sight
Of eager eyes doth through the virgin night
  Perplex her innocence with cherished fear.
  O cruel thou, with sweets to ripen here
In wintry cloisters what can know but blight.
    Wilt leave her now to scorn ?   The lictor's blows

To-morrow shall be merciless.   The light
Dies on the altar!   Nay, swift through the night,
   Comes pitiful the queen of young desire,
      That reddened in a dream this chaste white rose,
   And lights with silver torch the fallen fire.

ROME, *May*, 1891.

AFTER RUYSDAEL

THROUGH briery ways, from underneath
   The far-off sadness of the gold
That fades above the sun, the waves
   Swift to our very feet are rolled.

Above, beyond, to either side,
   The sombre woods bend overhead;
And underneath, the wild brown waves
   Leap joyously, with lightsome tread,

From rock to rock, and laugh and sing,
   Like lonely maids in woods at play;
Till in the cold, still pool below,
   A-sudden checked, they stand at bay,

Like girls who, in their mood of joy,
   To this more solemn woodland glide,
And with some brief, sweet terror touched,
   Stand wistful, trembling, tender-eyed.

What half-felt sense of something gone,
   What sadness in the moveless woods; .
What sorrow haunts yon amber sky,
   That over all so darkly broods!

AFTER ALBERT CUYP

A sunset silence holds the patient land;
Against the sun the stolid cattle stand;
Framed hazy, in the gold that slips
Between the sails of lazy ships,
And floods with level, yellow light
The broad, green meadow grasses bright.

NEAR AMSTERDAM

AFTER ALBERT CUYP

Sober gray skies and ponderous clouds,
  With gaps between of pallid blues;
Bluff breezes stirring the brown canal;
  A broad, flat meadow's myriad hues

Of soft and changeful breadths of green,
  Barred with the silvery grass that bows
By straight canals, and dotted o'er
  With black and white of basking cows;

And distant sails of hidden ships
  The ceaseless windmills show or hide,
Through languid willows white they gleam,
  And over red-tiled houses glide.

Two sturdy lads with wooden shoes
  Go clumping down the reed-fringed dyke,
And tow a broad-bowed boat, where dreams
  The quaint, sweet virgin of Van Eyck.

And slipt from out the revel high,
　Where gay Franz Hals has bid him sit,
Above the bridge, his lazy pipe
　Smokes placidly the stout De Witt.

AFTER TENIERS

A QUIET curve of sombre brown water,
　Flecked with duck-weed and dotted with leaves;
A low brick cottage, where shadows nestle
　'Neath velvet edges of well-thatched eaves.

In front a space, with its gaudy dahlias
　And solid shade of the branching lime,
Where, soberly gay, two boors are drinking
　In the deep'ning gloom of the evening time.

1870.

MILAN

DA VINCI'S CHRIST

ALL day long, year after year,
　Maid and man and priest and lay
Wander in from crowded streets,
　And through the long, cool gallery stray.

And with them, in the fading light,
　We loiter past the pictured wall,
Till lo ! a face before us comes,
　And something wistful seems to fall

From two strange eyes that speak to all;
  For here a priest, and there a maid,
Two lads, a soldier, and a *bonne*,
  Before the rail their steps have stayed.

What message bore this awful face,
  Through all the waning centuries fled?
What says it to the gazer now?
  What said it to the myriad dead

Who came and went like us to-day,
  And, pausing here in silence, all
In silence laid their weight of sins
  Before this still confessional?

A face more sad man never dreamed,
  A face more sweet man never wrought;
So solemn-sad, so solemn-sweet,
  Serenely set in quiet thought.

The silent sunlight slips away,
  The soldiers pass, the *bonne* goes by;
The painter drapes his copy in,
  And stops his work and heaves a sigh.

And followed by those eyes, that have
  The patience of eternity,
We carry to the bustling street
  Their loving *Benedicite*.

1870.

BRUGES: QUAI DES AUGUSTINS

AFTER VAN DER VEER

WITHIN the sad, deserted street,
  We stand a little space to gaze,
Beneath the high-walled garden's shade,
  Amid the twilight's growing haze.

The still depths of the dark canal,
  Between gray walls of ancient stone,
Stir not to any wind that blows,
  And seem so silent, so alone,

We wonder at the lazy swans
  That o'er the water dare to glide,
And marvel at the lads who cast
  Their pebbles from the bridge's side.

Quaint houses bound the darksome wave,
  Time-tinted, yellow, umber, gray,
With gaping gargoyles overhead,
  And underneath sweet gardens gay,

With ivy, flung like cloaks of green
  Upon the worn and mottled wall;
Forgotten centuries ago
  By burgher dames at even-fall.

Across the narrow space of flowers,
  A maid in scarlet petticoat
Comes with the shining pail of brass,
  And bends above the moveless moat;

And breaks her image with the pail,
  And scares the swans, and trips away,
And leaves the stern, gray, sombre street
  To silence and the waning day.

1870.

TO THE SEA AT DAWN

THE morn exults in new-born light
  And, black athwart its gold,
The broken fragments of the night
  Rock in their cradles old.

Ho, sturdy wooer of the great!
  What need to mock thy power
With feeble woman-tales that prate
  Of manhood's yielding hour?

The Norseland fury in us craves
  To feel thy billows leap;
Claims kinship with yon bounding waves,
  Calls cousin with the deep.

The vigor of thy strident song,
  Thy rhythmic marches gay,
Rang music to thy kinsmen strong
  Where'er their hero way:

As when, upon the Spaniards' flight,
  Was loosed thy stormiest power
For God and right and England's might,
  In England's darkest hour;

Or when across the death-watched wave
  Our stern sea-eagle swooped,
And where the bravest led the brave
  His fierce young eaglets trooped.

O poet, lord of many a mood,
  Like him of Arthur's hall,
That knight so bold in battle rude,
  So soft at woman's call,

Thy vassal waves this summer morn,
  Far o'er thy weary length,
Freight with the strength of sweetness born,
  The sweetness born of strength;

And let them whisper love for me
  By one remembered beach,—
Love stronger than thy wildest sea,
  Kind as thy gentlest speech.

AT SEA, *May* 30, 1888.

SUNSET AT SEA

ADOWN the thronged deck of the steamer
The babble of voices fails slowly,
As if unseen fingers of silence
Were laid on the lips of the speakers.
A blazon of azure-flecked crimson,
White-starred with the quick-leaping foam-jets,
Falls swift on the shuddering ocean;
While gather o'erhead to the zenith
Imperious splendors of scarlet.

Slow fadeth the color that troubles
The soul with mysterious terror,
Till unto the sky and the waters
Is born the cool quiet of purples
That calm the stirred heart of the seer.
The peace which is past understanding,
Which only the heart can interpret,
Comes clad in the shadows of twilight
With meanings elusive and tender,
That die at the mere touch of thought, and
Are frail as the firstlings of April.
The peace which is past understanding:
Ethereal, viewless, and solemn,
Mysterious gift of the evening,
A love dew that comes, how we know not,
And freshens all life, how we wist not;
Till down to the paling horizon
Are poured the night shadows, while ever
The huge striving bulk of the steamer
Hurls on through the dark and the ocean.

AT SEA, *June* 1, 1888.

THE WAVES AT MIDNIGHT

THE CLIFFS, NEWPORT

SEEN in the night by
Their snows, as they crush,
Evermore saying—
Hush — hush — hush —
They fall, and they die,
Break, and perish, without reply.

And are not and are,
And come back again
With the sob and throb
Of a constant pain,
And snatch from afar
The tremulous light of a single star.

Always the cliffs hear,
How mournfully sweet
Their murmurous music,
Their cry of defeat,
As near and more near
They shiver and die in darkness drear.

Bleaker the cliffs be,
And blacker the night,
Where tender with sorrow,
Where eager for light,
The waves of life's sea
Wail, crushed at an answerless cliff-wall
    for me.

1889.

THE RISING TIDE

An idle man, I stroll at eve,
  Where move the waters to and fro;
Full soon their added gains will leave
  Small space for me to come and go.

Already in the clogging sand
  I walk with dull, retarded feet;
Yet still is sweet the lessening strand,
  And still the lessening light is sweet.

Newport, *October*, 1891.

EVENING BY THE SEA

With noble waste of lazy hours
  I loitered, till I saw the moon,
A rosy pearl, hang vast and strange
  Above the long gray dune!

And hither, thither, as I went,
  My ancient friend the sea beside,
Whatever tune my spirit sang
  The dear old comrade tried.

Bar Harbor, 1892.

BEAVER TAIL ROCKS

CANONICUT

Fare forth my soul, fare forth, and take thy own;
  The silver morning and the golden eve
  Wait, as the virgins waited to receive
The bridegroom and the bride, with roses strown;

Fare forth and lift her veil,— the bride is joy alone!
　To thee the friendly hours with her shall bring
　The changeless trust that bird and poet sing;
　Her dower to-day shall be the asters sown
On breezy uplands; hers the vigor brought
　Upon the north wind's wing, and hers for thee
　A stately heritage of land and sea,
And all that nature hath, and all the great have
　　thought,
　While low she whispers like a sea-born shell
　Things that thy love may hear but never tell.

1889.

THE CARRY

NIPIGON

BLUE is the sky overhead,
Blue with the northland's pallor,
Never a cloud in sight,
Naught but the moon's gray sickle;
And ever around me, gray,
Ashes, and rock, and lichen.
Far as the sick eye searches
Ghastly trunks, that were trees once,
Up to their bony branches
Carry the gray of ruin.
Lo! where across the mountain
Swept the scythe of the wind-fall,
Moss of a century's making
Lies on this death-swath lonely,
Where in grim heaps the wood sachems,
Like to the strange dead of battle,

Stay, with their limbs ever rigid
Set in the doom-hour of anguish.
Far and away o'er this waste land
Wanders a trail through gray boulders,
Brown to the distant horizon.

1870.

IDLENESS

THERE is no dearer lover of lost hours
　　　　Than I.
I can be idler than the idlest flowers;
　　　　More idly lie
Than noonday lilies languidly afloat,
And water pillowed in a windless moat.
　And I can be
Stiller than some gray stone
That hath no motion known.
　It seems to me
That my still idleness doth make my own
　All magic gifts of joy's simplicity.

RISTIGOUCHE RIVER, 1892.

THE LOST PHILOPENA

TO M. G. M.

MORE blest is he who gives than who receives,
　For he that gives doth always something get:
　Angelic usurers that interest set:
And what we give is like the cloak of leaves

Which to the beggared earth the great trees' fling,
Thoughtless of gain in chilly autumn days:
The mystic husbandry of nature's ways
    Shall fetch it back in greenery of the Spring.
One tender gift there is, my little maid,
    That doth the giver and receiver bless,
    And shall with obligation none distress;
Coin of the heart in God's just balance weighed;
    Wherefore, sweet spendthrift, still be prodigal,
    And freely squander what thou hast from all.

LUCERNE, *July*, 1891.

GOOD-NIGHT

GOOD-NIGHT. Good-night. Ah, good the night
That wraps thee in its silver light.
Good-night. No night is good for me
That does not hold a thought of thee.
            Good-night.

Good-night. Be every night as sweet
As that which made our love complete,
Till that last night when death shall be
One brief " Good-night," for thee and me.
            Good-night.

NEWPORT, 1890.

21*

COME IN

" COME in."   I stand, and know in thought
  The honest kiss, the waiting word,
The love with friendship interwrought,
  The face serene by welcome stirred.

BAR HARBOR, 1892.

LOSS

LIFE may moult many feathers, yet delight
To soar and çircle in a heaven of joy;
The pinion robbed must learn more swift employ,
Till the thinned feathers end our eager flight.

BAR HARBOR, 1892.

A GRAVEYARD

As beats the unrestful sea some ice-clad isle
Set in the sorrowful night of arctic seas,
Some lorn domain of endless silences,
So, echoless, unanswered, falleth here
The great voiced city's roar of fretful life.

ROME, 1891.

OCTOBER

Stay, gentle sunshine, stay;
  Sweet west wind, bide awhile;
Nay, linger, and my maid
  Shall bribe you with a smile.

Sweet sun and west wind, stay,
  You know not what you miss;
Nay, linger, and my maid
  Shall pay you with a kiss.

1890.

SEPTEMBER

Sir Goldenrod stands by and grieves
  Where Queen September goeth by:
Her viewless feet disturb the leaves,
  And with her south the thrushes fly,
Or loiter 'mid the rustling sheaves,
  And search and fail, and wonder why.
The burgher cat-tails stiffly bow
  Beside the marsh.   The asters cast
Their purple coronets, and below
  The brown ferns shiver in the blast,
And all the fretted pool aglow
  Repeats the cold, clear, yellow sky.
The dear, loved summer days are past,
  And tranquil goes the Queen to die.

1889.

YOU AND I

WHAT would you say
If you were I,
And I were near,
And no one by;
If you were I?

What would you do
If you were I,
And night were dark,
And none were nigh?
What would you do?

'What would I say
If I were you,
And none were near,
And love were true?
What would I say?

What would I do?
Just only this.
And on my cheek
Soft lit a kiss.
This did she do!

I heard a cry,
And through the night
Saw far away
A gleam of white,
And there was I!

> But not again
> This she was I;
> Yet still I loved,
> And years went by.
> Ah, not again!

·1890.

THE CHRIST OF THE SNOWS

A NORWEGIAN LEGEND

SET wine on the table
  And bread on the plate;
Cast logs on the ashes,
  And reverent wait.

The wine of love's sweetness
  Set out in thy breast,
And the white bread of welcome,
  To comfort the Guest.

For surely He cometh,
  Now midnight is near;
The wild winds, like wolf packs,
  Have fled in their fear,

Or hid in far fiords,
  Or died on the floes:
For surely He cometh,
  Our Christ of the Snows.

Along by the portal,
  Half joy and half fear,
Wait man, maid, and matron
  The step none shall hear;

The babe at the doorway,
  And age with eyes dim,—
They whom birth near or death near
  Make closest to Him.

The clock tolleth midnight:
  Cast open the door;
Shrink back ere He passeth,
  Kneel all on the floor.

The stillness of terror
  Possesseth the night,
From star-haunted heaven
  To snow spaces white.

Lo! shaken by ghost gods
  Who angrily fly,
The banners of Odin
  Flame red on the sky.

The last note hath stricken:
  Did He pass? Was He here?
Is it sorrow or joy that
  Shall rule the new year?

The mother who watcheth
  ' The face of the child
Saith, Ah, He was with us,—
  The baby hath smiled!

The virgin who bends o'er
  The cup on the board
Cries, Lo! the wine trembled,—
  'T was surely the Lord!

Sing Christmas, sweet Christmas,
  All good men below;
Sing Christmas that bringeth
  Our Christ of the Snow.

1880.

ST. CHRISTOPHER

FOR A CHILD

THERE was none so tall as this giant bold.
He had a name that could not be told,
A name so crooked no Christian men
Could say it over and speak again.
One day he came where a good man prayed
All alone in the forest shade.
Then the giant in wonder said:
"Why do you bend the knee and head?"
"I bend," he said, "because I be
The weakest thing that you can see.
To Christ who is so good and strong,
I pray for help to do no wrong."
"Ho," said the giant, "when I see
One strong enough to conquer me,
I shall be glad to bend my knees,
Which are as stout as any trees."

"But," said the good man, sad and old,
"Yon stream is deep, the water cold.
Prayer is the Spirit's work for some.
Work is the prayer of the body dumb."
"If that be prayer," said the giant tall,
"The maimed and sick, the weak and small,
Across the stream and to and fro,
I shall carry and come and go,
Until the time when I shall see
Thy strong Christ come to humble me."
So all day long, with patient hand,
He bore the weak from strand to strand.
At last, one eve, when winds were wild,
He heard the voice of a little child
Saying, "Giant, art thou asleep?
Carry me over the river deep."
On his shoulder broad he set the child,
And laughed to see how the infant smiled.
Up to his waist the giant strode,
While fierce around the water flowed;
His great back shook, his great knees bent,
As staggering through the waves he went.
"Why is this?" he cried aloud;
"Why should my great back be bowed?"
Spake from his shoulder, sweet and clear,
A voice,—'t was like a bird's to hear,—
"I am the Christ to whom men pray
When comes the morn and wanes the day."
"No," said the giant, "a child art thou.
Not to a babe shall proud men bow!"
He set the child on the farther land,
And wiped his brow with shaking hand.
"In truth," he cried, "the load was great;

Wherefore art thou this heavy weight ? "
The little child said, "I was heavy to thee
Because the world's sins rest on me."
"If thou canst carry them all on thee,
Who art but a little child to see,
Thou must be strong, and I be weak,
And thou must be the one I seek."
Therefore the giant, day by day,
Still kept his work, and learned to pray.
And his pagan name that none should hear
Was changed to Giant Christopher.

1887.

POEMS OF OCCASION

POEMS OF OCCASION

A DOCTOR'S CENTURY

READ AT THE CENTENNIAL DINNER OF THE COLLEGE
OF PHYSICIANS OF PHILADELPHIA, 1887

A Doctor's century dead and gone!
    Good-night to those one hundred years,
To all the memories they bear
    Of honest help for pains or tears;

To them that like St. Christopher,
    When North and South were sad with graves,
Bore the true Christ of charity
    Across the battles' crimson waves.

Good-night to all the shining line,
    Our peerage,— yes, our lords of thought;
Their blazonry, unspotted lives
    Which all the ways of honor taught.

A gentler word, as proud a thought,
  For those who won no larger prize
Than humble days well lived can win
  From thankful hearts and weeping eyes.

Too grave my song; a lighter mood
  Shall bid us scan our honored roll,
For jolly jesters gay and good,
  Who healed the flesh and charmed the soul,

And took their punch, and took the jokes
  Would make our prudish conscience tingle,
Then bore their devious lanterns home,
  And slept, or heard the night-bell jingle.

Our Century 's dead; God rest his soul!
  Without a doctor or a nurse,
Without a "post," without a dose,
  He 's off on Time's old rattling hearse.

What sad disorder laid him out
  To all pathologists is dim;
An intercurrent malady,—
  Bacterium chronos, finished him!

Our new-born century, pert and proud,
  Like some young doctor fresh from college,
Disturbs our prudent age with doubts
  And misty might of foggy knowledge.

Ah, but to come again and share
  The gains his calmer days shall store,
For them that in a hundred years
  Shall see our "science grown to more,"

Perchance as ghosts consultant we
   May stand beside some fleshly fellow,
And marvel what on earth he means,
   When this new century's old and mellow.

Take then the thought that wisdom fades,
   That knowledge dies of newer truth,
That only duty simply done
   Walks always with the step of youth.

A grander morning floods our skies
   With higher aims and larger light;
Give welcome to the century new,
   And to the past a glad good-night.

MINERVA MEDICA

VERSES READ AT THE DINNER COMMEMORATIVE OF
THE FIFTIETH YEAR OF THE DOCTORATE OF
D. HAYES AGNEW, M. D., APRIL 6, 1888

GOOD CHAIRMAN, BROTHERS, FRIENDS, AND GUESTS,—
   all ye who come with praise
To honor for our ancient guild a life of blameless days,
If from the well-worn road of toil I step aside to find
A poet's roses for the wreath your kindly wishes bind,
Be certain that their fragrance types, amid your laurel
   leaves,
The gentle love a tender heart in duty's chaplet weaves.

I can't exactly set the date,—the Chairman he will
    know,—
But it was on a chilly night, some month or two ago.
Within, the back-log warmed my toes; without, the frozen
    rain,
Storm-driven by the angry wind, clashed on my window-
    pane.
I lit a pipe, stirred up the fire, and, dry with thirst for
    knowledge,
Plunged headlong in an essay by a Fellow of the College.
But, sir, I 've often seen of late that this especial thirst
Is not of all its varied forms the keenest or the
    worst.
At all events, that gentleman — that pleasant College
    Fellow —
He must have been of all of us the juiciest and most
    mellow.
You ask his name, degree, and fame; you want to know
    that rare man ?
It was n't you,— nor you,— nor you,— no, sir, 't was not
    the Chairman !
For minutes ten I drank of him; quenched was my ardent
    thirst ;
Another minute, and my veins with knowledge, sir, had
    burst ;
A moment more, my head fell back, my lazy eyelids
    closed,
And on my lap that Fellow's book at equal peace re-
    posed.
Then I remembered me the night that essay first was
    read,
And how we thought it could n't all have come from one
    man's head.

At nine the College heard a snore and saw the Chairman
    start,—
A snore as of an actor shy rehearsing for his part.
At ten, a shameless chorus around the hall had run,
The Chairman dreamed a feeble joke, and said the noes
    had won.
At twelve the Treasurer fell asleep, the wakeful Censors
    slumbered,
The Secretary's minutes grew to hours quite unnumbered.
At six A. M. that Fellow paused, perchance a page to
    turn,
And up I got, and cried, "I move the College do
    adjourn!"
They did n't, sir; they sat all day.   It made my flesh to
    creep.
All night they sat;—that could n't be.   Goodness! was
    I asleep?
Was I asleep?   With less effect that Fellow might have
    tried
Codeia, Morphia, Urethan, Chloral, Paraldehyde.
In vain my servant called aloud, "Sir, here 's a solemn
    letter
To say they want a song from you, for lack of some one
    better.
The Chairman says his man will wait, while you sit down
    and write;
He says he 's not in any haste,— and make it something
    light;
He says you need n't vex yourself to try to be effulgent,
Because, he says, champagne enough will keep them all
    indulgent."
I slept — at least I think I slept — an hour by estimation,
But if I slept, I must have had unconscious cerebration,

23

For on my desk, the morrow morn, I found. this ordered
    verse;
Pray take it as you take your wife,—"for better or for
    worse."

A golden wedding: fifty earnest years
    This spring-tide day from that do sadly part,
When, 'mid a learned throng, one shy, grave lad,
    Half conscious, won the Mistress of our Art.

Still at his side the tranquil goddess stood,
    Unseen of men, and claimed the student boy;
Touched with her cool, sweet lips his ruddy cheek,
    And bade him follow her through grief and joy.

"Be mine," she whispered in his startled ear,
    "Be mine, to-day, as Paré once was mine;
Like Hunter mine, and all who nobly won
    The fadeless honors of that shining line.

"Be mine," she said, "the calm of honest eyes,
    The steadfast forehead, and the constant soul;
Mine the firm heart on simple duty bent,
    And mine the manly gift of self-control.

"Not in my service is the harvest won
    That gilds the child of barter and of trade;
That steady hand, that ever-pitying touch,
    Not in my helping shall be thus repaid.

"But I will take you where the great have gone,
    And I will set your feet in honor's ways;
Friends I will give, and length of crowded years,
    And crown your manhood with a nation's praise.

"These will I give, and more; the poor man's home,
  The anguished sufferer in the clutch of pain,
The camp, the field, the long, sad, waiting ward,
  Shall seek your kindly face, nor seek in vain;

"For, as the sculptor-years shall chisel deep
  The lines of pity 'neath the brow of thought,
Below your whitening hair the hurt shall read
  How well you learned what I my best have taught."

The busy footsteps of your toiling stand
  Upon the noisy century's sharp divide,
And at your side, to-night, I see her still,
  The gracious woman, strong and tender-eyed.

O stately Mistress of our sacred Art,
  Changeless and beautiful and wise and brave,
Full fifty years have gone since first your lips
  To noblest uses pledged that forehead grave.

As round the board our merry glasses rang,
  His golden-wedding chimes I heard to-night;
We know its offspring; lo, from sea to sea
  His pupil children bless his living light.

What be the marriage-gifts that we can give?
  What lacks he that on well-used years attends?
All that we have to give are his to-day,—
  Love, honor and obedience, troops of friends.

VERSES

READ ON THE PRESENTATION BY S. WEIR MITCHELL TO THE PHILADELPHIA COLLEGE OF PHYSICIANS OF SARAH W. WHITMAN'S PORTRAIT OF OLIVER WENDELL HOLMES, M. D.

We call them great who have the magic art
To summon tears and stir the human heart,
With fictive grief to bring the soul annoy,
And leave a dew-drop in the rose of joy.
A nobler purpose had the Masters wise
Who from your walls look down with kindly eyes.
Theirs the firm hand and theirs the ready brain
Strong for the battle with disease and pain.
Large were their lives: these scholars, gentle, brave,
Knew all of man from cradle unto grave.
What note of torment had they failed to hear?
All grief's stern gamut knew each pitying ear.
Nor theirs the useless sympathy that stands
Beside the suffering with defenceless hands;
Divinely wise, their pity had the art
To teach the brain the ardor of the heart.
These left a meaner for a nobler George;
These trod the red snows by the Valley Forge,
Saw the wild birth-throes of a nation's life,
The long-drawn misery and the doubtful strife:
Yea, and on darker fields they left their dead
Where grass-grown streets heard but the bearer's tread,
While the sad death-roll of those fatal days
Left small reward beyond the poor man's praise.

Lo! Shadowy greetings from each canvas come,
Lips seem to move now for a century dumb:
From tongues long hushed the sound of welcome falls,
"Place, place for Holmes upon these honored walls."
The lights are out, the festal flowers fade,
Our guests are gone, the great hall wrapped in shade.
Lone in the midst this silent picture stands,
Ringed with the learning of a score of lands.
From dusty tomes in many a tongue I hear
A gentle Babel,—"Welcome, Brother dear.
Yea, though Apollo won thy larger hours,
And stole our fruit, and only left us flowers,
The poet's rank thy title here completes—
Doctor and Poet,—so were Goldsmith,—Keats."
The voices failing murmur to an end
With "Welcome, Doctor, Scholar, Poet, Friend."

In elder days of quiet wiser folks,
When the great Hub had not so many spokes,
Two wandering gods, upon the Common, found
A weary schoolboy sleeping on the ground.
Swift to his brain their eager message went,
Swift to his heart each ardent claim was sent:
"Be mine," Minerva cried. "This tender hand
Skilled in the art of arts shall understand
With magic touch the demon pain to lay.
From skill to skill and on to clearer day
Far through the years shall fare that ample brain
To read the riddles of disease and pain."
" Nay, mine the boy," Apollo cried aloud,
" His the glad errand, beautiful and proud,
To wing the arrows of delightful mirth,
To slay with jests the sadder things of earth.

At his gay science melancholy dies,
At his clear laugh each morbid fancy flies.
Rich is the quiver I shall give his bow,
The eagle's pinion some bold shafts shall know ;
Swift to its mark the angry arrow-song
Shall find the centre of a nation's wrong;
Or in a people's heart one tingling shot
Pleads not in vain against the war-ship's lot.
Yea, I will see that for a gentler flight
The dove's soft feathers send his darts aright
When smiles and pathos, kindly wedded, chant
The plaintive lay of that unmarried aunt;
Or sails his Nautilus the sea of time,
Blown by the breezes of immortal rhyme,
Or with a Godspeed from her poet's brain,
Sweet Clémence trips adown the Rue de Seine.
The humming-bird shall plume the quivering song,
Blithe, gay, and restless, never dull or long,
Where gayly passionate his soul is set
To sing the Katydid's supreme regret,
Or creaking jokes, through never-ending days,
Rolls the quaint story of the Deacon's chaise.
Away with tears !   When this glad poet sings,
The angel Laughter spreads her broadest wings.
By land and sea where'er St. George's cross
And the starred banner in the breezes toss,
The merry music of his wholesome mirth
Sends rippling smiles around our English earth."

" Not mine," Minerva cried, " to spoil thy joy ;
Divide the honors,—let us share the boy ! "

April, 1892.

A DECANTER OF MADEIRA, AGED 86, TO GEORGE BANCROFT, AGED 86

GREETING:

I

GOOD master, you and I were born
  In " Teacup days " of hoop and hood,
And when the silver cue hung down,
  And toasts were drunk, and wine was good;

II

When kin of mine (a jolly brood)
  From sideboards looked, and knew full well
What courage they had given the beau,
  How generous made the blushing belle.

III

Ah, me! what gossip could I prate
  Of days when doors were locked at dinners!
Believe me, I have kissed the lips
  Of many pretty saints — or sinners.

IV

Lip service have I done, alack!
  I don't repent, but come what may,
What ready lips, sir, I have kissed,
  Be sure at least I shall not say.

V

Two honest gentlemen are we,—
  I Demi John, whole George are you;
When Nature grew us one in years
  She meant to make a generous brew.

VI

She bade me store for festal hours
  The sun our south side vineyard knew;
To sterner tasks she set your life,
  As statesman, writer, scholar, grew.

VII

Years eighty-six have come and gone;
  At last we meet.   Your health to-night.
Take from this board of friendly hearts
  The memory of a proud delight.

VIII

The days that went have made you wise,
  There 's wisdom in my rare bouquet.
I 'm rather paler than I was;
  And, on my soul, you 're growing gray.

IX

I like to think, when Toper Time
  Has drained the last of me and you,
Some here shall say, They both were good,—
  The wine we drank, the man we knew.

October 3, 1886, *Newport.*

NOTES

❧

FRANCIS DRAKE.

THE difficulty of realizing to-day the feelings and mo-
tives of the men of another era is well illustrated in the
incidents on which I have based the dramatic poem of
" Francis Drake." In the poetical telling of it I have
adhered with reasonable fidelity to the somewhat vary-
ing statements given in " The World Encompassed "
(1628), Hakluyt Society, No. 16; the extracts of evidence
as to the trial of Doughty from the Harleian manuscripts,
in the same volume; Barrow's life of Drake; and an ad-
mirable but brief biography of the great sea-captain by
Julius Corbett, in the series, " English Men of Action." I
have had neither desire nor intention to make of this
strange story an acting drama. Doughty, as he is drawn
by Mr. Corbett, must have been, as he says, an Iago of rare
type. A scholar, a soldier, a gentleman of the Inner Tem-
ple, more or less learned in Hebrew, Greek, and Latin,
he seems to have had great power to attract the affections
of men. That he betrayed his friend's trust, and was
guilty of mutiny, and even of contemplating darker
crime, appears probable, although as to the details of this
sad story we know little, but small fragments of the evidence given on the trial having been preserved. The
historian, more than the poet, may well be perplexed at

the nobler characteristics which appear in this singular
being on the approach of death. It is here that the
judgments of to-day fail us before the account of the
quiet, cheerful talk[1] at dinner while the headsman waits.
An immense curiosity fills us as to what was said. Then,
there is the sacrament taken with Drake, the final embrace, the remarkable words of quotation from Sir Thomas More,[2] omitted in the poem, and at last the axe and
block. It is worthy of note that there is no woman in
this tragic story.

[1] "They dined, also at the same table together, as cheerfully in
sobriety as ever in their lives they had done aforetime; each cheer-
ing up the other, and, taking their leave, by drinking each to other,
as if some journey only had been in hand." ("The World Encompassed," p. 67. Hakluyt Society's edition.)

[2] Doughty is credited in one account of his death with saying to
the executioner, when about to lay his head on the block, "As good
Sir Thomas More said, 'I fear thou wilt have little honesty [*i. e.*
credit] of so short a neck.'"

CUP OF YOUTH.

I have accepted the popular version of Galileo's famous
call to Rome to answer for his intellectual views. Much
doubt has of late been thrown upon the received story of
the peril to which his visit subjected him.

Long after the period in question grave men of science
held to the possibility of reviving youth, and also believed
in the transmutability of metals.

Galileo, trained as a physician, used the pendulum as
a measurer of the pulse, causing it to beat even time
with any special pulse by raising or lowering the weight
or bob. Thus the length of the pendulum became a con-
ventional measure of the rate of the pulse. Counting it

with the aid of a watch, although first practised in the reign of Anne, was never common until the present century.

That "frail English boy" was William Harvey, the discoverer of the circulation of the blood.

THE VIOLIN.

The belief that it is sinful to touch that which the shadow of the cross falls upon is a medieval fancy, but I cannot now recall where I have seen it mentioned.

I am indebted to Professor T. F. Crane, of Cornell University, for the strange legendary story of the thirty pieces of silver. I have, 'of course, taken great liberties with the old Latin version, as to which Professor Crane says:

" The legend of the thirty pieces of silver is found only in Gottfried of Viterbo's ' Pantheon,' a rare work reprinted in Scriptores Rerum Germanicorum, Ratisbon, 1726 (ed. Pistorius and Stoure). I have copied it from M. du Meril, Poésies Populaires Latines du Moyen Age, Paris, 1847, p. 321, also a scarce work. I do not know of any other accessible version, although the legend was copied from Gottfried by various legend-writers of the time. Where Gottfried got it I cannot tell."

FRANÇOIS VILLON.

François Villon, born 1431, poet, thief, vagabond, led a life of excesses, in which were sharp experiences of the prison and the torture-chamber. His ballad "Des Pendus" was written in 1461, whilst he was under sentence of death. Soon after he is lost to history, and becomes fair subject for the imagination. There is not the least foundation in any known facts for the story I have labelled with his name.

CERVANTES.

Cervantes, who lost a hand at Lepanto, was for five years a prisoner in Algiers, and on his release lived a life of sad vicissitudes, dying in want on the 23d of April, 1616, the day of Shakespeare's death. Where lie the bones of the creator of Don Quixote is wholly unknown.

HERNDON.

On Sept. 12, 1857, the Central America was lost at sea. Captain Herndon of the navy was in command. His tranquil courage preserved discipline up to the last, and until his passengers, officers, and crew were all in the boats. Seeing that the last boat was already overloaded, Captain Herndon refused to add to its danger, and, ordering it off, went down with his ship.

GRAVES OF REGICIDES.

The regicides buried in the church of St. Martin, at Vevey, are Broughton, Ludlow, and Phelps. The tombstones of the first two are visible. Phelps has recently been commemorated by a stone placed upon the wall by the American descendants of his family,— the Phelpses of New England and New Jersey. Ludlow and Broughton lived to a great age at Vevey, and so, also, I believe, did Phelps, of whom less is known.

KEARSARGE.

On Sunday morning, June 19, 1864, the noise of the cannons during the fight between the Kearsarge and the Alabama was heard in English churches near the Channel.

DOMINIQUE DE GOURGUES.

In 1565, Menendez, an officer of Philip II. in Florida, put to death, under circumstances of strange atrocity, two hundred and eighty French Huguenots, most of whom were driven by starvation to surrender at discretion. Dominique de Gourgues, a French soldier, avenged this massacre as I have described, devoting to this purpose his fortune, and exposing himself to the malice of his own King, Charles IX. I have used a poet's license in the introduction of a supernatural influence. The tale is told at length by my friend the late Francis Parkman, in his " Pioneers of France in the New World."